THE SMALLEST MAN

Frances Quinn grew up in London and read English at King's College, Cambridge, realising too late that the course would require more than lying around reading novels for three years. After snatching a degree from the jaws of laziness, she became a journalist, writing for magazines including *Prima*, *Good Housekeeping*, *She*, *Woman's Weekly* and *Ideal Home*, and later branched out into copywriting, producing words for everything from Waitrose pizza packaging to the EasyJet in-flight brochure.

She lives in Brighton, with her husband and two Tonkinese cats.

THE SMALLEST MAN

Frances Quinn

**SIMON &
SCHUSTER**

London · New York · Sydney · Toronto · New Delhi

First published in Great Britain by Simon & Schuster UK Ltd, 2021

Copyright © Frances Quinn, 2021

The right of Frances Quinn to be identified as author
of this work has been asserted in accordance with the
Copyright, Designs and Patents Act, 1988.

3 5 7 9 10 8 6 4 2

Simon & Schuster UK Ltd
1st Floor
222 Gray's Inn Road
London WC1X 8HB

Simon & Schuster Australia, Sydney
Simon & Schuster India, New Delhi

www.simonandschuster.co.uk
www.simonandschuster.com.au
www.simonandschuster.co.in

A CIP catalogue record for this book is available from the British Library

Hardback ISBN: 978-1-4711-9340-8
Trade Paperback ISBN: 978-1-4711-9341-5
eBook ISBN: 978-1-4711-9342-2
Audio ISBN: 978-1-4711-9596-9

Printed and bound in Great Britain by CPI Group (UK) Ltd, Croydon, CR0 4YY

To Björn, Benny, Agnetha and Frida, who have no idea
how much help they've been.

The year is 1625. King James is dead and England has a new king and queen: Charles, the serious, awkward second son forced onto the throne by the death of his more popular brother, and Henrietta Maria, the fifteen-year-old devoutly Catholic Princess of France.

Charles has inherited a country where cracks are beginning to show. After repeated clashes with his father, Parliament is spoiling for a fight, and Charles, like James, believes his God-given right to rule trumps their increasing demands for a say in England's affairs.

After years of war against the Catholic countries of France and Spain, and the Catholic-led attempt to kill King James in the Gunpowder Plot, English Catholics are hated and feared; they can be fined and even imprisoned for practising their faith. But Protestants are divided among themselves too: the growing Puritan movement want a Church shorn of the 'Catholic' trimmings of saints' days and elaborate ritual – and of bishops, who, being appointed by the king, allow royal control over the Church. And with Puritans strong in Parliament, religious differences are deepening the political rift.

Into this England come the new king and his bride – and their marriage becomes the seed of a crisis that will split the country in two, pit brother against brother, and ultimately lead the people of England to kill their king.

Part One

Chapter One

My name is Nat Davy. Perhaps you've heard of me? There was
a time when people up and down the land knew my name,
but that was long ago – and they knew only half the story.
It's been quite a life, the one I've had; I was there when they
turned the world upside down, and I was there, right at the
heart of it all, during the turbulent times that led us down
the road to that day. So I got to thinking that I should write
it all down, because there's been a lot said about those times,
and not all of it's right.

But when should my tale begin? Not when I was born,
a butcher's son, in a tiny cottage just like all the other tiny
cottages in Oakham. Who'd have thought then that I'd ever
have much of a story to tell? Perhaps it starts when people
began to nudge each other and stare as I walked with my
mother to market, or the first time someone whispered that
we were cursed. But I didn't know then. She said not to listen
to them, that I was just a slow starter and I'd grow in my own
good time, and I believed her. No, I think my story begins on
the day of the Oakham Fair, in the year of 1625. When I was
ten years old and I found out what I was.

The June sun rose early and we set out soon after dawn, my father striding out at a pace that left the rest of the family a little behind, as usual. When I was younger, he used to swing me up and sit me on his broad, solid shoulders. I felt like a king up there, looking out over the hedgerows and waving to the cows in the fields. And I remember – I'm almost sure I remember – him smiling up at me and saying 'My fine boy'. But as I got older, but no bigger, he stopped carrying me on his shoulders and walked ahead of us instead. My mother said it was just because he hated to dawdle, and I believed that too, back then.

Mother carried my baby sister on her hip that morning, Annie's fat little fingers locked in my mother's long brown curls, and my brother Sam walked with me. He was taller than I was, even though he was only eight, but he liked to gaze around, kick a pebble along or pick a blade of grass and make it whistle, and he never minded strolling at my pace.

We always heard the fair before we saw it: a swirl of shouts and music and song. It came only twice a year, and the rest of the time not much happened in Oakham, so our steps quickened when we heard that noise and caught the smell of smoke and hot roast pork. And that year, there was a special reason for the way my belly turned over as we got close.

I looked up at Sam; he was walking as though there was a string through the tip of his nose, drawing him towards the smell, and there was a blissful look in his eyes, as if he could already taste the meat.

'Where's the penny?' I whispered.

I'd made sure he had it when we left, but my brother had a talent for losing things. He opened his hand and showed me it.

'Tell me again,' he said, 'when do we—'

I whispered the plan again, for about the tenth time, and he nodded.

By the time we reached the edge of the green, the noise had splintered into a hundred different sounds, all fighting to be heard: snatches of music from a fiddle band, stallholders hollering their wares, laughter gusting out from the ale tents.

We're here. It's really going to happen.

My mother hitched Annie higher on her hip and issued her instructions.

'You two, stay close to me. Do not wander off. And Nat, don't speak to anyone and don't let anyone hear you speak. There are strangers here, from all over.'

She said the same every fair day. I didn't know, then, why she didn't want anyone who didn't know me to hear me talk.

My father strode off, and we followed close behind. As we approached the green, a big group of lads appeared from the opposite direction. They jostled past, and I got separated from my mother and Sam. I tried to catch them up, but I couldn't push my way through the crowd, and then suddenly they weren't there. I was in a forest of legs, and I couldn't see my way through. I tried to jump up and catch a glimpse of my mother's blue dress, but it was hopeless, I couldn't see past all the people.

Where are they?

The crowd was pushing and jostling, and people couldn't even see me in front of them. Just when I was certain I'd be knocked off my feet and trampled, I heard my mother call my name, and then there she was, pushing through the crowd, Annie in her arms and Sam close behind her.

'There you are! This is no good, it's so crowded this year – Sam, put him up on your shoulders.'

As Sam swung me up, my father appeared, his face a picture of irritation.

'I told you this would happen,' he said. 'Now come on, let's get going.'

He turned to carve our path through the crowd. Now I was on Sam's shoulders, I could stretch up and see it all: burly wrestlers grunting and grappling, their skins shiny with goose grease; a juggler swirling wooden clubs that surely must be tied to his hands with invisible string; a man swallowing fire; a fiddle band calling silly, giggling girls and red-faced boys up to dance. A pink pig turned on a spit, charring the hairs on its nose and dripping glistening fat into the flames, and over all the other noise came the shouts of the fair people listing the wonders hidden in the tents: a sheep that could count to ten; a man with two noses; a child as black as coal. But I was looking for only one thing, and there was no sign of it.

She had to be there; they'd said she'd be there. But we'd walked right round the fair, and there was only a last line of tents to go.

Maybe she'd escaped, run back to the forest.

Then Sam tapped my leg, nodding towards a stripy tent, and I caught the words the man outside was calling out:

'The one and only faerie woman! See her walk and dance!'

I leaned down and whispered in his ear, 'Got the penny?'

He rolled his eyes, and patted his pocket. Panic flashed across his face.

'It was the other side,' I said.

He felt in the other pocket, and his shoulders relaxed.

'I was just joking you,' he said, and I pinched his ear to make him think I believed him.

My plan was to sneak away while my father lifted the iron ball and my mother was watching him. But he liked to wait for it to draw a good audience, and we walked round the green again before we finally went across. A skinny lad who looked as though he'd have trouble lifting a spoon, let alone the iron ball, was chancing his luck; the crowd laughed as he heaved the ball as far as his knees, held it with shaking arms, then dropped it. Still my father didn't move.

'Aren't you going up?' asked my mother.

'I'll wait a while yet,' he replied. 'Let the lads have their fun first.'

I wished he'd hurry up. There were little fishes swimming round in my belly at the thought of what was going to happen, and I wanted to get on with it. I looked down to check Sam was ready, but of course he wasn't watching at all. His gaze was fixed on a moon-faced woman beside him, or to be more accurate, on the pie she was eating. As she bit into it, a flake of pastry broke off and floated to the ground. Sam's eyes followed it all the way down, then flicked back to her mouth and watched her chew. That was exactly what I'd been worried about: Sam would never let me down on purpose but he was easily distracted, and the longer we stood there waiting, the harder it would be to keep his attention sharp. Or as sharp as it ever got. And if we missed our chance, we might not get another one.

I pinched his shoulder and whispered: 'Be ready!'

He rummaged in his pocket again.

'Ready.'

At last, after three more hopefuls had failed, my father winked at my mother and said:

'Time to show them how it's done.'

My father was as strong as an ox; he could heft the ball straight up if he wanted to. But he'd put on a show first. He made a big performance of rolling up his sleeves, and gave the ball an experimental little lift, then shook his head and put it down again.

'Now,' I whispered to Sam.

Gripping my legs, he turned and began weaving through the crowd. I glanced back; every head faced forward, watching my father circle the ball as though he was preparing to take it by surprise. Mother was going to be furious when she realised we were gone, but it would be worth it. Or perhaps she'd be so pleased and surprised she'd forget to be angry. It depended how quickly it worked. I'd thought about that a lot. Would the transformation happen there and then or later? Perhaps while I slept? Which meant we'd still get a wallop that night, but I could suffer that if everything was different in the morning.

As we got near the tent, a flap at the back opened, and a boy held it aside for the people who'd been inside to come out. I craned my neck to peer in, but he dropped the canvas too quickly.

The barkers had made a big fuss about the faerie woman when they came to drum up custom for the fair.

'First time in Oakham – captured from the forest!' they'd shouted. 'Thirty-eight years old, and only three foot high! A ha'penny to see her walk and dance!'

All that week, I thought about her. Faeries could grant wishes, everyone knew that. What if I asked her to make me grow? 'It'll happen in its own good time,' my mother kept saying, but it hadn't, not even a little bit.

It wasn't that my size had no advantages. I was a nosy child and I'd discovered that, because I looked no older than baby Annie, I could watch people quite unnoticed, and nobody cared what I heard them say. So I'd look and listen and tell my mother that old Ma Tyrell didn't really like her son's new wife, because I'd seen how her fingers twitched when she said the girl's name, like she itched to give her a pinch. Or that the baker was cheating people with lightweight loaves, after I heard him scold his apprentice for forgetting to keep his thumb on the scale when he thought no one was listening. My mother used to shake her head and say I had wisdom beyond my years.

But I didn't want wisdom beyond my years. I wanted to be like other boys: to climb the tallest trees, and run the fastest, and skim pebbles all the way across the pond. I wanted to help with the harvest like Sam did. And I wanted to be big enough to fight Jack Edgecombe from the dairy, who'd told everybody he'd seen me out riding Ma Tyrell's dog like it was a horse. Which was not true. Sam punched him on the nose for that but I wanted to be able to do it myself. So I made up my mind to see the faerie.

I'd been working up the courage to steal a ha'penny from the pouch my father kept under the mattress, but then Sam found a penny, just lying in the road. He'd have handed it straight to Mother, but I wasn't going to let that happen; if I could persuade him to keep it, I knew he'd share it. Sam was like that, soft as a baby mouse's belly. So I kept talking about the saffron buns and jam tarts and apple turnovers there'd be at the fair, until his conscience was no match for his stomach. It was bad of me; if Mother found out, there'd be trouble, and she always whacked him a bit harder. But I wanted the faerie to make me grow more than I'd ever wanted anything.

Sam's generosity had its limits though, and he refused to spend his share coming in with me. For a ha'penny, he'd worked out, he could get two saffron buns, an apple turnover and a go on the hoopla, with the chance of winning a ginger-bread man. I'd told him the faerie would probably be able to summon up any amount of buns and pastries by magic, but he couldn't bring himself to chance food he could see and smell against the powers of a creature he hadn't even glimpsed, so we agreed he'd wait outside.

As the fair man ushered the next four people in, we stood behind a family with two daughters, and a gangly young man in the company of two dairymaids, one plump and pink, the other tall and sharp-looking, like a heron. I supposed I'd be going in with them. As we waited, Sam kept a jealous eye on the hoopla stall, growling with irritation when a little girl won and chose a gingerbread man as her prize.

The boy stuck his head out of the tent and the man beck-oned the family in front of us across. The last people had only been in there a few minutes; what if the dairymaids had wishes too, and the time ran out before she got to me? If I was stuck behind them, she wouldn't even see me. I thought for a minute then whispered in Sam's ear.

'I can't,' he said. 'I don't know them.'

'Go on...'

He sighed and tapped the arm of the thin dairymaid.

'Pardon me, miss. My brother wants to see the faerie but

our mother says I'm not to leave him alone, and we've only half a penny to spend. Will you take him in?'

'Of course we will,' she said, lifting me off Sam's shoulders and balancing me on her bony hip. 'Look at those curls – what a little sweetie.'

Sam's grin told me I was going to suffer him calling me 'little sweetie' for weeks.

'How old is he?' said the pink dairymaid, chucking me under the chin with a surprisingly rough-skinned finger.

Sam's face flushed; he was hopeless at lying.

'Not very old,' he mumbled. 'About two, probably.'

They didn't question that and after another few minutes of the dairymaids clucking at me, the fair man called us forward. The fishes in my belly were doing somersaults now.

Make sure you say the wish in time.

It was hot and dark inside, with only a couple of lanterns for light, and it took a few seconds before I saw the cage. The faerie was sitting inside it, hunched over a little stool.

The fair boy cracked a long wooden stick against the bars.

'Up,' he said.

She stood, keeping her eyes on the ground. She didn't look like I'd thought a faerie would. She was about three feet tall, like a child, but she wasn't a child; her face looked tired, like my mother's. Her brown hair was stringy with sweat and there was no sign of wings.

'I've seen better ones than that,' said the pink dairymaid. 'Last year they had one tied up. Said it could bite.'

'It might still be dangerous,' said the young man, slipping his arm round the pink dairymaid's waist. He rattled the bars. The faerie didn't move.

'Walk,' said the fair boy.

Still looking at the ground, the faerie paced round the four sides of the cage.

'Make it dance,' said the pink dairymaid.

The fair boy slid the stick through the bars and gave the faerie a vicious little jab. She began a clumsy jig, hopping from one foot to the other with her shoulders bowed and her empty eyes looking straight ahead as though we weren't there.

'Call that dancing?' said the young man. 'My dog dances better than that.'

He smirked at the dairymaids, and the bony one gave a screechy laugh, right in my ear.

I had to get my wish in, before the time ran out. But if the faerie could do magic, why was she letting herself be kept in a cage and poked with sticks? I'd practised how to ask politely but my words tumbled out in a rush.

'Pardon me my name is Nat Davy and I've come to ask if you can grant a wish.'

The dairymaid nearly dropped me; the others turned and stared. The faerie walked to the front of the cage, narrowing her eyes as though she thought she knew me from somewhere. I asked the dairymaid to put me down, then walked to the cage and looked up at the faerie. I was starting to get a cold feeling that this wasn't going to turn out the way I'd hoped, but I couldn't go away without trying.

'Please, can you grant wishes?' I said.

She leaned forward and whispered something, but I didn't catch it because at the same time, the fair boy said, 'How old are you?'

Something about the way he said it made me not want to tell, but it didn't seem a good idea to lie in front of the faerie.

'I'm ten.'

The faerie came close to the bars and this time I heard what she whispered.

'Get out of here.'

The fair boy yelled out, 'Dan! In here!'

'Run,' said the faerie. 'Now.'

But as the man pushed through the curtain, the boy took hold of my arm.

'You won't believe this,' he said. 'This one's ten years old. Just said so. Talks as clear as you or me.'

The man looked down at me.

'He yours?' he asked the dairymaid.

'No, his brother asked us to bring him in. Said he was two.'

The man's knees creaked as he stooped. His bumpy nose was patterned with little red streaks and his hot breath smelt of onions. I stepped back but the boy still had hold of my arm.

'Tiny for ten,' said the boy.

'And perfectly formed,' said the man, looking me up and down.

He turned to the dairymaids and the young man, who'd only just managed to close their astonished mouths.

'Time's up, folks. And here...' He fished in the pouch at his waist. 'Half your money back, since you didn't see the whole show. Quick, or I'll change my mind.'

He held on to my arm as the boy showed them out, then fetched a tall stool from behind the cage and stood me on it. I wanted to jump down from it and run, but the fair boy would be faster than me. The man walked right round me, peering.

'Come on, let him go,' said the faerie. 'He's just a child.'

'Shut up, you,' said the fair man.

'So do we just take him?' said the boy, and my insides turned to water.

'Nah, he'd be too easy to find,' said the man. 'We wouldn't be able to show him anywhere from here to Oxford if we took him.'

Show me?

The man shrugged.

'But I reckon the parents'll give him up easy enough. He's pretty but he can't be much use to them, not that size. So, young man, where are your mother and father?'

A memory came into my head then, of the day my father's best fighting dog, Jasper, got hurt. He could still walk but he wouldn't be able to fight again. 'If a dog can't earn its keep, it's no use to me,' my father said, and he sharpened his big knife, walked into the woods with Jasper and came back without him. The fair man was right; I wasn't any use either. Sam had been helping in the fields since he was six. When I asked Mother why I couldn't go, she said:

'You'll go when you grow.'

But I hadn't grown. And suddenly I was certain about one thing: I had to keep the fair man away from my father.

'They're at the eating tents,' I said. 'I'll show you.'

He lifted me down. As my feet touched the floor, I sank my teeth into his leathery arm.

'You little sod!'

I scrabbled at the flap at the back of the tent, my fingers too small to get a grip on the heavy canvas. Any second now, I'd feel his hand on my neck and smell his hot onion breath.

But then the canvas parted and I tumbled out, almost falling on my face in the dirt. Behind me I heard the faerie cheer.

'Sam,' I shouted, 'quick, get me away.'

For once, he didn't hesitate. He saw my face, scooped me up and ran, as the fair man appeared at the tent flap.

'Hurry, he's coming!'

But the man just stood there, looking at us, then went back inside.

We didn't see any more of the fair. When my mother caught up with us, she marched us straight home, leaving my father in the ale tent. She stomped ahead with Annie clutched to her shoulder, walking so crossly that Annie's little head swayed from side to side like cow parsley blowing in the wind. Every twenty yards or so, she'd shout back at us. Did we realise how dangerous it was to wander off like that? Were we idiots, or what? Hadn't we listened to a word she said? If we thought we were coming next time, we could think again. And now, look, we'd made our sister cry.

It seemed to me more likely that Mother's shouting had made Annie cry, but I judged it best to keep that thought to myself.

That night, I lay awake next to Sam, thinking about the woman in the cage. She wasn't a faerie. Beside the matter of being in a cage and poked with sticks, when she danced I'd seen a big hole in the sole of her shoe; what kind of faerie didn't know enough magic to fix that? But if she wasn't a faerie, what was she? It was as though she was an ordinary person, but smaller. Like she hadn't grown. Like me.

Thirty-eight years old, the barkers had said. It had never crossed my mind that a person could get to be that old and still be as small as a child. I'd wanted to hurry things along, but it hadn't occurred to me that my mother was wrong; I wasn't just a late starter. I might never grow.

That morning, I'd woken up smiling, so sure that soon I'd be like all the other boys. In my mind, I'd tried on their long legs and strong, wiry arms, and pictured myself doing the things they did, and seeing my father look at me proudly, like he used to do. I wanted it so badly, and I was so close to having it. Could it really be true that it wasn't going to happen? Not tomorrow, not ever?

It couldn't be true. I wouldn't believe it. But as I lay there in the dark, listening to my father's rasping snores and Annie snuffling like a piglet, I kept remembering the way the little woman looked at me. She'd seen that I was like her. The boy and the man had seen it too. That was why the man wanted me. To put me in a cage, and make people pay to see me, because I was something strange.

Chapter Two

Our house was different when my father was in it. It was only one room, with a table and two chairs, and our pallets stacked in the corner, yet during the day I hardly noticed how small it was. But when he walked through the door carrying his apron, all bloody from a day spent cutting up meat, the house shrank. He was a big man, but it wasn't just his body that took up a lot of room, it was his whole self.

The day after the fair he came home earlier than usual. Sam had gone for milk from the dairy and Mother was sewing, telling me a story about when she was a girl. I'd been lost in my thoughts all day; she kept asking what was the matter, but I said there was nothing. I didn't want to tell her and see in her face that she'd known all along what I was. But of course she had. That was why she didn't want me to speak to anyone at the fair.

She got up to start making dinner.

'Wait a bit,' he said, pulling a coin from the pouch at his waist. 'Here, Nat, go to the baker's and get four seed cakes. Don't let them give you stale ones.'

Mother turned and looked at him.

'I've some good news,' he said.

I didn't ask what the news was. It would only be about the dogs: someone had agreed to sell him a good fighter, or someone else's best fighter had been killed.

The bakery wasn't busy, but the baker was deep in conversation with the blacksmith's wife, so I waited my turn. The blacksmith's wife had her youngest child with her; she was about Annie's age and, like my sister, just getting used to her legs. Seeing a possible playmate, she fixed me with a determined expression and stomped unsteadily towards me, but at the last, she wobbled. I stepped forward to stop her falling, but at that moment, her mother turned and, seeing me, snatched her away. I wasn't surprised; people often seemed afraid of me touching them. But I wondered, that day, did they all know what my mother knew? That I wasn't a late starter at all, but someone like the faerie, who would never, ever grow?

As I left the bakery, Jack Edgecombe was lurking at the end of the street with two other boys. If he had an audience, he never missed a chance to repeat his stupid story about me riding Ma Tyrell's dog, or pretend I was so small he couldn't see me. Usually I answered him back – he wasn't what you'd call quick-witted, Jack, so most times I'd leave him floundering for an answer and make his friends smirk at him instead of me. But that day I took the long way home.

I went to push open our front door, then stopped; inside, my mother was shouting at my father.

'You can't do this,' she said. 'I won't let you.'

She never argued with him. Never. There was no point; once he'd made up his mind he never gave in. But she was cleverer than he was. When she wanted to change his mind about something, she had a way of seeming to agree with him but then mentioning the thing again later, in a way that made it sound like what she wanted was his idea and he'd been clever for suggesting it. Sometimes she had to have a few goes, but she'd usually get her way and he'd end up pleased with himself. 'You catch more flies with honey than vinegar,' I heard her say once to a neighbour who was having trouble with her own husband, 'and you don't have to wear the ribbon to be the winner.' It made me feel safe, knowing she was really in charge, not him.

But now she was arguing with him. A little cold worm of fear squirmed in my stomach, because that meant whatever was happening was something she didn't know how to talk him out of. I pushed the door a little and put my ear against the opening.

'I've decided,' he said, slamming his hand on the table. 'And that's that.'

'You can't do this, John. You *can't*.'

'You must see it makes sense. He can't earn his keep here, you know that.'

They were talking about me. She said something about how I hardly cost anything to keep, but I only half heard. In my mind I saw my father walking into the forest with Jasper and coming back without him, and I understood. The fair man had found me. I never discovered how, but it can't have been hard. Everyone in Oakham knew whose child I was.

'I won't let him be put on show like a freak,' said my mother, and now there was a horrible pleading sound in her voice.

'Lucy, he *is* a bloody freak.'

My hand dropped from the door.

'Think about Sam and Annie,' he said. 'When they want to marry. Who'll have them if people think they could have a child like Nat? Whatever cursed him, they'll think it cursed the whole family.'

I'd heard people say we were cursed before – once Jack Edgecombe even said a witch had stolen my mother's real baby and left me in its place – but my mother always told me they were talking nonsense. I waited for her to say it then, but she didn't.

'It's for the best,' he said. 'And Swires' ten shillings will pay our rent for the year.'

'The rent wouldn't be a worry if you didn't owe so much at the Red Lion.'

Swires must be the fair man, but why would he pay our rent? Then she said it. Quite quietly, but I heard every word.

'How can you think of *selling* him? He's your son.'

'So you say.'

'Not that again. I've told you over and over—'

'That's enough.' He slammed his hand on the table again. 'I won't hear a word more. He'll go with Swires.'

She wouldn't let him do that. Not send me away, to be in a cage.

Tell him. Tell him he can't do that.

After perhaps a minute, she spoke.

'All right. But not now. When the fair comes again in September. Give me a chance to prepare him.'

My father sighed heavily.

'I daresay Swires'll wait. He seems keen enough to have him. But don't think you can change my mind. In September, he goes.'

Chapter Three

In the weeks that followed, neither my father nor my mother told me what had been decided. I told myself I'd heard wrong. I told myself I'd dreamed it all. But I knew I hadn't, because sometimes, I'd look up and catch her brushing away tears. And he, when he looked at me at all, couldn't meet my eye.

I couldn't stop thinking about the faerie, all alone in her cage. Had her father sent her to the fair too? Had she been there since she was a girl? Surely my mother wouldn't let that happen to me. But perhaps the faerie had thought that too, and now there she was, and that was her life.

No. That couldn't be right. My mother would not do that. That day, when I'd waited for her to say he couldn't send me away, and she hadn't, that was just because she knew if she argued, he'd dig his heels in. Now she'd be thinking up a way to change his mind, without him even noticing she'd done it. *You catch more flies with honey than with vinegar.*

But I kept remembering how he sounded when he said I was a freak. He wanted to be rid of me; what if there was nothing she could say to change that? What if the only way to change that was to grow?

* * *

'Are you sure this is going to work?'

Sam looked from me to the tree where he was looping a rope around two low branches.

'Yes. Come on, lift me up.'

He sighed.

'Don't blame me if you end up all long and thin like a worm.'

He hooked the rope under my arms, taking my weight in his. As he eased his hands away, I dropped, gasping as the ropes pulled tight around my chest and under my arms; it was hard to breathe.

'Are you sure—'

'I'm all right. Tie the rocks on.'

We'd collected them the day before: six heavy ones. Sam attached one sack to my ankle. As he let go of it, pain jolted through my leg and into my back. He winced as he let go of the second sack and I cried out. The weight pulled the rope even tighter, biting into my skin.

'I'll get you down—'

'No, I'm all right. Talk to me, so I don't think about it.'

'What shall I say?'

'I don't know... tell me a story. A silly one – that one about the pigs, that Mother used to tell us.'

Sam was hopeless with stories. He could never remember what order things happened in, so he had to keep going back and saying, 'No, wait a minute, the second house was made of wood... or was it straw?'

The pain came in hot stabs.

Remember the faerie. Remember the cage.

'Then the pig, no, the wolf... Nat, you look funny. I think you should get down. You've probably grown loads already.' He glanced at the mark we'd made on the tree, to check against afterwards, and back at me. 'Well, a bit, anyway.'

'No, carry on with the story.'

'All right. Well, the third pig...'

His voice came from far away. There was a roaring in my ears and when I looked down he was at the end of a grey tunnel and its walls were closing in.

'You shouldn't have got me down.'

Dust billowed up from the straw as I stamped around. Why did he have to do that? I could have held on for longer.

'I thought you were dead.'

'You idiot, of course I wasn't dead.'

'Well, you looked dead. Your eyes were closed and you were all white. Anyway, you probably would have been dead, if I hadn't got you down.'

I stood beside the mark on the tree. Sam's face told me the result.

'Not even an inch?'

He shook his head, avoiding my eye.

'Half an inch?'

'I don't know... it could be.'

As I've said before, lying was not Sam's strong point.

'It's all right for you,' he said. 'It's not you who'd have got the whacking if you'd died.'

'I wasn't going to die. Next time, just leave me—'

'Are you joking? I'm not putting you up there again. Why can't you just wait to grow, like Mother says?'

I hadn't told Sam when I worked out what I was. He was my little brother. He was the only person in the world who made me feel tall. How could I have him feeling sorry for me?

'All right,' I said. 'You help me try again with the stretching, and I'll give you my bread, every day for a week.'

'No. It was horrible seeing you go all white like that. I'm not doing it again.'

If he was prepared to turn down extra food, nothing was going to change his mind. I would have to think of something else.

As it turned out, my mother had an idea of her own. After dinner the next day, she waited until no one was around, then handed me a piece of bread.

'Let's see if we can feed you up a bit. Get you growing.'

The next afternoon she sneaked me an early bowl of the broth she was cooking for dinner, and from then on she found a way to give me a bit of extra food every day. As children do, I accepted my good luck without asking where it came from. It was only when I was older and looked back that I understood: all that summer she'd gone hungry, to try to make me grow so she didn't have to let my father sell me to the fair man. But it made no difference. The summer slid towards its end, and still I got no taller.

Chapter Four

A lot of things can change the course of your life. For me, it was a shilling. I always imagine it to be a bright, shiny one, but I never saw it. All the same, I have that shilling to thank for everything that happened: good and bad.

As September approached and my mother still said nothing about the fair man, I told myself she must have found a way to change my father's mind. Then one night I woke, needing to go outside; we didn't have a pot indoors in the summer. As I surfaced from sleep, I realised my mother was crying softly in the dark. Beside her, my father sighed.

'Lucy, the boy has to go,' he said quietly. 'And like I said, if you don't tell him tomorrow, I will.'

He turned over, the straw pallet crunching beneath his weight, and began to snore. But she was still awake and every now and then she made a smothered sound, between a hiccup and a sigh, like Annie did after she'd been bawling for ages and finally stopped. As though there were a few last cries left inside that had to squeeze themselves out.

I don't know what frightened me more: my father's words or those stifled sobs from my mother. I sat up and yawned so she'd think I'd just woken, and went outside. After I'd done my business behind the house, I clambered up the woodpile by the door and perched on top. My hands pleated and unpleated the linen of my nightshift as my father's words echoed in my head.

The boy has to go.

He was going to sell me to the fair man; she couldn't stop him. I felt light, and insubstantial, as though my bones had melted away and I was filled with air. It couldn't be true, it just couldn't be. They couldn't send me away, all on my own, to live with strangers, and get poked with sticks, and never come home again. I didn't want to be a baby, but my eyes filled up with tears, and I sat there as they dripped onto my shift.

The door opened.

'Nat?' whispered my mother. 'What are you doing out here?'

I couldn't say what I'd heard. She'd have to tell me then, and that would make it real. I hurriedly wiped my eyes with my hand.

'I woke up,' I said. 'I wanted to see the moon.'

She sat beside me and looked up.

'It's a big one tonight. Nearly full.'

She put her arm round me and I leaned into her warm, soft shoulder. She hugged me tight, and then said, 'Nat...'

I looked up. *Don't say it. Please don't say it.* But she just shook her head.

'Nothing. It doesn't matter.'

We sat there looking at the moon for a long time. Seeing me tuck my feet under my nightshift when they got cold, she held her hands out for them.

'I want you to remember something, Nat,' she said, as she rubbed my feet warm again. 'You're small on the outside. But inside you're as big as everyone else. You show people that and you won't go far wrong in life.'

Her voice wobbled when she said the last part, and then she patted my feet and said we should go indoors and try to get back to sleep. But I didn't sleep again that night. I don't believe she did either.

Lying there in the dark, I thought and thought about how to stop them letting the fair man take me, but it wasn't until the birds started singing and streaks of light came slanting in under the door that I got the idea. I wasn't going to grow, that was clear now. I'd managed to persuade Sam to try the harness thing once more, but it hadn't worked, even though this time I'd made myself stay up there longer by taking short little breaths and counting to ten, over and over again. All I got for that was a sore back and angry red weals on my ankles. But what if I could show them that, even if I didn't grow, I could still be useful? That being small didn't matter as much as they thought? Surely then they wouldn't send me away?

The harvest was good that year. The wheat stood well over three feet tall and the field stretched out like a big puddle of gold, the ears waving gently in the breeze. I'd had to scramble up a tree to see the cutters on the other side, swinging their sickles wide to get a purchase on each bunch of wheat, then sawing backwards and forwards to cut it down. The women and children followed behind, gathering the stalks into sheaves and propping them together in threes to dry in the sunshine.

I'd heard all about it from Sam so I knew what to do, though I hadn't expected the sheaves to be so tall.

Sam was in the far corner, working on his own, under instructions to stay there so I could sneak across, hidden in the crop, and start helping him before anyone noticed and sent me home. Once the cutters and pickers saw I could do as well as anyone else, my father would realise I was useful after all.

I made a good start, but once I was in from the edge, the wheat grew so thickly I had to push the wiry stalks apart to move through it, and so tall that the way ahead was hidden. Eventually, voices told me I was near the border of the uncut wheat: men joking about something, women chattering, children singing a song about frogs in a meadow. I was still aiming for Sam's corner, but weren't the men's voices closer than they ought to be? As I tried to get my bearings, a scythe came swathing through the stalks. I shouted but it was too late; the man's arm carried on swinging towards me.

There have been a number of times in my life when I thought my last moment had come: that was the first. So when I opened my eyes to see the face of a girl with golden hair, naturally I thought I'd gone to heaven and she was an angel.

'He's awake,' said the angel, in a surprisingly ordinary voice.

A ring of people with worried faces leaned over me: Sam, some of the cutters and a lady who looked like the angel, but older. Instead of slicing my head clean off, the man had only hit me with the sickle's handle and knocked me out. Later I'd have a bump the size of a walnut, but I wasn't dead.

'You'd better take him home,' said the girl with the golden hair. 'He still looks pale.'

'Yes, miss,' said Sam, and swung me across his shoulder.

'I can walk,' I protested, but he ignored me.

When we reached the road there was a carriage standing there, with two white horses tossing their heads and scattering clouds of harvest flies. We'd seen it before; it came from Burley, the big house on the hill. The richest man in Rutland, the Duke of Buckingham, lived there, so the angel girl must be his daughter and the lady his wife.

'She heard you scream,' said Sam. 'That's why they stopped.'

'I did not scream. I shouted.'

He was making me sound like a girl.

'What were you doing there anyway? You were nowhere near my corner.'

'I couldn't see, could I?'

He sighed.

'Mother's going to kill me for this. And I bet I don't get any dinner.'

At first we couldn't work out why she didn't get angry. She just smeared goose grease on my swelling forehead, pulled out our pallet and made me lie down. When my father came in she told him the story, her words tumbling out in a rush, and made it sound as though it had all been the man with the sickle's fault. Sam's eyes widened but I saw what she was doing. My father had said she had to tell me about the fair man that day but with all the fuss he didn't remember, and another day went by. She was still hoping and hoping that at the last minute she'd find a way to talk him out of it.

* * *

She was making stew when he came home the next day. He walked in, looking unusually cheerful, and said, 'So, is Nat ready for his big adventure?'

My insides turned to water.

'John, I haven't—'

'The boy gave you the message? That he's to go tomorrow morning?'

The cooking pot crashed to the floor and hot stew splashed up, bits of carrot and swede and gobbets of gravy spattering the wall. Annie started bawling. Sam said, 'Where's he going?' and at the same time my mother said, 'You can't—'

My father put up his hand.

'No, Lucy. No arguments this time.' He threw his bloodied apron down on the table. 'I'm going to feed the dogs.'

My mother knelt in front of me and took my hands. She was crying now and I couldn't watch her try to explain.

'It's all right,' I said. 'I know where I'm going. I heard him say it.'

'Where are you going?' said Sam. He looked at my mother. 'Where's he going?'

'I tried to change his mind,' she said. Her words were mixed up with sobs and she was breathing as though she couldn't get enough air. 'I didn't think he'd really do it. Perhaps he still won't, perhaps when you get there, he'll see—'

I shook my head.

'I heard him. I'm a freak. And people think we're cursed, because of me.'

'What?' said Sam. 'What are you talking about?'

'You're not a freak,' my mother said, stroking my cheek.

30

'Do you hear me? You are not a freak.' Her face was wet all over with tears and they still kept spilling out of her eyes. 'I'll get you back, I will. I'll think of something, I promise. And—'

My father walked in, wiping his hands on a cloth.

'Make sure you have his things ready tonight. Don't want to keep them waiting at the big house.'

All three of us turned to stare at him.

'What?' said my mother.

'The message I sent – with the boy from the Red Lion.'

'I didn't get any message,' she said.

'Little sod, I gave him a farthing for that. Well, it's good news. The duke wants to take him to London. It's a big chance for the boy, so stop that bloody weeping.'

The girl with the golden hair had told her father about me, my father explained, and now he wanted me to go and live in their house in London.

'But what's he to do there?' asked my mother.

'Be a sort of page, the duke said. Wearing fancy clothes and you know, attending on them. And he'll sleep in a proper bed and get three good meals a day.'

'But he's so young,' said my mother. 'London's a long way away, and—'

'There's no pleasing you, woman, is there? I find this fine opportunity for the boy and you're still complaining. Well, it's this or Swires.'

I didn't want to leave my family and live with strangers. But my father meant what he said and, more than anything, I didn't want to be put in a cage and poked with sticks.

'I'll go,' I said. 'I'll go to London.'

* * *

Sam came with me when I went to say goodbye to the dogs. They were sleeping off their dinners in the shed and Blackie, Patch and One-Eye just lifted their heads, then went back to dozing. But Growler padded up and licked my hand. I stroked his big, hard head and pressed the feel of it into my memory. I was trying to do that with everything – the smell of my mother's stew, the way our front door creaked, the funny face Annie made when she was eating something she liked – so I could keep home in my head and take it with me.

'I don't understand,' Sam said. 'Why have you got to go?'

'Because I'm small.'

'But you've always been small. That's just how you are.'

'And I'm no use.'

He shrugged.

'You were useless in the wheatfield. But it'll be different when you grow.'

I couldn't tell him, even then.

'Well anyway,' I said. 'You heard what Father said. It's a big chance. And once I've been there a while maybe there'd be something there for you as well. I could keep a lookout.'

His face brightened.

'In the kitchens, maybe?'

'Maybe.'

'You promise?' he said. 'You won't just forget about me, when you get there?'

'Don't be stupid, of course I won't.'

I meant it, then.

* * *

Next morning, they stood outside the house, Sam waving, my mother sobbing. They were still there when we turned the corner and took the road towards the big house, where I was to get on a coach to London. My father lifted me onto his shoulders, just the way he used to, saying we'd never get there otherwise, and as we walked he told me about my new life.

'It's a different world down there,' he said. 'There'll be things the likes of us have never seen. Some reckon the duke's the most powerful man in England – I shouldn't even be surprised if the king and queen dine at his house. Just think – my son breathing the same air as the King of England.'

I wanted to ask if I'd be allowed to come home one day. After a year, maybe? Or two? Or if I'd have to stay there for always. But I didn't want my father to think I wasn't grateful he hadn't sold me to the fair. Sometimes over the past few months, I'd wondered: did he wish I'd never been born? But now here he was, willing to miss out on the ten shillings that would have paid a year's rent. Then I was glad I hadn't said anything, because my father said:

'You've done well for yourself, Nat, that's for sure.'

I sat up straighter on his shoulders then, because that was the first time in a long while that my father had sounded proud of me.

Everyone called it the big house; I thought that just meant it was bigger than our house, maybe even as big as the church. But it was as big as all the houses in Oakham put together. We went round to the back, where my father reached up to lift me from his shoulders. I wanted to cling on and never let go, but I remembered how he'd sounded when he said I'd done well for myself, and let him put me down. He knocked on a big wooden door and a woman came.

'My son Nat,' said my father, 'as arranged.'

He patted me on the head, quite fondly, before he walked away.

But you're wondering, I expect, about the shilling. The one that changed the course of my life. I didn't see it, but I heard it, chinking into my father's hand.

'Six, seven, eight, nine, ten…' said the woman at the door, counting out coins. 'There we are… eleven shillings.'

Chapter Five

As he walked down the hill, my father must have reckoned he'd done well. Not only had he got rid of a son who was no use, but he'd got an extra shilling for him. Later, it gave me some satisfaction to realise he'd been cheated; if he'd known where I was really going, he could have asked more. But at the time what I thought was how stupid I'd been, to believe he'd given up the fair man's ten shillings because the duke's offer was a good opportunity for me. He'd just got a better price, and if he'd sounded proud, it was only of the fact that I hadn't turned out to be totally worthless after all.

I had never been all alone among strangers before, and my belly tied itself into a knot as I looked around. People were coming and going, carrying bundles and boxes; I jumped back as a boy staggered past carrying a pile of clothes so high he couldn't see over it. Something slithered down from the heap and fell on me, and there was so much shiny, slippery fabric that I couldn't get out from under it.

'When will you learn to be careful?' the woman who'd answered the door said to the boy. 'You know there'll be hell to pay if that gown's dirtied.'

She lifted the dress off and peered at me.

'Goodness, you are a tiny one. Good job you are though, since we've only two hours to get your clothes ready. Now, let's give his lordship a look at you. He said to bring you straight away.'

The angel girl and her mother were sitting by an enormous fireplace – you could have cooked a whole pig in it – and the man standing beside them wore the finest clothes I'd ever seen, so I knew he must be the duke. There was more lace on his doublet than the rector's wife had on her best frock, and she was reckoned to have the fanciest taste in Oakham. He was tall too, with long black hair and a small pointy beard, and there was something about the way he stood that made him look very pleased with himself.

'Ah, here we are!' he said. He turned to the duchess. 'You were right. Perfect.'

He bent and put his face close to mine. His skin smelt of something sweet, like flowers. I held my legs stiff so they wouldn't tremble as he touched my hair, pulling out a curl between two of his fingers.

'Very pretty,' he said, and looked up at the woman who'd brought me in. 'Blue for the clothes. And gold thread in the lace – that will look well with the hair.'

'Very good, my lord.'

'And get him clean, Marjorie. We don't want to tickle the queen's delicate little nose with the stink of the dog shed, do we?'

I plucked up my courage to speak as I followed Marjorie down a passageway.

'Pardon me, but what did he mean? About the queen?'

'Didn't you know? You're going to live with the new queen, when you get to London.'

I stopped and looked up at her.

'Why?'

She bent down and ruffled my hair in quite an annoying way.

'Because you're such a pretty little thing, and the duke wants a present for her, that's why. Now, let's get on, there's no time to hang about.'

She must be simple. You couldn't give a person as a present. And anyway, my father had said I was going to live at the duke's house in London. She must have misunderstood.

The seamstresses, a thin woman with very blue eyes, and a sulky-looking girl, sat surrounded by shelves of fabric in every colour I'd ever seen, and some I hadn't: rich gold that shimmered as though it was moving; a deep green like fresh oak leaves; the bright red of holly berries; palest pink, like the inside of a snail's shell.

'Blue, he says. And gold in the lace,' said Marjorie.

The thin woman pulled a box down, and rooted about inside it.

'Gold, gold . . .' She plucked out a roll of lace. 'This'll do perfectly.'

'And something plain for travelling,' said Marjorie.

The girl rolled her eyes.

'In two hours?'

'Stop complaining, Lizzie,' said the woman. 'Sooner we get on with it, sooner it's done.'

She stood me on a table and measured me, calling out numbers that the girl wrote down, her tongue between her lips. Then the woman pulled out a roll of fabric that was the colour the sky goes on a clear night, just when the stars are coming out. She held it against me, and nodded.

'Lucky we don't need a lot, I've only a yard and a half left.' She picked up a pair of scissors. 'You can take him now. Best get him washed before we try anything on.'

'But my mother washed my face before I left home,' I protested, gripping my breeches with one hand and my shirt with the other. 'And I don't stink of the dog shed, I hardly ever go in there.'

'His lordship wants you washed,' said Marjorie. 'So either you take that shirt and breeches off, or I do. What's it to be?'

I stood shivering in my undershirt and drawers as she scrubbed me with a rough linen cloth, dipping it in a bowl of cold water and wringing it out hard, as if it had done something to upset her. By the time she administered the final attack, tipping my head back and giving my face and ears a good rub, I felt as though I'd been licked all over by a giant cat. I reached for my clothes, but she snatched them away.

'Fit for nothing but burning, those are. Come on, we'll see how the seamstresses are getting on.'

Perched on the table in the seamstresses' room, I caught sight of my reflection in the window. They'd made a doublet like the duke's, with a wide collar trimmed with lace. There were tiny gold buttons down the front, and breeches in the same material, soft like the fur on a newborn puppy. The boy in

THE SMALLEST MAN

the glass didn't look like me, but when I moved my hand, he moved his too.

While the seamstress was fussing with the doublet's hem, I brought my arm up to my nose. The fabric smelt of nothing. I thought of my old clothes, waiting to be burned. They didn't have the stink of the dog shed, I was sure of that, but if I buried my nose in them, I'd smell home. I pictured my family there, without me, and screwed up my eyes so I wouldn't cry.

Chapter Six

Three days later I got my first glimpse of the city where I was to live. Once, Sam and me stirred up an anthill with a stick and the ants came teeming out, scurrying in all directions, as though every one of them had a different place they needed to get to, and quickly. That, to the eyes of a boy who'd never been outside our small market town, was what London looked like: people everywhere, all going about their particular business, most of them in a hurry. A couple of men dressed in fancy clothes like the duke's crossed the road in front of the coach, the feathers on their hats dancing in time; two apprentice boys in aprons, their faces pimpled with sweat, lugged a wooden chest; women bustled along with shopping baskets laden with parcels. A girl passed by with a basket on her head, piled high with apples, shouting that they were 'fresh this morning from Kent', and a man dragged a big fat donkey, and called out, 'Fresh milk, asses' milk, best milk for your babies', over and over, like a song. Not one single face was familiar.

As we trundled on – so slowly even I could have walked faster – the streets narrowed, lined with buildings that leaned towards each other so the tops of their roofs almost touched. The sunlight disappeared and the air thickened. If the duke objected to the smell of our dog shed (which as far as I knew he'd never been inside anyway), how could he bear the stink of London? It was like a fog you couldn't see, a mixture of smoke and dung and rotting food, with the dark, musty smell of mud and water. It got up into my nose so I could almost taste it, and yet the people walking around didn't seem to notice; they just went about their business as though they were breathing the same ordinary air we had at home.

'This place seems to get bigger every time we come,' said Joseph, the duke's servant, who'd travelled with me. The duke and duchess rode in a bigger coach in front, and a wagon piled high with boxes and crates wobbled along behind. Joseph yawned so widely I expected to catch sight of his breakfast, and leaned back in his seat, stretching out his long legs in front of him. How did he come to be so tired? He'd not only slept through most of the journey, but snored his way through the two nights we'd spent at inns along the way. I'd barely slept at either place, partly because it was so strange to be away from home, and partly because Joseph's snoring was so loud I might just as well have laid my head down in the middle of Oakham's town square on market day.

Since he was awake now, I took the chance to ask if he knew why I was being taken to London. I was sure Marjorie had been mistaken about me being a present for the queen, but he said it was right.

'The queen don't like his lordship, see, on account of the way the king hangs on his every word, and the duke only has to snap his fingers to get whatever he wants. And there's no love lost there, because his lordship don't like her either. Mind you, nor does the king.'

'But why's he giving me to her if he doesn't like her?'

'Makes him look good, doesn't it? She's always complaining he's stirring up the king against her, but there he is, giving her a nice little present. Who comes up smelling of roses then?'

He tapped the side of his head.

'Smart, his lordship is. Come from nothing – well, as good as nothing. His father was a gentleman but only barely, and his mother hadn't a penny to her name. But he got himself so well in with old King James, you'd have thought they were father and son. Which if you ask me is how the king would've liked it – never had much time for Prince Charles, what with his stuttering and stammering, and his strait-laced ways. He'd have liked a son with a bit of a swagger to him, and the master's got that all right.'

Prince Charles was the king now. We'd said prayers for him in church, when the old king died, and people talked about how he wasn't supposed to be the king, his brother was, but his brother had died. I'd felt sad for him then, imagining what it would be like if Sam died, and I felt sad for him again now. I knew what it was like to be a disappointment to your father.

'And now the master's just as well in with him,' Joseph went on. 'Soon as he saw the end was coming, he starts praising him up, and giving him bits of advice. Before you know it, the prince is counting on him like a long-lost brother, and when he takes the throne, the master's right there beside him. They say his majesty won't decide what to eat for breakfast without consulting him first. So if the queen's got any sense, she'll thank him prettily for you, and make up her mind to get along with him as best she can.'

He sat up and looked out as we rumbled through another gate and turned into a broad road. The huddled, overhanging buildings disappeared and we passed fine big houses made of stone, with rows of windows.

'Here we are. This is the duke's house, on the left.'

The house he pointed to was the biggest of them all, built of pale grey stone. It was surrounded by a wall and to the side were trees, lots of them.

'This is just the back. Front's on the river. And that's the orchard at the side. Lovely, it is, specially in spring.' He leaned back. 'You'll have to see it all later though, we're to go straight to get you measured up.'

'But they already made me new clothes.'

'Not for clothes, lad. They've got to measure you up for the pie.'

Chapter Seven

I was a frightened little boy, who knew nothing about London but what my father had told me: that it was a different world, and the people there weren't like us. And I'd already seen that those eleven shillings chinking into his hand meant they could do what they liked with me. So in my innocence, I honestly believed they were going to bake me in a pie for the queen to eat. I thought that must be what they meant about giving me to her as a present.

So I had to get away. Wait for a minute when no one was watching, and run as fast as I could. Which wasn't very fast, but if I could get few minutes' start on them, I might be able to hide somewhere and wait until they stopped looking. I didn't know what I was going to do then: I had no money and nowhere to go.

Joseph lifted me from the coach and as he reached back in for his cloak, I took my chance and ran, darting back the way we'd come, to a courtyard with a big tree in the middle. There were four ways out; I chose the nearest, a narrow path between two buildings, just as the duke's shout came from behind me:

'Find him. Now.'

Running feet pounded towards me. Where could I hide? I ran towards the nearest door.

Don't be locked, please don't be locked.

The latch was high up. I stood on tiptoe, stretched my fingers, but I couldn't reach it. I looked around; there was nowhere else. Crouching down, I bent my legs like a frog, then jumped up as high as I could, stretching my fingers. The latch rattled out of its slot. I pushed the door and tumbled inside as it opened.

The room was piled high with sacks of flour, stone jars and wooden casks. I put my ear to the door. The footsteps stopped; they were in the courtyard.

Go another way, don't come this way.

'He can't have got far,' said a man.

'No,' said Joseph. 'But he's a shrimpy little bugger, he'll have hid himself somewhere. I'll have a quick look down here, you carry on that way.'

One set of footsteps, coming closer. He was in the lane. I squeezed behind a row of barrels in the corner, just as the footsteps stopped outside. The door creaked open: Joseph. I held my breath, my eye pressed to the tiny gap between two of the barrels. As long as I didn't move, he wouldn't see me.

He peered around, gave the flour sacks a kick, and seemed about to leave again. As he opened the door, a shaft of sunlight fell across the floor. He glanced down, and smiled. I followed his eyes to my footprints in the dust. I ran but of course he caught me, plucking me up by the back of my jacket, and holding me in the air.

'Let me go,' I shouted. 'You can't put me in a pie!'

'Is that so? We'll see what his lordship has to say about that.'

The duke looked down at me with the same expression he'd had when he'd said that thing about the queen's delicate little nose. Like something was funny, but he couldn't quite be bothered to laugh.

'What were you going to do?' he said. 'Run all the way back to Oakham?'

By now I was trembling. I kept remembering the bakery in Oakham, and the way the air in front of the ovens shimmered in the heat.

'Please, don't put me in a pie, sir.'

'Why not? I paid good money for you, didn't I?'

'Let me go home, my father will give it back.'

I was almost sure he would.

'And then what would I fill the pie with? Can't let the queen go hungry, can we?'

He must have seen my terror but he just looked at me, his head on one side, a little smile twisting his lips, then turned to Joseph.

'Do we have any beef, Joseph?'

'I expect so, sir.'

'Hmm. Perhaps we should make a beef pie for the queen.' He tapped the corner of his mouth with one long finger, then shook his head. 'No, her majesty isn't keen on beef. And I want this pie to be a treat for her.'

'Please, sir. Let me go home.'

'Perhaps fish?' he said, as if he hadn't heard me. 'But it's so hard to get good fresh fish at this time of year. No, it can't be fish.'

He looked down at me again, with that same half-smile. Then he threw his head back and laughed, and Joseph laughed too.

'They say some bad things about me,' the duke said, 'but no one's yet accused me of eating children. Take him to the bakehouse, Joseph – you can explain on the way.'

'Be careful – drop this and the duke'll have your guts for garters.'

I recognised the cook's sharp tones as the pie, with me in it, was slowly lifted. The heat of the kitchens retreated as we moved towards a swirl of voices. It sounded like a lot of people – over a hundred, the cook said. She'd told me no one was going to eat me, or even put me in the oven. The duke had been laughing at me; the pie was just a pastry box, already cooked, no gravy or anything, and I had to lie in it, dressed in the fine blue clothes, until it was put in front of the queen. Then she'd open it and find me in there. They wouldn't even eat the pastry. I'd asked the cook, and she'd sniffed and said no, they'd just throw that away, it was a terrible waste of food, but she wasn't there to reason why, she was just the person who had to work her fingers to the bone for their whims and fancies, wasn't she? I couldn't believe it was true, that they'd waste all that pastry – it would have fed us at home for a week – but then I couldn't believe anyone would consider it a nice surprise to find a boy in what they thought was their dinner either. But the cook told me they were always putting things in pies that weren't really pies.

'A dozen larks I had to get for the duchess's birthday. Had a devil of a job getting them all sealed in, then she took the lid off, and they flew up to the roof timbers and shat on the company.'

As the pie was placed down, the duke spoke.

'A gift for her majesty.'

The voice that replied was light and clear, but she pronounced the words peculiarly. I remembered Joseph saying she was French.

'Thank you, but I have aten – eaten – enough.'

'Ah, but this is something special. Lift the lid and see.'

The corner of the lid nearest my feet was broken away. 'Hold your breath,' the duke had instructed me. 'Don't move until my signal.' I hoped he wouldn't be too long about it.

'A doll?' She sounded cross. 'You think I am a child, who plays with dolls?'

'No, your majesty. Take off the rest and see.'

The remainder of the pastry lifted away in one piece and a face looked down at me. I didn't know the queen was so young. She was just a girl, perhaps fourteen or fifteen. Her eyes and hair were dark and wound through her hair were strings of pearls. She wasn't pretty exactly, but she had the kind of face that looked like it smiled a lot. She wasn't smiling then though; she looked as cross as she'd sounded.

The duke coughed, and I sat up. She jumped, clapping her hands to her mouth. As the duke plucked me out and stood me on the table, a gasp went round the room and a hundred voices started talking at once.

'A little man,' he said. 'Ten years old, and perfectly formed in every way.'

You'd have thought he'd put me together with his own hands.

'Bow to her majesty.'

As I bowed, crumbs of pastry floated down onto the table. *Should I pick them up?* Then people started clapping, and when I looked up, the queen was smiling.

'*Un parfait petit homme,*' she said. 'I have never seen one so little.'

'T-t-ten?' said a man dressed in black, sitting next to her. 'B-but he can't be!'

'But he is, your majesty,' said the duke.

The king. King Charles himself. Right there in front of me. I guessed he must be at least ten years older than her, and his long face and thin lips looked unlikely to smile much at all. As he stuttered over his words, he closed his eyes for a second, as if shutting out all the faces made it easier to speak. Beside the duke, who'd changed into a doublet spangled with beads that caught the light, he looked like a pigeon with a peacock, and I remembered what Joseph had said about the old king wishing the duke was his son.

'A true miracle of nature,' the duke went on. 'The parents are of ordinary size, and I believe he has two or three siblings, also quite normal.'

The queen smiled at me.

'How – what – are you called?'

I felt a hundred eyes on me as I opened my mouth to answer, and my voice came out wobbly.

'Nathaniel Davy, your majesty.'

'And from where do you come?'

'From Oakham.'

'A town in Rutland,' said the duke. 'It's in the middle of the country.'

'And the smallest county in England,' said the king. 'So small, and he's from my smallest county.'

He looked around the room, and after a second, there was a burst of laughter. I glanced back: every face behind me was laughing, throwing their heads back as though he'd just made the funniest joke in the whole world. The duke laughed harder than anyone; he even wiped an imaginary tear from his eye. The king smiled, but then his face fell when he saw the queen wasn't laughing. He leaned across to her and I heard him say quietly:

'I should have thought you might be pleased that you came tonight, despite your headache. Perhaps you see now that George wishes to be your friend, and has nothing but our best interests at heart.'

'Yours, perhaps,' she said. 'His own, certainly. Not mine.'

He sighed, and turned away from her.

'Her m-majesty seems to be having her usual difficulty in finding the right English word,' he said to the duke. 'But I am sure she wishes to express her thanks for the g-gift.'

Both of them looked at her; she flushed red but said thank you, quite politely. As the duke bowed, irritation flickered across her face. She knew why he was being nice to her, even if the king didn't. I thought to myself – and though I didn't know it then, I'd often think it again – that the king wasn't as clever as you might expect a king to be.

That night, for the first time, I slept alone, in a chamber that was just for me. Exhausted by the terrors of the day, I thought sleep would come quickly, but it was strange to lie without

Sam snoring gently beside me and, despite the heavy coverlet, I was cold with fear. All I'd ever known was life in our little house, with my mother and father and Sam and Annie. Now I was all alone in a world where I didn't know anyone, and as I lay there in the dark, I wondered what was going to become of me.

Chapter Eight

My new home, the palace of Whitehall, sprawled along the riverside for half a mile, with so many buildings, and courtyards and gardens and little streets running between them, that it was like a village in itself. It was so big that the king and queen didn't even live together; she'd brought all her own servants and priests and ladies in waiting over from France with her, and she lived with them on one side of the palace while he lived on his side with all his people. I supposed that was because they didn't like each other. I didn't find out until later it was just what kings and queens did.

That first morning, when a servant took me to the chamber where the queen and her ladies spent their days, we walked and walked through halls and galleries and passageways and I tried to memorise the twists and turns, certain I'd never find my way back again. Finally, we reached a tall double door that opened to the servant's knock. I jumped back with a yelp: there was a giant standing there. He was as tall as one and a half men but thin, with long, spindly legs that ended in the biggest feet I'd ever seen. I had to bend my neck back to look up at his face; it wore a melancholy expression, as though he'd just heard bad news and expected more at any moment. He leaned forward, very slowly – there was a long way to go – and shook my hand. I half expected it to be crushed in his but the handshake was surprisingly gentle.

'Jeremiah Hobley, the queen's doorkeeper. Pleased to make your acquaintance. I hope you won't find it too cold here. There's a stiff old wind blows off that river, gets right into your bones. Beats me why they want to live here, damp as it is, but there's no knowing with people of fashion, is there?'

I didn't know if there was or not, but I said no, to be polite.

Straightening up, seemingly joint by joint, he beckoned me in. 'Come inside then, lad, or the cold will creep in with you.'

At the far end of the room, the queen sat on a big chair, with a red canopy hung with gold tassels. It was on a platform with steps all round, and a dozen ladies were sitting around her, some sewing, one in a window seat, plucking at a lute. They all looked up as I came in and one said:

'Oh, he's so tiny! Look at his sweet little face.'

The others were talking what I supposed must be French. I didn't understand the words but it wasn't hard to tell they were saying much the same thing. Sam would have laughed his head off if he'd heard them. The queen smiled and beckoned to me, and the ladies crowded around, clucking and cooing. One crouched down and stroked my hair, as if I was a cat.

'What are you going to call him?' she asked. 'What about… Lord Minimus?'

'My name's Nat,' I said.

Then I thought, should I have said that? Perhaps the queen was allowed to change my name if she wanted to, like my father did when he bought a new dog. But the queen said, in her funny French accent, that I had a perfectly good name already. A movement caught my eye; there was a small black dog sitting on her lap. She lifted it up onto its back legs so it was standing like a person. It was the ugliest dog I'd ever seen; its nose was squashed flat, and its eyes bulged out from droopy folds of fur.

'This is Bonbon,' the queen said, stroking its wrinkly head. 'Bonbon, say hello to Nathaniel.'

The dog stared at me with a look that said life had disappointed it so far, and it wasn't expecting my arrival to bring any improvement to the situation. And then a strange creature poked its head up behind the queen's shoulder; about as big as a rabbit, but shaped like a person, and covered in brown fur, everywhere except its face and hands. And behind it came another one. The first one clambered down onto the arm of the chair, stood up and looked at me with shiny black eyes. Suddenly it opened its mouth and made a huffing noise at me, showing sharp yellow teeth. I jumped back, almost tumbling off the step, and the ladies laughed.

'This naughty pair are Bruno and Bella,' said the queen.

'What are they?' I asked.

I was trying to make sense of their funny little hands and feet, which looked so much like a person's: were they people who'd been bewitched in some way?

'They're monkeys,' she said, which didn't enlighten me much because I didn't know what a monkey was. Not wanting to look foolish, I decided to ask someone later, and in the meantime keep well away from them. If they were bewitched, they'd most likely be cross about it, and I didn't like the look of those teeth.

'So,' said the queen, counting on her fingers as though she was ticking off a list, 'we must have a little bed made for you, and a chair, and some lovely clothes. Can you dance?'

'I don't think so.'

At home there was dancing round the maypole at Whitsuntide, but my mother never let me join in, in case I got trampled on.

'Monsieur Lefevre can teach you. And you must have the other lessons too. Reading and writing, and of course French.'

I wasn't sure about the reading and writing. Sam went to the village school for a while and came home shaking his head, saying letters and numbers made his eyes hurt. But I didn't want to seem ungrateful and I liked the sound of the bed.

'Thank you very much,' I said. 'But what am I to do here?'

'You are to be my dwarf,' she said, and that was the first time I knew that there was a name for what I was.

Those first weeks, I missed home so much it was like an ache in my belly. I missed my mother, and Sam and Annie, and being able to walk around Oakham and know every face. The palace was so big and full of people that when I walked its long corridors, full of strange faces peering down at me, I felt smaller than I ever had at home. Every single bit of the day was different and strange to me: when I woke in the morning I missed Sam's warm back against mine, and when the day ended at a dinner table laden with goose and partridge and syllabub and tansies, I longed for a bowl of my mother's stew, eaten by the fire.

What I missed most, though, was the hope I used to have. I

wished I could turn back time to the day when I still believed I was going to grow long legs and strong arms, and be able to do all the things other boys did. When I didn't know what I was and I didn't know my father wanted to be rid of me.

But that life was gone, and I couldn't have it back. And so when my knees trembled at the thought of all the faces looking at me, or when I woke in the night and missed Sam's soft snore, I would make myself think of the faerie in the cage. At home, I had been no use, and being no use had almost got me a life like hers. If I was no use at the palace either, they might send me home and, if they did, my father wouldn't hesitate to double his money and sell me to the fair man anyway. So I made up my mind to do my best with the strange new role life had handed me.

Several times a day, the queen and her ladies went to mass; in those hours I took my lessons. The rest of the time, they sat and gossiped, or sewed, or taught tricks to their dogs and the monkeys. And me? I became a doll for them to play with. They sewed me costumes, of satin and velvet and lace, exclaiming over how pretty I looked in them, and when the fancy took them, they picked me up and dandled me on their knees, chucking me under the chin until my cheeks burned hot. They laughed then and said how sweet it was that I was shy, and if you have ever been, or known, a ten-year-old boy, you'll understand how little I welcomed those attentions. But I learned to watch out for the simpering expression that usually prefaced my being plucked up with no control over my destination, so I could step well back and distract them with a song. I applied myself to my dancing lessons, and performed the results to great applause, and when I wasn't singing or dancing, I capered about with the dogs and the monkeys, and said silly things that made the queen and her ladies laugh.

When the queen received important visitors, I would be stood on a stool to recite a poem for them, and one day, I was even lent out as a cure for indigestion. The French ambassador was troubled with a stomach ache, and during his time at the Spanish court, he'd learned that the comical sight of dwarves capering about, while a person was eating, was considered good for the digestion. At his request I was sent to his apartments, where I performed a few cartwheels and did a little jig, during which the ambassador despatched the best part of a capon, a good portion of roast beef, a partridge and an entire dish of syllabub, belching violently between mouthfuls and loosening his breeches three times, then pronounced himself cured. I was glad to be of help, and even more so when he gave me sixpence for my trouble.

If you'd seen me there, singing and dancing, and smiling until my cheeks ached, you'd have thought I was the happiest boy in Christendom. And every morning, I told myself I was lucky. I had so nearly ended up in a cage at the fair, and now here I was, waking on linen sheets in a bed the queen had ordered to be made just for me. I had more new clothes than I could count, fresh underlinens every day, and even a servant of my own, to see to it my chamber was clean and tidy, the rushes freshly laid, and the fire already blazing when I rose in the morning. They got me through the day, those thoughts. But still, every night, as I lay down to sleep, I longed for home.

Chapter Nine

I must have been at the palace for a month, perhaps two, when I saw Charles Crofts for the first time. I was sitting in the window seat, wondering what Sam was doing at home and wishing I was there with him, when a shout from outside made look me down to the gardens below. Half a dozen lads of about my age were chasing around; a tall boy with curly black hair had snatched a hat off one of the others' heads and was holding it out of his reach, laughing. I asked Marie, one of the queen's ladies, who they were and she told me the tall boy was the son of William Crofts, the queen's Master of Horse, and the one who was like him but shorter and stockier was his brother, David. The others she couldn't name, but said they were the sons of noblemen 'sent here to learn about life, and how the world works.' They had lessons in shooting and archery in the tilt yard, she told me, and kept a horse each in the queen's stables.

I watched them quite often from the window after that, and found myself looking out for them when we were out walking in the gardens or when the queen sent me on errands around the palace. Crofts would always be larking around, plucking his brother's hat off and throwing it into a tree or kicking the fair-haired boy's backside and dodging away so it seemed someone else had done it. He was the tallest of them all, and the leader; the others jostled each other and pretended to spar but no one did that with him, and when they rode their horses along the riverside, Crofts' big black stallion always left the others behind. Once, I saw them climb the biggest tree in the orchard, a tall oak with hardly any low branches. I'd often thought that even Sam, who was the best tree climber in Oakham, would have had trouble with that oak, but Crofts' strong arms pulled him up as though it was nothing at all. He was the kind of boy my father would have liked to have for a son.

Before long, all I thought about was what it would be like to be one of them. To be with boys my own age, fighting and running and larking about. And to learn to ride and shoot, instead of sitting in the chamber all day with women and monkeys and dogs, being dressed up and petted and told I was sweet. I told myself again and again that I was lucky to have the life I'd been given, when things might have gone so differently. But still I kept thinking, what a life theirs must be.

I couldn't have it, I knew that. But I was so lonely that I started to wonder, could I at least be friends with them? We were the same age, after all, and sometimes the boys in Oakham had let me join in a game of catch-as-catch-can or fox's footsteps, as long as the numbers were uneven so neither team got stuck with me instead of someone good. And I knew by then that I could make people laugh, with the way I told a story, or mimicked someone's way of talking. Maybe that would be enough to make them like me.

On the afternoon of the queen's birthday, when she was away getting ready for the evening's festivities, I took my chance and slipped down to the gardens. The Crofts brothers weren't there but the others were squatting on one of the gravel paths, playing knucklebones. The fair-haired boy looked up, and I pointed to the stones.

'Can I play?'

They looked at each other.

'Do you even know how to do it?' said one.

'Of course.'

I was good at Knucklebones; it was one of the few games the boys in Oakham played that didn't require strength or speed, and I'd practised and practised flipping the stones up and catching them. By the time the Crofts brothers came striding down the path a bit later, I'd won three games.

'What's this?' said Crofts, nodding at me.

'Nat. He's the one that was in the pie,' said Matthew, the fair-haired boy.

'I know that. What's he doing here?'

Matthew looked uncertainly at me and the others glanced at each other. I nodded to the window above.

'I saw you from the chamber,' I said. 'It gets boring up there.'

'Don't you get fed sweetmeats all day long, like the monkeys?' said Crofts. 'That can't be too bad.'

'I could bring some down,' I said. 'There's always loads, they wouldn't even notice.'

'And what happens if we're playing a game and you fall over and hurt yourself? You'd go running off to the queen, and we'd get the blame.'

'I wouldn't do that.'

He laughed.

'Of course you would.'

'I wouldn't. I'm not a telltale.'

'You swear?'

'I swear.'

He shrugged.

'What are you then?'

'What?'

'They say you're ten.'

'I'm nearly eleven.'

'Then why do you look like that?'

Heat rose in my face.

'I'm ... just small. I'm a dwarf.'

It was the first time I ever said that word out loud and it was like a stone in my mouth.

'You look like a baby.' He glanced round at the others and smirked. 'Bet you still wear a tailclout.'

Before I could answer, he snatched me up and tipped me upside down. I hung, helpless, by my ankles as he poked at my backside, then shook his head.

'Nope,' he said. 'Got to be fair, no tailclout there.' His voice bubbled with laughter as he put me down. 'I'm surprised they let you use the pisspot though – could be dangerous for you.' He mimed someone toppling into a pot, and sang out, 'Help, I'm drowning in piss,' in a squeaky voice, waving his arms.

The other boys were laughing now. And I stood there with a stupid smile on my face. Pretending I thought it was funny too, as my cheeks burned with humiliation. Still hoping they'd let me be their friend.

'Right,' said Crofts. 'You have to pass a test.'

'All right,' I said. 'What?'

He thought for a moment, narrowing his eyes. Then he looked towards the orchard, and smiled to himself.

'Let's see if you can climb a tree. Come on.'

They ran off and I followed, like a pathetic little puppy. I knew, even before I caught them up, where I'd find them. By the time I got there, they were all sitting in the big oak tree, the one even Sam would have struggled to climb. Above its broad, straight trunk, the first branches were well out of my reach. Crofts smirked down at me.

'Come on then, pie boy. What are you waiting for?'

I jumped up and spread my arms across the trunk, digging my fingers into the rough bark, the way I'd seen boys at home do when there were no low branches to reach for. Bracing my legs against the tree, I clung on for a couple of seconds and tried to push myself up, but my arms wouldn't reach and I fell, skinning my palms on the bark.

'That the best you can do?' said Crofts.

I threw myself at the tree again and held on. But as soon as I tried to edge upwards I lost my grip and slid to the ground.

'Our little sister could do better than that,' said Crofts' brother. 'Maybe you should try something smaller. Like a rose bush.'

I should have walked away then, but I wanted to be friends with them so badly. Time and again I tried, while they whooped with laughter. Eventually I spotted a hole to tuck my foot into. By the time I hauled myself up to the lowest branch, my palms were bleeding and my legs shook from the effort. I looked down; the ground was very far away.

Crofts swung down and dropped lightly onto the grass.

'Right,' he said, looking up at me. 'Now jump down.'

He knew I couldn't.

'It's too high,' I said.

'It's too high,' he whined in a baby's voice. 'Well, isn't that a shame?'

I started to climb down, but as I stretched to reach the nearest branch, he pulled himself up into the tree again.

'If that's too high, try this,' he said, lifting me easily and perching me even higher up. I could see, without even testing, that the nearest branches were too far for my arms to reach; I was stuck.

They stood underneath the tree and looked up, laughing. Crofts mimed falling into the pot again and I was treated to another chorus of 'I'm drowning in piss'. Stupidly, for a second I let myself think of how I'd longed to be their friend, and to my horror, tears pricked my eyes. *Do not cry.* I dug my nails into my palms. *Do not cry.*

Matthew said, 'I think we should get him down now. What if he tells the queen?'

Crofts looked up at me.

'Not a telltale, are you, pie boy? You said you weren't.'

You planned it like this. From the start.

'No,' I said. 'I won't.'

'So you'll say you climbed up there yourself, won't you?'

I nodded, and they walked away, laughing. Crofts turned round.

'Just so you know,' he said, 'you're a freak. And we don't keep company with freaks.'

I sat there, stupid and sick at heart, my face burning at the memory of Crofts poking at my backside, and their laughter at my pathetic attempts to climb the tree. A freak. Well, I'd heard that before. Why did I think they'd accept me, when my own father couldn't? And how ashamed of me would he be now, if he'd seen it all?

It was Jeremiah, the doorkeeper who I'd thought was a giant, who rescued me. With the queen away from the chamber everyone was about their own business that afternoon, but he noticed I wasn't there when dinner started and came to look for me. I was shivering by then, my feet and hands numb with cold. Before I'd say what happened I made him promise not to tell the queen. I wasn't going to let Crofts say I'd told tales. And even then, I didn't tell him everything; I was too ashamed.

'He's a bad lot, that Crofts boy,' he said. 'I've seen how he is with horses, and that tells you a lot about a person.' He peered down at me. 'I should think you're hungry?'

I nodded.

'We've missed our dinner, but I think I can scrape something together.' He tapped the side of his nose. 'Got a friend in the kitchens.'

With long, loping strides I had to trot to keep up with, he led the way to a little store room, lined on three sides with shelves stacked high with stone jars.

'Nice and cosy in here. Gets the warmth from the ovens. Sit yourself down on the floor and I'll be back directly. It might be thin pickings tonight but I'll see what I can find.'

The thin pickings turned out to be two meat pies, half a loaf of bread, a piece of cheese as big as a man's hand, five thick slices of cold roast beef and the same of ham, a lump of butter and two mugs of small beer. To avoid any questions about that afternoon, I asked Jeremiah how he came to be at the palace. As he chewed his way steadily through the beef, then the ham and finally the cheese, accompanied by hunks of bread torn from the loaf and thickly buttered, he explained he'd been a groom in a big house in Kent.

'Worked with horses all my life. Then the old king bought a mare off the master of the house, and I delivered her. Skittish little thing, but if I say it myself, I have a way with horses. They saw that in the stables here and offered me a place. Back home, things had got a bit... well, what with one thing and another, I'd been thinking about a change, and so I took it.'

'But you don't do that now?'

'No, the queen picked me out after I brought her horse up for her one morning. Said I was a wonder of nature and she wanted her visitors to see me.'

'Didn't you mind?'

'I did, yes. I loved working with the horses, still go down to the stables to see them when I can. But I'd learned by then, when you look like this' – he gestured at his long, spindly legs – 'you're more precarious than other people, and you're best to take your chances as they come.' He reached for a pie, and ate it in four bites, licking gravy from his fingers. 'But I daresay you've discovered that for yourself.'

I found myself telling him about how my father had wanted to get rid of me because I was no use, and about trying to show I could be useful after all.

'But it didn't work,' I said. 'And then he got a better offer from the duke and that's how I ended up here.'

'And you wish things had been different.'

'I just want to be like other boys.'

'Well, lad, you've had a lesson in life today, I'm afraid. See, you and me, we know that in our hearts and our heads we're just like everyone else. But most people can't see further than the outside, and sometimes it makes them nasty. There isn't much we can do about it, except stay away from the nasty ones. That's my advice to you, and I hope you'll take it.'

Chapter Ten

I was happy to take Jeremiah's advice; I wanted nothing more to do with Crofts and his friends. But it was impossible to avoid them completely. If I was with the queen and her ladies, they limited themselves to sniggering at me, but if I was alone Crofts would call out 'Here comes the freak!' or 'Look, it's the queen's little dolly.' Then he'd plant himself in front of me and block my way when I tried to go round him, so all I could do was look at my feet and wait until he walked off, laughing with the others. He never touched me; he knew he didn't have to. When he stood there, looking down at me and smiling at my helplessness, I felt like an insect he could squash with one foot. And I wished, more than anything, that I could just go home and forget I'd ever seen Crofts and his friends. Sometimes, at night, I would look out of my chamber window at the moon, and think of my mother's words. *You're small on the outside. But inside you're as big as everyone else. You show people that and you won't go far wrong in life.* But how could I show people that, when they looked at me and saw the queen's little doll-boy?

It was at about that time that I began to realise there was

someone else at court who was as lonely and homesick as me. Queen Henrietta Maria was still only a girl, barely five years older than I was. The youngest daughter of the King of France, she'd been sent away from her home and family to marry a man she'd never met, who didn't like her much, and she had the Duke of Buckingham stirring the pot to make sure it stayed that way.

Two or three times a week, they dined together in the Great Hall – it was a kind of spectacle that anyone who wanted to came to watch. I saw how she dreaded those dinners; she'd hardly say a word in the hours before them, and when the time came to leave her quarters, she stiffened her neck and held her chin up, as if she was making herself ready to face an enemy. Sometimes the entire meal passed without her and the king exchanging a glance, let alone a word. More often, he'd speak but only to criticise. 'It has come to my notice,' he would say, or 'I am given to understand that…', and she'd roll her eyes and say 'From who, I wonder?' He complained that her dress was too plain and, on another occasion, not plain enough; that her English was still poor; that she was too friendly with her maids and ought to keep a proper distance, like his mother. He had a way of looking down his long nose at her, as though she was a particularly stupid child he was reprimanding, and then the duke, sitting beside him, would chime in with a remark of his own, always loudly enough for everyone to hear.

She'd always answer back – the time he said she should be more like his mother, she told him his mother was only a Danish princess, and didn't compare to one from France. But when she was upset her English tended to desert her, and that made the king crosser, even though he understood French perfectly well. The evenings invariably ended with him red-faced and stuttering over his words, and the queen flinging back a tirade in her own language, while the duke looked on, like a cat who'd just been presented with a large bowl of cream and had no doubt there was more where that came from.

At the beginning, I thought she at least had a home on our side of the palace, where she was surrounded by the people she'd brought with her from France. But as my daily lessons progressed and I came to understand their language better, I realised there was precious little comfort there either. All they talked about was how the king hadn't kept promises that they claimed were part of the marriage negotiations – things like lifting the laws against Catholics, and building chapels in all the palaces, open to any Catholics who wanted to come. Even I, young as I was, knew that couldn't happen; no one liked the idea of a Catholic queen anyway, and any sniff of her turning the king that way would have people thinking he was going to take us back to the days of Bloody Mary, with heretics being hunted out and burned. But her priests and advisors kept on and on at her, telling her she had to make the king do it, that the pope himself had trusted her and her alone with the job of saving the English Catholics. To her face, they blamed the king and duke, but when she wasn't there, they complained about her, and just like at home, no one noticed I was listening. She wasn't doing enough, they said. She was letting him get away with it, and letting down her country and her faith.

The day I really understood how things were for her was a

few months after I'd arrived. The evening before had ended with another falling out and when a message came that morning, I happened to glance across as she opened it. She flinched at the words, and as she folded the paper her hands trembled. For the rest of the morning she was quiet, and when Bonbon jumped up and started chewing the lace on her dress, soaking it with drool, she didn't even notice.

That afternoon, we went to walk in the gardens. As usual the ladies were chattering like demented sparrows, and there's only so much talk about the relative merits of satin and taffeta a boy can stand, so I walked down to one of the landing stages and sat there to watch the boats, and daydream that I was back in Oakham. It was a Wednesday, I remember, because I was thinking that my mother would be walking back from market. She often used to buy an apple for us to share on the way back, a bite for me, a bite for her, and I wondered if she might be eating an apple and thinking of me as she walked home that day.

A few minutes later, the queen came and sat on a bench just along the bank. She gazed out over the water, but she wasn't seeing the wherries and barges; her thoughts were somewhere else. I sat there, half hidden by the steps, as she unfolded the message from that morning and read it, then reached down and pulled Bonbon onto her lap.

'See what he calls me?' she said quietly. 'A silly little girl.' She buried her face in Bonbon's fur for a moment, then lifted her head and looked down at her with a sad little smile. 'What would they think at home if they saw me now, Bonbon? The Queen of England, telling her troubles to a dog.'

She didn't look like the Queen of England though, sitting

there alone, her face as pale as a winter sky. She looked like the young girl she was, lonely and far from home.

'There you are.'

The queen jumped and wiped her eyes as Madame St George, who was in charge of all the ladies, bustled up and caught sight of the paper.

'What does he say? Why has it taken so long?'

'It isn't about the chapel,' said the queen. 'He gave me his answer on that last night.' She imitated the pompous tone the king often used to her, her mouth pinched as though she'd sucked a lemon: 'It will be built when it's built, and in the meantime, if the rooms here are not big enough, we are at liberty to worship in the garden.'

'Unbelievable!' Madame St George threw her bony arms wide. 'This is an insult to your faith, and we cannot stand for it. Perhaps you didn't make it plain enough – you must insist.'

'Mamie, I have tried. But how can I persuade him when he can hardly bear to be in the same room with me?'

She read from the letter. She wasn't mimicking him now, her voice was small and flat:

I wish you to know that from now on, when I lie with you, it is for the sake of my duty to the country, and not from any affection or desire for you.

'Affection and desire?' said Madame St George. 'What does this have to do with affection and desire? Princesses of the blood do not marry for love, you know that.'

'But don't you remember the letters he sent? He was so impatient for me to arrive – he said he was longing to begin our life together. I didn't seek to marry for love but I thought I had found it all the same. Now he doesn't even like me.'

She must feel like I did, on the day of the Oakham Fair, when I thought I was going to get the thing I most wanted, and instead everything turned bad.

Madame St George bent down in front of the queen, and took her hands.

'Listen to me. You must forget this nonsense of liking and not liking, and accept the responsibility God has given you. The Catholics of England are depending on you. Will you see them continue to be persecuted, forced to deny their faith?'

'No, but I—'

'Then you must make him see. He promised to change the laws, but after all this time, we see no change at all. He promised you chapels – where are they? He does not even pay your people as the settlement requires.'

She pursed her lips and smoothed a wrinkle in her skirt.

'You know I think nothing of money, but it is an affront to *you* that we are not paid and your court is not maintained in the correct style.'

'I know. You're right.'

Madame St George stood up, and the queen did the same.

'Forgive me, I was being silly,' she said. 'I won't let everyone down, I promise.'

She had no one, really, other than that ugly little dog and the monkeys. If I missed my family and my old life, how much lonelier was it for her, even further from home, with the king and the duke finding fault with her on one side and her own people on the other? So after that, I made it my business to notice when she was quieter than usual, when she'd stare out of the window as though she was seeing somewhere else. Then I'd perch on the steps of her chair and do my best to cheer her up. She liked to hear stories about life in Oakham, like the night a rat dropped out of the roof onto my father's face, and he jumped up and got his foot jammed in the pisspot (I didn't say pisspot, I knew better by then). And one day I picked up a bit of her sewing, draped it round my shoulders like a cloak, and swished it about, standing with my hand on my hip and one foot forward, toes pointed as if to show off a finely turned calf, smirking a little half-smile. She looked at me quizzically at first, then burst into laughter:

'The duke in miniature!' She wagged a finger at me – 'Nathaniel, that is wicked!' – but she was still laughing, and from then on, when she was quiet and sad, I'd impersonate the duke, and make him say the silliest things I could think of. It wasn't much, but I just wanted her to know there was someone on her side.

Chapter Eleven

My efforts to cheer up the queen were heartfelt, but they weren't much against the nastiness she got from the king and the duke, and the constant nagging from her side that she ought to be persuading the king to do more for the Catholics. I watched her become more and more unhappy, but I didn't expect what happened that autumn.

It was a trip to the gallows at Tyburn that brought matters to a head. I'd been there a couple of times with Jeremiah, who very much enjoyed a hanging, and had an uncanny knack of predicting, even before the ropes were round their necks, which were 'snappers', whose necks would break and grant them a quick death, and which were 'dancers', who'd dangle, jerking in agony for half an hour or more. Like most boys of my age, I was entertained by any gruesome spectacle, so I was pleased when, on the first sunny morning after a week of rain, Madame St George suggested a walk to Tyburn. That morning, I'd had an encounter with Charles Crofts, in which he'd said my mother must have been a witch to give birth to a freak like me. So when they discussed the excursion, I was too busy imagining how it would feel to be big enough to punch him on the nose to take much notice. It didn't occur to me that there might be any other reason for the jaunt than a hanging, even though I'd never known the queen to attend one before.

It was a mile or so through the parkland, a long walk for legs as short as mine, but Jeremiah kindly kept me company at the rear of the party. As we approached the gallows I was disappointed to see no crowds; had someone mistaken the date? But up ahead of us, the queen and her ladies walked on, right up to the spot, then knelt and began to say prayers. Seeing my puzzlement, Jeremiah whispered that they were praying for the souls of Catholic martyrs who'd been hung there.

'It's not my place to say so,' he said, looking at the passers-by casting curious glances, 'but I think there'll be trouble over this. If the king hears of it, I don't like to imagine what'll happen.'

Of course he heard of it; the duke had ears everywhere. That evening, the king marched into the chamber, his face red and his beard quivering.

'N-now you have gone too far!' he said. 'Kneeling at T-T-Tyburn! What were you thinking of?'

Her little chin went up and she stood and faced him.

'How and where I pray is my own concern. Or have your promises about my faith been cast to the wind now, like all the others in the marriage settlement?'

'My concern is what you prayed for.'

'Since you ask, we prayed for the souls of our Catholic martyrs.'

'You prayed for the men who plotted to blow up Parliament, and kill my father.'

She rolled her eyes.

'I can assure you we did not. Your informant has—'

'And to walk there barefoot like penitents? Did you not see what trouble that would cause? The people already suspect you, must you make them hate you too?'

They hadn't prayed for the men behind the Gunpowder Plot, nor walked there barefoot. But if the duke said they did, the king would believe it. She appealed to her ladies to confirm the truth, but he shook his head.

'Do not compound your difficulties by lying. I have it on good authority you did.'

'Your good authority has misinformed you—'

'Enough,' he said, his hands clenched into fists by his sides. He turned to us.

'Leave. All of you.'

We looked at each other, unsure what to do.

'N-n-now. Or I will s-s-summon guards to remove you.'

The news rippled through the court in minutes: the queen's people were being sent home. All of them, from Madame St George, the priests and the advisors, to the lowliest serving maid, had to go. The king had decided – with a little help from the duke, naturally – that it was their influence that was making difficulties between him and her.

Outside, one of the king's secretaries confirmed it was true. His voice was drowned by shouts of protest but then a piteous cry from the window above pierced the clamour. We all looked up. The queen would have been furious when he said what he was going to do, and tried to argue him out of it, but clearly he'd stood firm. That cry – that must have been the moment she realised he was serious. Then came the most terrible sobbing, as she begged him not to do it. We didn't hear his reply, but I could picture him, standing there with his arms folded and his mouth all tight like a cat's backside. She appeared at the window; he slammed it shut. She banged on the glass so hard it shattered. People gasped, and she started to shout to us but the king caught hold of her, pulling her away. She clutched the window frame and then looked down, wide-eyed, as her hand turned red with blood. He dragged her away and she disappeared out of sight. We stood there, staring up at the window, but she didn't appear again.

That night she took to her bed, crying and refusing to eat or see anyone. Eventually, the king agreed she could keep two priests, her dresser, a cook, a baker and her dressmaker, but the rest were to go. Their complaints about wages owed were ignored, so her so-called friends helped themselves to her wardrobe instead. I don't know if it was true – so many rumours flew about over those few days – but people said she was left with a single dress by the time they'd finished.

The day she returned to the chamber, with her poor hand bandaged, it was a different place, and she was different too. Her French ladies in waiting were replaced by English ones, and among them were the duke's mother, his wife, his sister and his niece, so she was surrounded by his spies. Sitting up on her canopied chair, she looked smaller somehow, and though she answered politely when they addressed her, she barely spoke of her own accord. I did my best to make her laugh with a story about my father's dogs, and she smiled now and then, but it was at parts of the story that weren't funny, so I knew she wasn't really listening.

In the weeks after that, she grew paler and thinner and quieter. Sometimes it was as though she wasn't really there at all. I didn't try to amuse her anymore; there was no point. All I could do was make the steps of her chair my usual sitting place, so she'd always have a friendly face nearby. I hoped it would make her feel less alone.

Chapter Twelve

As the months rolled on, I began to get accustomed to my new life, but I still missed my family. When we sat down to dinner, and the servants brought in plate after plate of meat, filling the hall with rich, savoury smells, I remembered the way Sam's nose almost twitched that day when we walked to the fair, and pictured his eyes growing wide at the sight of such a feast. I wondered what my mother would think of the silks and velvets the queen and her ladies wore, and I smiled sometimes to imagine Annie's face if she saw the monkeys playing. When I thought of my father, though, I just heard that shilling chinking into his hand.

No matter how much I wanted to avoid them, I still came across Crofts and his gang with monotonous frequency. Some days, I'd be bowling along quite happily, not even thinking about being small, and then they'd appear, or I'd hear a shout of 'Pie boy!' And after each encounter, I walked away feeling smaller and more useless.

I didn't even need to see them to feel a tight clump of humiliation in my belly. When we walked in the orchards, the sight of the big oak tree set off Crofts' laughter in my head, and when I danced for the queen in yet another fancy costume, it was as though he was there, grinning at me. I hated him. And yet in my heart, I still wished I could be like him.

'Lad, you've got to stop this,' Jeremiah said one morning, after I'd ranted about how I'd like to be big enough to give Crofts a black eye, like any other boy would. 'You're the way God made you, same as I am, and it's no use wishing we were otherwise. I've a few more years behind me than you have, and I can tell you, trouble finds the likes of us easy enough, so you're best not to look for it. Keep your head down, and what people throw at you will fly right over it.'

I didn't argue with what he said. Since the day he plucked me down from the tree, he'd become a good friend, and he meant it kindly. But I still kept remembering what my mother told me that night just before I left Oakham: that on the inside, I was as big as anyone else. *You show people that and you won't go far wrong in life.* My mother was the wisest person I knew, and if she was right, then surely there had to be a way to show Crofts, and everyone else, that I wasn't a doll, I was a boy like any other?

I gave it a lot of thought over those months but short of a magic spell to make me bigger or Crofts smaller, so I could fight him, I couldn't see a way. And I'd lost my faith in magic spells a long time ago. But that spring, quite out of the blue, I spotted my chance. After the French were sent home, the king decided the queen should show herself to the people more, so we went to the races in Hyde Park. There were two horses in each race, and in the last the riders were a tall man with broad shoulders and a powerful chest – not unlike my father – and a skinny youth who looked as though a strong gust of wind could knock him flat. The boy's horse bolted away at the start, to cheers from the crowd, but the man quickly gained on them, driving his horse past and leaving them yards behind. People were starting to turn away, losing interest, when, just as it looked like the race was won, the skinny lad put his head down and used his whole body to urge the horse on. Suddenly, it summoned a burst of speed. Coming up behind the man's horse, it drew alongside it, until they were matching each other stride for stride. The crowd roared and I found myself holding my breath as, in the last few hundred yards, the boy pulled ahead and won the race. Afterwards, the big man walked over to congratulate him. His playful smack on the back nearly sent the boy flying, and yet on horseback, they'd been equal.

That's how I could do it.

High up on a horse, I'd be as close as I could get to being equal with everyone else. If I could learn to ride and beat Crofts in a race, I'd humiliate him like he humiliated me – the son of the queen's Master of Horse, beaten by her dwarf. And I'd show everyone I wasn't just a little doll to be dandled and petted.

I'd never ridden – to tell the truth, I'd never even been close to a horse – but I had the ideal teacher, didn't I? Jeremiah knew everything about horses, there was no one better. And he was always at the stables, talking to the grooms, so he'd be able to get us a horse to practise with.

I couldn't wait to tell him my idea, but I'd reckoned without his tendency to see doom lurking round every corner. At some length, and with many sad shakings of his head, he warned that it was highly unlikely someone of my size could learn to ride, and even trying would almost certainly result in my death.

'You could easily be killed, falling from a horse. If your back doesn't snap like a twig, you can be kicked in the head, even trampled into the ground. There'd be nothing left of you but bits of bone.'

'But people fall off horses all the time. They don't all die.'

'Yes, but someone bigger, with longer legs and arms, they've got more chance to save themselves. You'll tumble off like a pea from a stick.'

In the end I persuaded him to let me try, but only by telling a lie. My mother, I knew, wouldn't approve of that – she was very strict about lying – but I told myself she'd understand, if she knew I was doing it so I could show people I was big on the inside. So I told Jeremiah I'd forget about the race and just see if I could learn to ride well enough to go out in the park with the queen and her ladies, who rarely exceeded a speed they could achieve on their own two legs. After warning me it would take months and months, if I could even do it at all, he agreed.

Later that day, the queen sent me on an errand to the other side of the palace. I was grinning to myself as I strolled back through the gardens. I wasn't the least bit worried by Jeremiah's fears for me: he routinely saw danger in anything from the odd shape of a cloud to a strangely gamey flavour in the meat served at dinner, but his fears never materialised into more than a passing thunderstorm or a bout of indigestion. And once he saw I could do it, he'd realise I could race Crofts after all, wouldn't he?

As I passed by the stables, Crofts and two of his gang were coming out of the yard.

'Pie boy – out on your own?' Crofts called out. 'Did you fall out of the queen's pocket?'

I hadn't planned on issuing the challenge so soon, but I was so pleased with my plan that I had a sudden rush of courage, and before I knew it, the words were out of my mouth. Crofts' usual smirk was replaced by a puzzled frown as he looked at the other boys, then back to me.

'You want to what?'

'Race you. At Hyde Park.'

'You, race me? Have you bumped your head or something?'

'You should do it,' said Will. 'It'd be funny.'

'Don't be silly,' said Crofts. 'He can't ride a horse.'

'I reckon he can,' said Matthew. 'He wouldn't be asking you otherwise, would he? But if he wins, you're going to look really stupid.'

'If he *wins*? Against me?' Crofts looked down at me. 'I'm not racing against you, you little squirt.'

'Why not? If you're so sure you'd beat me?'

He rolled his eyes.

'Because it would be ridiculous, that's why. Now go back and play with the nice ladies in the chamber.'

He moved to walk away, but I stood my ground.

'If you're refusing my challenge, you must be scared I'd beat you,' I said.

Matthew laughed; Crofts glared at him. He looked back down at me, and shrugged his shoulders.

'All right, you little freak. I'll do it. At the autumn meeting, we'll race.'

Their sniggers followed me as I walked away, but I didn't care. He didn't believe I could beat him, but I'd disconcerted him and, for the first time, I'd ended an encounter without the hard clump of humiliation in my belly. I couldn't wait to get started on my lessons.

I'd told Jeremiah I wanted to keep the lessons secret as a surprise for the queen – though really it was to avoid an audience of Crofts and his friends – so we decided to get up at dawn and go out into the parkland while no one was around. I waited, hopping from foot to foot, too excited to keep still, until Jeremiah appeared from the stables, leading a grey horse.

'This is Shadow. She's a good steady mount, nice and calm.'

Close to, it was bigger than I expected. I looked up at it, and it looked down at me, as though it wasn't quite sure what I was.

'Right then,' said Jeremiah. 'First we'll make some adjustments to the saddle.' He laid a battered sheepskin across the shiny leather, then pulled some thick cloths from his pocket, and rolled them up. 'Now, I know you don't like to be picked up, and later on we'll find a better way, but it'll save us trouble just now if I lift you on.'

The saddle had a front and back that came straight up, but there was a lot of room between me and the front and back parts. Jeremiah tucked the rolls of cloth in so I was wedged between them, and shortened the straps as much as he could, but my feet only just reached the stirrups. The horse took a few frisky steps backwards, making me wobble and grab its neck. If it took it into its head to run, I'd be thrown off like a leaf in the wind.

Jeremiah saw the fear in my face.

'Are you sure you want to do this?' he said. 'It's dangerous, as I told you, and there'd be no shame in changing your mind.'

I remembered how I'd walked away from Crofts the day before, with my head held high.

Do you want to show him, or not?

'I want to do it,' I said. 'Let's get started.'

Very slowly, Jeremiah walked the horse up and down. I sat rigid, my hands gripping the reins.

Look straight ahead; don't look down.

'Well done, Nat,' said Jeremiah, after about ten minutes that felt like as many hours. 'You've got a good line there, but try to remember to breathe, that'll help you find your seat.'

He lengthened his stride, walking a little ahead, and it was all I could do not to flatten myself against the horse's glossy neck and cling on with my arms round its throat. He'd talked the night before about how you had to tell the horse what to do by shifting your weight – 'Put simply, you talk to it through your backside' – but I was so afraid of losing what little purchase I had on the saddle, I couldn't move at all.

I glanced down; the ground was even further away than I'd imagined. The sight made me lose concentration for a moment, and I couldn't hold my balance. I slid to one side, and when I tried to shift my weight back, I couldn't drag myself up. The ground loomed up at me; hooves thundered out their threat to trample me. I couldn't hold on. I slipped, and I must have yelled out.

'I've got you!' Jeremiah said, grabbing the neck of my doublet and swinging me away from the horse. 'You're all right, I've got you.'

It all happened so quickly; even when he stood me on the ground, I was still expecting the thud of a hoof on my head. I leaned down and pretended to brush dust off my breeches, so he wouldn't see the terror on my face.

'Do you want to stop?' he said.

There was nothing I wanted more; the thought of getting back up on the horse made me feel sick.

Think of Crofts, think of him laughing at you if you give up.

'No. I can do it. Put me back on.'

We stayed out for an hour. I was stiff with fear and never more than a couple of minutes passed before I lost my balance and slid off. Jeremiah caught me every time, but the same sick fear drenched me over and over again, as I imagined hooves smashing into my skull. And that was when we were going no faster than a man could walk. I remembered Crofts galloping on his stallion. *How are you ever going to be able to do that?*

Chapter Thirteen

A few months after the French courtiers left, the queen decided to have her portrait painted, to send to her family. I think it was a comfort to her, to know they'd think of her when they looked at it. I hadn't left anything behind that would remind my family of me, and it made me wonder if they ever thought of me now. I thought of them often: a chilly night would remind me of evenings sitting by the fire while my mother told us stories, and when the court poets stood up and recited endless streams of words about the king, I'd remember the silly rhymes me and Sam used to make up about people we knew. It all seemed so far away now, but I hoped they did still think of me sometimes.

The painter of the picture was a Mr Van Dyck, who'd come all the way from Holland. It was his idea that the queen should have me and Bruno the monkey in the painting with her.

'Very curious,' he said, stooping to peer at me so closely I could have counted the pores on his nose. 'So little and yet well shaped. And with the monkey, it will work perfectly for the picture – a glimpse of your life here.' ·

I didn't mind; Mr Van Dyck insisted no one else be in the room while he painted, so for a few hours now and then, I escaped the endless wittering of the ladies in the chamber, which was just as irritating in English as it had been in French.

We assembled in a room on the river side of the palace, where the light was good. The queen wore a blue satin gown; I had a new doublet and breeches in red velvet, and Bruno had a collar to match. Mr Van Dyck positioned me beside the queen, and tried to get Bruno to perch on the back of a chair. But the plan didn't appeal to Bruno, who shinned up the curtains and sat on the pelmet, baring his teeth and shrieking heartfelt monkey curses down at Mr Van Dyck.

'I paint the ape in afterwards,' he said, waving his brush. 'Otherwise we lose the light.'

He worked in silence for a long time, looking at the queen and then back to the canvas. Then he stood back, and looked at me.

'Come forward,' he said. 'There, a little in front.'

He went back behind his easel and resumed painting, peering round it at me now and then.

'So,' he said, after a while, 'how did you come to live here at Whitehall, little fellow?'

'My father sold me to the Duke of Buckingham. My mother didn't want him to, but he did it anyway.'

The queen looked down at me.

'You were not in service with the duke?'

'No, your majesty. He bought me as a present for you.'

'I did not know... But you are happy here, all the same?'

'Yes, your majesty,' I said. 'I just miss my family sometimes.'

'Look to the front,' Mr Van Dyck said, pointing his brush at me. 'I have to get the eyes.'

Now I couldn't see the queen's face. Had I sounded ungrateful? Was she cross? Even now, I could still be sent home.

After a few minutes, she spoke again.

'When you tell those stories, about your home and your family – I thought you had left them long ago.'

'No, I left them to come here.'

I didn't say any more, in case she could tell that thinking about that day made me sad. Mr Van Dyck was screwing his eyes up, staring at the canvas, then stepping back, muttering. When he dipped his brush into the paint, and started again, she said, almost in a whisper:

'I miss my family too. Every day.'

It must be all right to say it then, now she'd said it.

'I miss my mother,' I said. 'And my brother.'

'You have only one?'

'And a sister. But she's just a baby.'

'I have three brothers and three sisters,' she said. 'I miss them all, but mostly Gaston. He's only a year older than me, we played together.'

'What did you play?' I asked, looking up at her. I was curious to know if princes and princesses played the same games we did.

Mr Van Dyck snapped his fingers.

'Face the front. I have many talents, but I cannot see your face through the back of your head.'

'Oh, Gaston was always making up games. Usually they were games only he could win, but I didn't mind.'

She told me about the palace where they lived, and the

toys they had – there was a doll's house that sounded bigger than our cottage – and how Gaston used to play tricks on the masters who gave them their lessons. She was laughing as she told a story about him putting honey in the schoolroom ink, when Mr Van Dyck clapped his hands.

'Enough for today. The light is fading.'

I walked to the window, where Bruno was still sitting up on the pelmet, chewing a tassel he'd bitten off the curtain. The queen followed, and between us we convinced him to leave his perch. As he scampered away, still clutching the tassel, she looked down at me.

'So you are like me,' she said. 'The subject of a bargain. Bought and sold, and sent away.'

I hadn't thought of it that way before. I'd been sold for eleven shillings, and her father had sold her for the promise of an alliance with England and toleration for the Catholics. How pleased my father would have been to know he'd done better than the King of France; at least he'd got his price.

'It was so nice to talk about home,' she went on. 'I can't speak of it to anyone else, not now. Everything I say goes straight to the duke's ear, and he tells the king it means I will never learn to love England. But I think you understand.'

'I think about home a lot,' I said, adding hastily, 'but it doesn't mean I want to go back.'

'Nor I. I was proud to come here, and I want to be a good queen. I just didn't know it would be so lonely.'

She smiled down at me.

'But today I felt a little bit less alone. So thank you, Nathaniel.'

Chapter Fourteen

Every morning at dawn, I sneaked out into the parkland with Jeremiah for a riding lesson, and every day, I cursed myself for challenging Crofts before I knew what was ahead of me. I tried to follow Jeremiah's patient instructions, but my fear made me sit stiff as a twig, and time and time again I lost my balance and slid off. Because I was so small and his hands were so big, he always caught me, so my limbs were still intact, but I hated myself for being so small and scared and useless.

Every night, I would tell myself, tomorrow will be different – tomorrow I'll be better. But every morning, I woke with the same fear cramping my belly, and when I sat in the saddle, I was as useless as the day before. I only kept getting back on because each day I did meant another day before I had to accept that I was what Crofts said I was: the queen's little dolly, good for nothing but dancing a jig or spouting a silly rhyme. And then face his scorn.

As Jeremiah had said, Shadow was a good steady mount, and she patiently bore my tumbles, slowing to a stop after I fell off into Jeremiah's hands, then waiting for him to lift me back into the saddle. One day, as I stood beside her after yet another fall, she reached her head down and nuzzled mine, as if to say, come on then, get back on.

'She likes you,' said Jeremiah. 'Horses always know a good person from a bad one.'

We'd been about to go in but, touched by the horse's show of affection, I decided to have one more go. Jeremiah was adjusting the saddle when a horsefly settled on Shadow's neck. She shook her head, and it must have bitten her; she darted forward, too fast for Jeremiah to grab the rein, and took off across the grass. I didn't have a chance to get my balance, and as she sped up, I started to slip. I tried to pull myself up, but it was too late, I was off balance, my own weight dragging me down.

'Whoa,' shouted Jeremiah, but the bite had spooked Shadow and she just kept running. In panic I grabbed at the front of the saddle, but it was no use, I was sliding off.

You could be trampled into the ground.

'Hold on!' Jeremiah shouted.

I tried to keep my leg anchored over the saddle, but my foot was slipping. My scrabbling to pull myself back up must have frightened Shadow and she bucked. I slid sideways off the saddle and I could see the ground coming towards me and the mud spraying up from the hooves that would kick me.

Nothing left of you but bits of bone.

I lost contact with the saddle and the world turned upside down. I landed on my side with a thump that knocked the air from my lungs. Pain shot through my leg and I crumpled myself into a ball, waiting for a flailing hoof to crack my skull.

'Nat!'

I peeled my hands from my eyes. Shadow was standing

ten feet away, and Jeremiah was running towards me, his coat streaming out behind him and his long arms flailing like the sails of a windmill. Every bit of me hurt. He knelt beside me, his face white.

'I thought you were a goner.'

I sat up and took a breath, wincing as my ribs protested.

'I'm all right,' I said. 'And I know what it is now. I've got to fall.'

'What?'

'I've got to lose my fear. I can't do that if you catch me.'

'Don't be daft. The queen wouldn't want you to hurt your-self.'

I looked away from his kindly smile.

'I'm not doing this to ride with the queen,' I said. 'I lied to you. I've challenged Crofts to a race.'

'You ... well, you can just unchallenge him. Nat, you're brave enough to do it, but brave won't be enough. You're too small, and that's the truth of it.'

'I thought you were my friend.'

'I am, and that's why I won't let you kill yourself with this foolish idea.'

'I'll do it by myself then.'

'No you won't. Because I'll be telling the lads in the stable not to let you take a horse out on your own. I'm not letting you hurt yourself, and that's that.'

Chapter Fifteen

Both of us sulked for a week, then Jeremiah knocked on my chamber door and asked if I wanted to have breakfast with him. He'd often forage a little feast for us from the kitchens to eat after our lessons, but we hadn't breakfasted together since the day I fell off Shadow.

'I have it on good authority there's apple pastries just out of the oven,' he said sheepishly. 'I didn't think you'd want to miss them.'

Though we were friends again, he was adamant he wouldn't help me race Crofts. But I was certain now that if I lost my fear, I'd improve. I'd had my dream of growing taller taken away from me; I wasn't going to let this one go too. I waited a few days, then one morning when we were eating breakfast, I asked about his life in Kent. It was easy to get him reminiscing about how beautiful the countryside was, and he was laughing as he told me about the funny sayings they had down there. Then I said:

'What was it like, when you grew so tall?'

He looked away.

'It's a long time ago. I don't remember it very well.'

'You told me once you were six foot tall when you were twelve.'

'That's about right.'

'Well, did people stare at you?'

'Not people that knew me, but if I went off the estate they did. I was a bit hard to miss.'

'Didn't you mind?'

'Like I said, it was a long time ago ...' He sighed. 'All right. Since you ask. They threw stones at me, the local lads. Called me a monster.' He sat back and stared up at the ceiling. 'And then a girl was attacked one night, and the village blamed me. She didn't say it was me, she didn't even say the man was tall. But I was the odd one, and that was good enough for them.'

'What happened?'

'Luckily for me, there'd been a big hunt that day, so we were still settling the horses well after dark, and there were six good people who could swear I was in the stables when it happened. Otherwise I don't know how it might have gone. And you know what, Nat?'

He looked at me; were there tears glistening in his eyes?

'After that the village women crossed the road if they saw me coming. Or they'd huddle together, as though I might take it into my head to grab them, right there in the middle of the street.'

'But they knew it wasn't you.'

He shrugged.

'It didn't matter. They'd decided I was a monster and that was that. Anyway.' He rubbed an enormous hand across his eyes. 'It's a long time ago.'

'I didn't mean to upset you.'

He smiled.

'No, lad, you weren't to know. But you're a crafty one, Nat – you meant to make me think, and you have. I understand it now: you want to show them you're not what they think you are. And the truth of it is, that's what I should have done, instead of just keeping my head down, and letting people believe what they wanted to.' He stood and brushed the crumbs of breakfast off his breeches, then looked at me for a long moment. 'All right. We'll give it a try. But if you die, and the queen puts me in the Tower, you'd better haunt the place and get me out.'

Chapter Sixteen

Every few weeks, I'd stand beside the queen, as Mr Van Dyck painted and muttered. She talked more and more about her family, and life in France, and after a time she began to ask me about English customs and sayings that she didn't understand.

'I will never master this language,' she said after I'd explained one day that raining cats and dogs just meant raining hard. 'But at least you don't laugh at me when I ask, like everyone else does.'

Most of all, she talked about Gaston, the brother she missed as much as I did Sam.

'Was he sad that you left?' I asked one afternoon, remembering Sam standing outside our house and waving until we couldn't see each other anymore.

'Yes, he was. He came all the way to the ship and we cried when we parted. But we always knew I would have to go away when I married, just like my sisters. They're braver than me though, and they seem to be happy. I thought it would be the same for me, but it isn't.'

She sounded so sad that I didn't think before I spoke.

'But that's not your fault,' I burst out. 'That's the duke's fault, and the king's for listening to him.'

I looked up: had I gone too far? When we talked about home, and our families, it was easy to forget she was the Queen of England, but she was, and he was the king, and I wasn't sure if it was all right to say what I'd said. Mr Van Dyck snapped his fingers.

'Please! Face the front.'

I held my breath, but she wasn't angry.

'I know you don't like the duke any more than I do,' she said. 'But what can I do, when the king likes him so well, and me so little?'

I didn't know how to answer that. I admired the way she held her own against the king and the duke, always fighting back when they criticised her, but it wasn't getting her anywhere. I'd noticed how the king would glance across to the duke when they argued, and get an encouraging nod. It wasn't hard to imagine the conversations that nod represented; the duke telling the king that he wouldn't take that kind of thing from any wife of his, and the king ought to keep his uppity little queen in line. So every time she fought back, she was playing into his hands. But there was another way – the one I'd seen work so many times on my father.

'I think you should do what the duke does,' I said. 'With the king, I mean.'

'What Buckingham does?'

'He never argues with him. He flatters him and tells him what he wants to hear.'

'So you think it's my fault then, that I should have been more pleasant to him?'

I risked Mr Van Dyck's clicking finger and turned round. I must have looked worried; she shook her head.

'No, I'm not angry. Nathaniel, no one speaks the truth to me. The duke and the king say I shouldn't keep causing trouble. My courtiers told me I should fight them harder. And look where listening to that has brought me. So tell me what you think.'

And so I found myself telling the Queen of England about my mother's belief that you catch more flies with honey than with vinegar, and you don't have to wear the ribbon to be the winner.

'Your mother sounds a very wise woman,' she said.

'Oh, she is. She's much wiser than my father, because he always thought he'd won, even when he hadn't.'

I smiled to myself, thinking of what my mother would say if she knew I was passing on her advice to the Queen of England.

'And you really think I can also do this?' said the queen. 'When the king doesn't even like me?'

'I don't know, your majesty. But I think if you don't try, well then...' I hesitated, but she nodded for me to go on. 'If you don't try, you've let the duke win. And he shouldn't win.'

She thought for a moment.

'You're right. What you suggest, I think it will be hard. But to let him win – perhaps that would be harder.' Mr Van Dyck gave an irritated sigh as she turned and looked down at me. 'I came here to be queen, and if I have to use honey, that's what I will do.'

* * *

99

Of course, it wasn't as easy as that. My mother had had years of doling out honey instead of vinegar, and even she couldn't always make it work. And she didn't have someone as clever as the duke trying to turn my father against her. With his help, the king and queen continued to fall out regularly, and the entire court knew they rarely spent the night together. But one evening, at one of the public dinners she used to hate so much, she said something to the king and, after a moment's hesitation, he laughed. He didn't laugh very often – never with her – and when the duke saw it, he looked like a man who'd lost a shilling and found a thimble. When she saw I'd noticed, she made a little sign with her finger, like a bee flying through the air.

Not long after that, she had her first triumph over the duke. By then, everyone in England knew he was all but running the country, and people didn't like it: there was a rhyme that went around, saying the king ruled the kingdom, but the duke ruled the king and the devil ruled the duke. Relations with the French had got worse, because – of course – the laws against Catholics hadn't been abolished, and when the King of France started persecuting French Protestants, the duke saw a way to make himself more popular. Some Protestants were under siege in the port of La Rochelle, and he persuaded the king that if they sent the navy to rescue them, the country would be grateful to their victorious monarch and his favourite advisor. The duke even decided to command the fleet himself, though to the best of my knowledge, the most commanding he'd ever done was to his tailor, about the placement of beads on his doublets.

At his farewell banquet, he couldn't resist trying to provoke the queen. He gave a speech about how they were going to sail to victory, and at the end, he turned to her and said:

'It is regrettable we must take this action against the family of our queen, but the French have shown we cannot trust their promises.'

The entire room held its breath; everyone was expecting her to give him an earful about how the French weren't the only ones who hadn't kept their promises. But she looked up at him, her face a picture of innocence, and said:

'I also regret the need for this fight. But I am Queen of England, and so of course I hope England will be victorious.'

He flinched as though she'd poked him in the eye with her spoon, but recovered quickly and bowed. The king patted her hand and said how wise she was becoming, and the duke had no choice but to smile one of his oily smiles and agree. When she glanced over at me a few minutes later, I lifted my finger and made the sign of a bee flying.

Chapter Seventeen

With the duke away, the queen took the chance to spend more time with the king, and that meant I could snatch some extra riding practice with Jeremiah during the day, walking Shadow further into the parkland around the palace to make sure no one saw us. And I turned out to be right; surviving that first fall chased away the crippling fear that made me sit so stiffly in the saddle. I still fell; bits of me were black and blue and some mornings my muscles ached so badly I could barely stand. But I'd learned to tumble away from Shadow's hooves and, week by week, the falls became less frequent. Because I was so small and light, Jeremiah had to come up with different ways to do things, and we had to try lots of tricks that didn't work before we found the ones that did. But when, one morning, I finally got Shadow to move off, walk and stop, all by myself, I almost burst with pride. I wished, that day, that my mother could have seen me.

Soon, we'd progressed from walking to trotting. But if I wanted to race against Crofts, I'd have to gallop, standing up in the saddle, and that last step still defeated me. Jeremiah tried every trick he could think of, but nothing worked.

Just when I thought I'd never get it, it was Shadow who showed me what to do. Probably by accident, but I don't know; she was a very clever horse. We set off at a trot, as usual, and as she went into a canter and I eased myself up, for some reason she kicked up her back legs. Usually when I lost my balance, I slid to one side, but the movement jolted me forward and without thinking about it I grabbed at her mane, winding my fingers into the thick, coarse hair. And I stayed on.

'Nat! That's it!' shouted Jeremiah as he loped along behind us. 'Just stay like that, you're there!'

When I pulled Shadow up beside him, he was dancing on the spot, waving his long arms in triumph. We'd circled the paddock at a gallop and though I'd wobbled once or twice, somehow, reaching forward and twining my hands into Shadow's mane had put me in just the right position to keep my balance.

From then on, we seized every possible moment. By the time the autumn race meeting was three weeks away, I could gallop the entire distance. Even Shadow was pleased with me, bending her head to nuzzle my shoulder when I slipped down off her back at the end of a ride. Jeremiah had attached a special strap to the saddle so now I slid down by myself, and we'd worked out what to do about getting on too. There'd be a mounting block with steps at the park, so we'd practised with the one at the stables early in the mornings, when only the grooms were around. Holding on to the strap, I could just about manage to scramble into the saddle from there. It wasn't elegant, but it would do.

* * *

Up there on Shadow's back, flying along, I felt equal to anyone, and as the races got closer, fear turned to excitement. My mother's advice about not having to wear the ribbon to be the winner might be working for the queen, but Crofts was never going to leave me alone unless I humiliated him the way he humiliated me. And I began to believe that I could, once and for all.

But the day before the races we went into the city, and as we came back on the royal barge, Crofts and the other boys were riding along the riverside. I watched as he pelted along ahead of the others, seemingly without the slightest effort, and my heart hit my boots. When I rode Shadow, we were a team, but Crofts rode as though his horse was part of him. How had I ever thought I could beat that?

I didn't realise he'd seen me watching but he must have guessed I was on the barge with the queen. As we walked up through the gardens, he was standing by the path, pretending to fiddle with his boot. He waited until the queen and her ladies had passed by before he stood and looked down at me.

'The queen's little dolly,' he said. 'Got your hobby horse ready for tomorrow?'

I went to walk on, but as usual he stood in front of me and blocked my way.

'You can't even ride a horse, can you?' he said.

'You'll find out tomorrow, won't you?'

'Are you serious? You really want to do this?'

'I said so, didn't I? And you accepted my challenge.'

He shrugged.

'Have it your own way, pie boy.'

As he turned to walk away, he said, 'Should be a good crowd tomorrow, three hundred or so. And they're all going to be laughing at you.'

That night I had a nightmare about the race. As I walked up to the mounting block, Shadow turned into Ma Tyrell's dog, from Oakham. Then she was a horse again, but I got on facing the wrong way, and she started running before I could turn round. I slipped off her rump and as the ground rushed towards me, I woke up, sweating. What if I fell off as soon as Shadow moved? What if I couldn't even manage to get on? As I lay there in the dark, I asked myself why I'd ever come up with such a stupid idea. I'd wanted to stop Crofts humiliating me, and now here I was, helping him to do it.

Chapter Eighteen

The day of the race was bright and sunny, drawing an even bigger crowd than usual. I'd barely slept after waking from my nightmare, and by morning my stomach was a knot that twisted tighter every time I thought about the race. Sitting in the stand with the king and queen's party, I looked out at the hundreds of spectators ranged behind the posts that marked out the circular course, and imagined the roar of all those people laughing at me.

It's no good; I can't do it.

Jeremiah had put my name and Crofts' down to race when we arrived that morning, but he could just as easily take us off the list again. I tapped his arm.

'What is it, lad?' He looked at me very seriously. 'Do you want to pull out? Because if you do, I'll not think any the less of you. You've been brave, and you've made yourself a better rider than many. There'd be no shame in leaving it at that.'

So he didn't think I could do it either. And who knew better than him?

'But listen to me.' His voice was gruff, almost cross. 'I know you. I know what you can do when you put your mind to it. You're the bravest boy I ever met, and to my mind it'd be a damn shame if you don't take the chance to show it.'

'Of course I'm doing it,' I said. 'I wasn't thinking of pulling out.'

'I thought not. Well, let's go and get ready, shall we?'

I kept my eyes straight ahead as I rode to the start, ignoring the curious murmurs.

'What if they won't let me race?' I said to Jeremiah. 'When they see me?'

'I've told them. You're the queen's dwarf, and she's given special permission.'

'But—'

'They're not going to take it into their heads to go and ask her, are they?'

Crofts was there waiting, with the other boys. The black stallion was even bigger than I remembered. It looked at Shadow and I could swear it smirked, just like its master. But when Crofts saw me, surprise flashed across his face, just for a second, before he recovered his usual mocking grin.

'So, pie boy, you can sit on a horse. And not even side saddle.'

I leaned down to fiddle with my boot so he wouldn't see my white face and shaking hands.

'How about I give you a head start?' he said, pointing at a place halfway round. 'As far as the second bend. Don't want people saying I had it too easy.'

'Nat doesn't need a head start,' said Jeremiah. 'He'll race you fair and square.'

'That's right,' I said, but my chest was tight and annoyingly my voice came out small and croaky.

Crofts threw back his head and laughed.

'Pie boy, you are cracked in the head.'

'Cracked!' echoed his brother, shaking with laughter.

Jeremiah was adjusting the stirrups. He stood up then, squeezed my shoulder and said very quietly, 'You'll show 'em, Nat. You'll show 'em.'

I took a breath.

'Are you ready?' I said to Crofts. 'Because I am.'

We'd agreed on three laps, but Crofts pulled ahead easily as soon as the rope went up. As he reached the halfway point, he was already so far in front I had no hope of catching him. Even after my nightmare, a small part of me had hoped I might beat him, but of course that was stupid. The best I could hope for was to get round as fast as I could without falling off. I'd prove I could ride and that would have to be enough.

Then, up ahead, he reined the stallion in and stopped. Taking a carrot from his pocket, he held it up, and leaned round to feed it, very slowly, to his horse. The crowd erupted into laughter. My cheeks burned but I urged Shadow on. Even if we couldn't win, I owed it to Jeremiah – and, I realised suddenly, to Shadow, who tried so hard for me – to do my best.

Crofts let us pass him and finish the first lap before he kicked the stallion into action again. I leaned into Shadow and she responded; for a few moments, we kept our lead, but he was coming up behind us, and though we were going faster than we'd ever done, he passed us again, looking back and giving me a cheery wave. I gritted my teeth and kept going.

Crofts looked back again, grinning. He slowed down, and this time, he wheeled his horse round in circles, as though it was dancing, while he waved and bowed to the laughing crowd. Then, over the pounding of Shadow's hooves, someone shouted:

'Come on, the little man! Come on!'

Good old Jeremiah.

But it wasn't. I was concentrating so hard on driving Shadow forward that it took a few minutes before the thought fell into place. Jeremiah would never have called me that. What I could hear was people cheering for me.

'Come on, dwarf!'

'You show him!'

Once again, Crofts let me pass him. This time I held the lead for a little longer, spurred on by the cheering, but it was a matter of moments before he came up behind us again, yelling:

'Come on, pie boy, is that the best you can do?'

One more lap to go. By now I was expecting him to stop again before the finish and, sure enough, he yanked back on the reins, turning round and starting to shout something at me. But he must have pulled too hard; the big black horse stopped so suddenly that he was hurled forward, flying over its head to hit the ground with a thud. There was a gasp from the crowd. For a second he lay there, then a sigh of relief rippled around as he clambered to his feet.

A cheer rang out as I passed him. But he was getting back up on his horse, and the finish still looked far away.

In my head Jeremiah's words pounded in time with Shadow's hooves. *You'll show 'em, you'll show 'em.* I kept my eyes on the end of the course, but Crofts was coming up behind me now.

'Out of the way, pie boy!' he shouted.

He was getting nearer, but Shadow kept up her speed.

'He's going to do it!' someone yelled. 'The dwarf's winning.'

We held our lead for a minute or so, but the black stallion was beginning to gain on us. He was going to pass us. He was still going to win. Shadow was running as fast as she could, but it wouldn't be enough. With fifty yards to go, Crofts drew level, and smirked across at me.

'Get your little pony,' – he kicked out at Shadow – 'out of my way.'

His foot hit her side, and it must have frightened her, or annoyed her. She skittered a little, and then from nowhere she found an extra burst of speed. I gripped her mane as we passed Crofts' horse, and got clear ahead of it. He shouted out and urged his horse on, but Shadow kept going, she didn't slow for a second. The finishing line drew nearer and nearer, and the crowd was shouting, but then Crofts started to draw level with us. *That's it. He's going to win.* I closed my eyes so I didn't have to see him pass us after all that. And then there was an enormous cheer, and I opened my eyes, and we'd won. By little more than a head, but we'd won.

Chapter Nineteen

Jeremiah was dancing up and down at the finish line.

'Did you hear the cheers, Nat? You did it!'

Crofts' face as he dismounted was one of the sweetest sights I ever saw. His friends ran up.

'He beat you,' said Will. He could hardly speak for laughing. 'The dwarf beat you.'

'I let him win,' said Crofts. 'Surely you saw that?'

'Didn't look like you were letting him win at the end there,' said Matthew. 'Looked like you couldn't get past him.'

'What? You can't really think—'

I strode over and stood in front of him, like he used to with me.

'Must be embarrassing,' I said. 'Being beaten by me.'

The other boys smirked.

'I *let* you win,' said Crofts.

'Why would you do that?' I asked. 'You said you'd beat me.'

The others looked at him. Crofts shook his head, and stalked away.

'You're thick, you lot,' he shouted over his shoulder, 'I let him win. Anyone can see that.'

The queen was talking to Jeremiah. I ran across, grinning all over my face. But my smile froze at what she was saying.

'How could you be so ... so ...' She was struggling for the right English word. That only happened now when she was really angry, or really upset. '...so foolish! He could have been killed.'

She saw Jeremiah catch my eye, and spun round.

'And you – what were you thinking, to put yourself in danger like that?'

I wasn't sure what to say. She was supposed to be pleased. She was supposed to be proud of me.

'I just ... I wanted to show I could do the things other boys do.'

'But you are not other boys. You are my dwarf.'

'I'm a dwarf. But I'm not a doll. That's what everyone sees, when they look at me, but your majesty, I'm not much younger than you were when you came here. I'm nearly a man, and nobody sees it.'

'And you thought to show it by risking your life?'

'I wasn't. It took months and months, but now I can ride as well as anyone.'

'Well, I forbid you to ride again.'

'But—'

'And anyone allowing you to take a horse from my stables will be dismissed immediately.'

She turned and stalked away.

'What are you doing?' said Jeremiah, when he came to my chamber that evening. 'It's dinner time.'

'I'm packing,' I said, though in truth I didn't know what to take. I'd brought nothing much of my own with me, and it felt like stealing to take the clothes the queen had had made for me.

'Nat, come on, don't be daft. You can't leave.'

'You said I couldn't learn to ride a horse, remember? I did that, now I'm doing this.'

I sounded braver than I felt. I had no idea where I could go; the only other place I knew was Oakham, and I wasn't going to go there and let my father double his money by selling me to the fair. But I kept telling myself I'd done one impossible thing, and if I had to, I'd do another. Learning to ride had started out as revenge on Crofts, and make no mistake, it was sweet to have beaten him. But discovering that, on Shadow's back, I really could be equal to anyone, that was sweeter. How could I give it up? And it wasn't just that. I'd believed the queen had come to see me as a friend, but I was wrong. She talked to me because she had no one else, but I was still just a little doll to her. It stung to think how stupid I'd been.

'She was only angry because she was frightened for you,' said Jeremiah. 'She's very fond of you, you know.'

'Just like she's fond of Bonbon, and the monkeys.'

'Nat, don't cut your nose off to spite your face. We're not like other people and it's not so easy to find our way in the world as it is for them. You've beaten the Crofts boy, like you wanted to, and beaten him well. And tonight, you'll sleep in a warm bed, with a full belly. Can't it be enough?'

I wavered then, I can't deny it. I thought of the faerie woman in her cage, and the people who'd called kind, gentle Jeremiah a monster. But I shook my head.

'I've made up my mind. I'm going tomorrow, at first light.'

He sighed.

'Well, I can't stop you. But don't go so early. Stay and have breakfast with me, for old times' sake?'

'All right,' I said. 'For old times' sake.'

We stretched out our breakfast for as long as we could. The thought of walking away from Jeremiah made me feel a sadness I hadn't known since I heard that eleventh shilling clinking into my father's hand. And for all I was angry with her, I'd miss the queen too. When at last we'd eaten the final crust of bread, and finished the dregs of the beer, he walked with me to the gates.

'You're sure you won't change your mind? It's a cold world out there,' he said, as our footsteps slowed.

I shook my head.

'There must be something out there I can do.'

'Well, if there is, lad, you'll find it. Of that I'm sure. But if you ever—'

'Hey! You there! Dwarf!' One of the queen's guards ran towards us. 'Everyone's looking for you!'

She must have found out I was going. I started running, but of course he caught me up in just a few steps.

'The queen wants to see you. At the stables.'

Chapter Twenty

As we walked to the stables, I kept thinking about what she'd said after the race, that anyone who let me take a horse would be dismissed. Was she going to ask who'd let me take Shadow out before, so she could get rid of them? It wasn't like her to be vindictive, but she'd been so angry, perhaps she would. And it would be all my fault.

She was standing there with Crofts' father, her Master of Horse. Surely she wasn't going to dismiss him too? For all I hated Crofts, I didn't want that. At least I could tell her his father hadn't known anything.

'Your majesty, I need to explain—'

'You explained yesterday.'

'But it wasn't—'

'You explained yesterday, but I was too angry to listen. You gave me a terrible fright, you know.'

'I know, I'm sorry, but—'

'But I've thought about what you said. I know how it is to be treated like a child when you are no longer one.'

I stared up at her.

'So,' she said, gesturing towards the stables. 'Choose. Which one would you like?'

'Your majesty?'

'Choose a horse. One of your own, to ride when you like.'

I walked across to the stable block, where Shadow was standing with her head out of the door, as though she'd listened to every word. I held up my hand and she stretched down to nuzzle it.

'I'll take this one,' I said.

I can't say that after that day no one ever treated me like a doll again. People still plucked me up off the ground without warning, and the queen never lost her delight in ordering me new costumes, and seeing me dress up in them. But my life did change. As well as giving me Shadow to ride, the queen arranged for me to take lessons in archery and shooting with Will, Matthew and the other boys, and even though they were ahead of me when I started, I practised and practised at both until I was as good as they were.

The Crofts brothers left court a few months after the race – I heard their father sent them to live with an uncle in Northumberland, to learn about managing an estate. Crofts' friends were different, once Crofts was gone, and we never spoke of how they'd treated me before. I didn't know then that he would come back into my life one day, and I was very much the happier for that.

The other thing that happened was I became quite famous. Hundreds of people had seen me in the race and because, even for a dwarf, I was so small, they were curious.

'Look at this,' said Jeremiah one morning, waving a news pamphlet at me. 'It's about you!'

My eyes widened as I read it:

THE SMALLEST MAN IN ENGLAND!

Spectators in Hyde Park last week were agape to see a dwarf of minuscule proportions take part in the races, and win. The tiny fellow goes by the name of Nathaniel Davy, and resides at the queen's court. Said to be twelve years old, he stands no taller than an infant - a veritable Miracle of Nature!

Shortly afterwards, one of the court poets wrote a long poem about me, and though it was really just a pile of nonsense, when it was printed, people flocked to buy it. And when we walked in the park, people nudged each other, saying, 'That's the queen's dwarf – the smallest man in England.' When I heard them, my stomach no longer churned with shame; I felt special, even proud. Sometimes I'd walk a little apart from the others, to make sure I'd be seen, exhibiting something of a swagger when people were watching.

I still missed my mother and Sam, but as time went by, I found myself thinking about Oakham less and less, and one day, as the towers and turrets of Whitehall came into sight after a long trip down the river to Hampton Court, I realised the palace had come to mean home to me now. I had left my old life behind, and it began to seem a distant memory.

My only wish was to see the queen happy too. During the months that the duke was away on the expedition to La

Rochelle, she and the king had had some time to get to know each other, unhindered by his poisonous interventions, and it looked as though my mother's advice was paying off. By the time the fleet limped home, chased off by the French with thousands of men lost, the two of them weren't exactly lovebirds, but they could stay in each other's company for an evening without war breaking out, and there was even a rumour the queen was expecting a child. It turned out not to be true, but we all saw – not to be too indelicate about it – that the necessary was taking place.

But once the duke got home, he slipped straight back into place like a greased eel. At the slightest sign the king might listen to her instead of him, he'd find a way to come between them, and the king always took his side. At heart, I think he was still the unloved son who'd been so pathetically grateful for the duke's approval, and he couldn't contemplate losing it, even for a moment. Even when London bubbled with rumours that the duke was plotting to take over the country and kick out the king, even when Parliament came right out and said he was the cause of all England's problems, the king's devotion to him didn't waver.

Despite the disastrous end to the campaign in La Rochelle, the following year the king agreed to a second attempt, certain that the duke would return victorious and be proclaimed as a hero. We journeyed down to Portsmouth for the king to inspect the fleet, and Buckingham walked us round the harbour, where lines of ships were swarming with men getting them ready to sail, and a crowd had gathered to watch. Wearing his smuggest smile, he pointed out the guns on one, and the gigantic sails on another, and the king nodded appreciatively, for all the world as though the two of them had years of sea battles under their belts.

Afterwards, when we were about to leave, I was standing near the duke, who was talking to a couple of navy officers. Just as the conversation came to an end, a thin man wearing a shabby brown coat darted out of the crowd.

'My lord,' he said, 'I must speak with you.'

The duke went to walk on, but the man caught his arm.

'You won't remember me, but I served you in the first expedition to La Rochelle. John Felton's my name.' He lifted his left arm; the sleeve hung empty from the elbow. 'That's where I got this. I haven't been able to find work since, sir, but I'm a good sailor, and if you'll take me with you I'll serve you well.'

The duke smiled. I'd seen that smile before, but the man hadn't. His shoulders relaxed; he thought the duke was going to help him. The duke glanced round at the two navy officers, then turned back to the man.

'We're going to fight the French,' he said. 'Not wave at them.'

The officers smirked and the poor man looked at the duke as though he was trying to make sense of his words. The duke leaned forward, and spoke very slowly, as if to an idiot.

'I've no use for you. If you wanted to fight, you should have taken better care to stay attached to your limbs.'

'But my lord... I've no way to live.'

'In that case,' said the duke, 'you will have to go hang.'

He strode off towards his carriage. The man stood there, watching it drive off. He didn't look angry, just puzzled, as though he'd expected things to go one way but they'd somehow gone another, and he wasn't quite sure how that had happened. Still staring at the coach, he repeated, 'But I've no way to live'.

I fished some money out of my purse, and went up to him.

'Here. It's not much, but it'll tide you over for a little while.'

He looked down at me, and the gold coins in my palm.

'You were with them,' he said. 'You could speak to him for me.'

'He wouldn't listen to me,' I said.

'But I have to go to sea. I've no way to live.'

I held out the money again.

'Please, take it. I wish I could help, but the duke's no more a friend of mine than he is of yours.'

He took the money then, and walked away.

The king went back to London, but the queen decided to spend some time in Wellingborough, to take the waters, which were said to help ladies wanting to become pregnant. She confided to me that she also wanted to get away from the king, whose endless praise of the duke's preparations for the campaign was trying her temper:

'All I hear is how wonderful his dear Buckingham has been, and all I see is how that man will ruin this country with his stupid games. But if I say a word, I play into his hands. So it's better to be somewhere else for a while.'

We were all sitting in the gardens when a letter came for the queen. She read the beginning, and gasped. She looked at me; by then we'd come to know each other so well I could usually read her thoughts in a glance, but that day, I couldn't. She was shocked, but there was something else in her eyes that I couldn't interpret.

We all watched as she read to the end of the letter, then read it again before she looked up.

'It's Buckingham,' she said. 'He's been killed.'

I understood then what I'd seen in her eyes. I felt the same; shocked but not sorry.

'I must go to him,' she said, and at first, confused, I thought she meant the duke, but then she caught my eye and wiggled her finger like a little bee flying, just a tiny bit that only I would notice. She'd seen her chance. The king would be distraught; if ever she was to make him depend on her as he'd done on the duke, now was the time. My mother would have been proud of her.

We didn't hear the full story until later. As the duke left his lodgings in the morning, a man had rushed forward and stabbed him. That one blow being all it took, he gave himself up and told his story. He'd been staying at an inn for the past few nights, he said, and there he'd drunk and eaten his fill. He mentioned a particularly good steak pie that had formed his dinner on the last night. That morning, he paid his bill, walked to an ironmonger's and spent his last ten pennies on a knife. His name was John Felton.

The death of the duke changed everything for the queen. By hurrying to the king's side when he needed comfort, then gradually taking the place of the duke as his friend, advisor and constant support, she made him love her. The change was astonishing to watch: he gazed at her like a spaniel at a lamb cutlet, constantly touching her arm or her cheek, as if reassuring himself she was real. Before long he was consulting her on every decision; impossible to imagine in the days when he treated her as a silly girl. But the change in him was nothing compared to the change in her. I thought at first she was playing at it, that now the duke was no longer there to be defeated, she was gaining the king's confidence as a way to make him help the English Catholics. But to my surprise – perhaps even to hers – over the months she grew to love him back. I didn't understand much about love in those days, but in later years I came to realise what changed was that he needed her, and she found she liked being needed.

By December that year, she was expecting their first child. By then the king consulted her on everything, and she was helping him negotiate peace with her homeland. And though she still hadn't been able to improve matters much for the Catholics, he'd had a beautiful chapel built for her, and she'd taken that as a sign there was hope for change. At the New Year feast, she shone with happiness. I sat back in my chair, tired from a morning ride on my very own horse, my belly full of goose and syllabub, and watched the king laugh as she whispered in his ear. It felt like a golden time for all of us. And for a while, it was.

We didn't know, of course, what was waiting.

Part Two

Chapter Twenty-one

You'll wonder how we didn't see it coming. Looking back, I wonder myself. But even when the trouble started, no one could have predicted where it was going. That the king and queen could end up at war with their own people? That the people could put their king on trial and sentence him to death? It was impossible, and if anyone had said it, I'd have thought they were soft in the head. And no one did, then, but it happened anyway.

I remember very clearly the day I realised things had changed. It was not long after my twenty-fourth birthday, the first sunny day of spring. The queen was visiting her children – they had six by then, and they lived out at Richmond, where the air was fresher, with a small army of nurses, tutors and cradle-rockers. I'd been in her service for fourteen years by that time, and since I'd turned eighteen she'd paid me a generous allowance. So that day, I took the chance to go into the city and buy a book from the seller in the Royal Exchange.

It was busy, as usual, and being in no hurry after I'd made my purchase, I stood in the upper gallery for a while, looking down at the comings and goings. Fashionable ladies strolled and chatted, trailed by maids laden down with parcels from the drapers and the furriers. Orange sellers, rat catchers and bird vendors yelled out their wares, and men of business with important-looking faces strode along the walkways between Cornhill and Threadneedle Street. A couple of lads in the aprons of apprentices were loitering by the fountain, and I watched them glance admiringly as a maid carrying a small heap of packages passed by. She didn't look at them, but her jaunty step said she knew perfectly well they were looking at her. A few yards on, she dropped one of the parcels, and the tallest lad rushed to pick it up for her. She smiled at him, looking up through her lashes, the look that every boy learns means he's in with a chance. A look that I'd long ago realised would never be directed at me. Though I was a man in years, I stood no higher then than when I left Oakham. I'd studied the young men at court until I could stride as manfully as any of them, and with the change in my features since my boyhood, I was rarely mistaken for a child anymore, but still, the only glances I drew from women were curious ones.

The closest I'd got to love – and it wasn't close at all – was an occasional visit to the stews of Southwark. In a conversation that had meandered down a great many euphemistic lanes, Jeremiah had recommended an accommodating Welsh girl called Tessa, who didn't mind what shape or size her customers were, so long as they paid in good hard cash and didn't take too long about the proceedings. Her cheerful good humour made what I was afraid would be a humiliating experience into a happy one, and whenever I returned, she did me the kindness of appearing pleased to see me. It was a pale imitation of what it must feel like to be loved, but it was all I could hope for. So although there were girls at Whitehall who caught my eye, I'd taught myself to enjoy a pretty face much as you might a painting, or a lovely view, and try my best not to want more. But watching how easily the boy had won that look, envy stung me, hard. I had a purse of gold at my waist, quite likely more than he'd earn in a month, but what would that count for, beside his long legs and broad chest?

Cross with myself for letting my guard down, and at the same time sincerely hoping the girl turned out to have a vicious temper or dull wits – ideally both – I tucked my book under my arm and made my way out. Outside on Cornhill, a pamphlet seller was shouting:

'Read about the papist queen's secret plans!'

On another day, I'd probably have ignored him; it wasn't news that the queen's religion made her unpopular. But I was in a bad humour already, and when I saw the way people were muttering and shaking their heads as they read the pamphlets, anger bubbled up inside me.

'Give me one of those,' I said, handing over a coin.

The seller looked at me curiously, but took my money. Underneath a crude sketch of the queen carrying a cross encrusted with jewels, the pamphlet said she was in league with the pope, and blamed her for the rebellion in Scotland the year before, saying it was on her instructions that the king had insisted the Scots use the English prayerbook, hoping it'd be a first step to turning them Catholic. And now she and the pope supposedly had an army in Ireland, ready to invade England and force people back to the Catholic faith. I thought back to the young girl who'd tried so hard to make a strange country her home; all these years later, she was still getting the blame for things that weren't her fault.

'How can you print this?' I said. 'It's all lies.'

'Oh, you say so, do you, little man?' said the seller. 'And how would you know?'

'That's her dwarf,' said a woman standing nearby. She looked down at me. 'So you're saying this ain't true?'

'Of course not. The queen loves this country.'

'So why's she writing secret letters to the pope?' demanded a red-faced man, brandishing his pamphlet. 'Says even the king doesn't know about them.'

'That's nonsense too,' I said.

'Why should we believe you, if you're in thick with her?' said the pamphlet seller.

'And he'll be a papist,' the woman chimed in. 'They all are, her lot.'

That I couldn't deny: to please the queen I'd been baptised a Catholic when I was thirteen. In the sheltered world of the court, it didn't seem to matter one way or the other. But I wasn't there now. The little crowd that had been standing reading the pamphlets closed in around me, and passers-by were stopping, eager to see what was going on. I glanced behind me; in a matter of moments the crowd had become two or three deep and I couldn't see a way through. The red-faced man pointed a fat finger at me and said:

'I bet you he's one of her spies – I've heard about it, she sends 'em out all round the town. Spying on honest people so they know who to round up when the time comes.'

'A papist spy!' someone yelled, and suddenly the whole crowd was shouting down at me, about the Irish, and spies, and plots and the pope. I tried to push my way through, but they shoved me back.

'Tell us the truth!' a woman shouted. 'When are the Irish coming?'

'We'll make him tell us!' said the pamphlet seller, and snatched me off the ground. He shook me like a rat, until my brain seemed to rattle inside my skull. Then the crowd pressed in, faces hard, hands grabbing at me.

They'll tear me apart.

I did the only thing I could think of: punched the pamphlet seller on the nose, as hard as I could. He was holding me up near his face, and the bone cracked as I hit home. Clapping one hand to his bleeding nose, he dropped me. Other hands clawed at me as I scrambled to my feet, but I ducked them and ran. I didn't stop until I was three streets away.

At the river, I had to lean against a post and get my breath back before I could hail a boat. The boatman nodded as I clambered in; I'd travelled with him before. Not one of the chatty ones, thank the Lord. As I looked back across the sun-spangled water, all I could think was, why didn't we know? The rebellion in Scotland was far away, but this was on our doorstep. For months, we'd heard reports of disturbances in the city, people gathering to rant about taxes and shout wild accusations about Catholic plots. Yet at Whitehall the balls and the masques and the dinners had gone on as they always did, and until that morning I'd had no idea how angry London was.

The queen's religion had always caused suspicion, but in the past it was tavern talk and whispers in the markets. This was different; there'd been pure hatred in the faces that looked down at me, just because I was linked to her. Even safe in the boat, it made my belly turn to water to think what they'd have done to me if I hadn't got away. And though they weren't yet brave enough to say whatever they liked about the king too, it was obvious to me, that day, that soon they would be. Everyone knew he wasn't loved by the people, even though at court we all pretended he was.

I hadn't liked him much myself, in the beginning, but over the years I'd come to see him differently. He was a good man, and an honest one, who truly wanted the best for his country. But he wasn't overburdened with sense, and every time he tried to do what he thought was right, it turned out wrong. Convinced he was gifted with wisdom, he'd battled with Parliament from the start, saying God had put him in charge, not them. When they demanded more of a say, he packed them all off home, but that meant grubbing around for taxes and loans he could raise without their say-so, until rich and poor alike thought he was bleeding them dry. And then he took it upon himself to tell people how they should worship on a Sunday morning. Myself, I doubted if God in his heaven cared what prayerbook people used, or where they stood the altar, but plenty of people on earth did, so even someone with lettuce for brains could see that was going to cause trouble. The Scots had refused to stand for it; what was he going to do if the English realised they could do the same?

As the boatman began to steer towards the jetty, I fished out the fare from my purse. He tipped his hat as I handed it over.

'See you again,' he said, and headed back the way we'd

come. I stood there, looking up the river towards the city. How did we not know? And how long would it be before people started looking this way – towards us?

Chapter Twenty-two

I didn't tell anyone what happened that day at the Exchange; I didn't want the queen to know about all that hatred boiling up against her. But it wasn't long before the mood in the city became impossible to ignore. Shopkeepers took to boarding up their premises and the rumours got wilder each week – one pamphlet said the queen was planning to poison the king and install young Prince Charles on the throne, a puppet king with her pulling the strings. Anonymous placards popped up all over the place, calling her a shrew who wore the king's breeches, and the pope's personal harlot.

And then one morning, a maid noticed marks on a window. The king and queen had spent the previous night together, as they often did by then, and, steps from where they'd been sleeping, someone had stood in the darkness and etched the words: 'God save the king. God damn the queen and all her offspring.' The king smashed the glass with his own hand, while she looked on, white-faced. What nobody said, but everybody was thinking, was if one person could get that close, so could more. And if a mob attacked, the sprawl of buildings, with a road running through the middle and jetties on the river, was impossible to defend. Sometimes, in the dark of the night, I would wake, certain I'd heard voices shouting, or the slap and grate of boats tying up, and I don't think I was the only one.

That's when people began to leave: first a maid here, a groom there, mostly those who had family outside London, but then anyone who could get a place elsewhere. The guard was doubled, then trebled, but still, courtiers took to tucking their valuables inside their clothing in case they had to up and leave in a hurry. And we all knew that, before long, it would become too dangerous for the king and queen to stay. The question was when. Would they leave quietly, or wait to be driven out? I hoped it would be the former, because I could still see that ring of angry faces pressing in around me, and hear the fury in their voices. But no one dared ask.

'We ought to give some thought to what we're going to do when they go,' said Jeremiah one morning, as we walked back from the stables.

It was a while since we'd talked; there was a new cook in the kitchens who he'd taken a fancy to – Sukie, she was called – and he spent his free time hanging around down there, hoping to catch a word or two with her.

'We'll go with them, won't we?' I said.

It hadn't occurred to me that there was a question about it. For a second, I remembered the old days, when I pretended I was happy so they wouldn't send me home. I *was* happy now, and this was home. Where was I going to go, if it wasn't with the queen?

'This isn't like when we go to Hampton Court for the summer, Nat. What this comes down to, for the likes of you and me, is picking a side. If we go, that tells anyone who cares to notice, we're for the queen – and we're against those that aren't. That puts us in danger as well. And you'd be in more danger than most. People who wouldn't recognise a single other person at court know who you are. You'd be a trophy – and if they got their hands on you, they wouldn't let you go.'

I thought of that day in the Exchange: the angry faces and the grabbing hands, the shouts about things that were nothing to do with me but made them hate me anyway.

'I've been thinking,' said Jeremiah. 'We could go down to Kent, where I was before. I could get back into the stables, I'm sure, and I reckon the lady of the house would be beside herself to have a footman who used to be the queen's own dwarf.' He looked down at his feet, then back at me, as a blush crept over his big old face. 'And, well, the thing is... I'm thinking to ask Sukie to marry me. I don't know for sure she'll say yes. But she's a country girl, from Essex, and I think if I could offer her a nice little cottage, it would improve my chances.'

The sheepish look on his face made me smile.

'I'm pleased for you,' I said. 'And of course she'll say yes, why wouldn't she? But would you really leave the queen?'

'I don't say I'd take the decision lightly, Nat. But it wants thinking about – and if you want my advice, you'll think about it sooner rather than later.'

Over the next few weeks, I did think about what Jeremiah said. But in the end it wasn't that that made up my mind. It was a visit from my father.

Chapter Twenty-three

He looked smaller than I remembered. The powerful chest that once reminded me of a cockerel strutting across the yard had become sunken and bony, and his wide shoulders were hunched, as though he was protecting himself from a chilly wind. He was holding a battered hat, turning it round and round in his fingers, and looking up, open-mouthed, at the painted ceiling of the great hall. The front of his left boot was encrusted with something dry and brown. I hoped it wasn't dog shit.

He jumped when I said hello, and his eyes widened at my fine clothes and buckled shoes.

'Look at you, you're like a proper gentleman. And all this …' He gestured around him. 'Bit different from Oakham, eh?'

Fourteen years. He'd left me at that door and walked away without once looking back, and now here he was, fourteen years later, all smiles.

Why are you here? I wanted to say it, but my mouth wouldn't spit out the words. So I asked how he'd got there, just for something to say.

'Walked down to Northampton, and took the stage wagon from there. Five days in all.'

I'd forgotten how long things take when you don't have money. *Now I really want to know why you've come.*

'So ... you been all right then?' he said. 'They treat you all right?'

He'd waited fourteen years to ask that. *What are you going to do if I say no? Offer to buy me back?*

'They treat me very well,' I said. 'But how are things at home? Is everyone all right there?'

He looked down, twisting his hat again.

'That's why I came. I thought you'd want to know. Your mother died.'

My mother. I realised, with a flush of shame, that I hadn't thought about her for a long time. I hadn't thought about any of them. But now I saw her, as clearly as yesterday, sitting beside me on the woodpile, telling me I was big on the inside, and not to forget it. I remembered those early months at Whitehall, when I'd longed to see her face again. Now I never would.

'She took a chill, and it went to her chest,' he said. 'As I say, I thought you'd want to know.'

It was a long way from Oakham to Northampton; he'd walked all those miles, then spent his money on a wagon ride, so he could tell me the news himself. Perhaps he'd changed. It had been a long time, after all.

'Thank you. For coming, I mean.'

'You were always her favourite,' he said. 'Apple of her eye. She talked about you all the time, after you went.'

Why hadn't I ever gone back to see them? In recent summers, we'd often stayed at Wellingborough and I could easily have travelled to Oakham from there. But I didn't want to by then. I was Nathaniel Davy, the queen's dwarf, and I didn't care to remember the shabby little cottage and the boy who was no use. I could have kept my promise to find Sam a place at court too, but as the years went on, I told myself he wouldn't like it, he'd be happier at home. The truth was I didn't want Sam, with his simple country ways, to embarrass me.

We talked about the rest of the family for a while. Little Annie was still at home with my father, but Sam was married with a child of his own. Envy pricked at me when I heard that. But it eased my guilt too. He'd made a life for himself in Oakham, so perhaps I'd been right, perhaps he was happier there.

There was news of the neighbours too. My old enemy, Jack Edgecombe, I was glad to hear, had married most unhappily, to one of the girls from the bakery. My father wasn't sure which one; I hoped it was the ugly one.

'You should see Sam's little girl – she's the spitting image of your mother,' he said. 'Curly-headed, just like she was. Sam's wife had a bad time of it having her, the midwife thought the baby would die, but your mother must have been watching over her from heaven that night.'

It took me a moment to realise what he'd said.

'How old did you say Sam's child was?' I asked.

'Sam's child?'

'You said she was two.'

'Did I? No, she's not two, no...'

He knew he'd been caught.

'When did Mother die?'

He looked down at his hands.

'Three years in August.'

'So you waited three years and then thought I might like to know?'

'It's taken me five days to get here.'

And I'd been stupid enough to think that meant something.

'What have you really come for?'

I knew, now, but I was going to make him say it.

'Things changed after the duke was killed,' he said.

Of course; no more dogfights up at the big house.

'Frank Herries, who used to run the fights at the White Horse, he hurt his back, so I took on his patch. Not as good money, but it kept me going. Then the place changed hands, and I was lucky to get a fight once a quarter. Well, you'll remember how much those dogs eat, Nat. I held on as long as I could, but last year I had to do away with them.'

Of course you did. Because they were no use to you.

'The butchery side of things isn't doing too well either. You don't realise it, I daresay, sitting here …' He waved an arm at the room. 'But times are hard in the country. I live as cheaply as I can, but …'

But it's hard to drink yourself stupid three times a week without a bit extra coming in.

He busied himself with picking a fleck of dirt from his hat as I opened my purse. I fished out a pile of coins and handed them up to him, taking care not to let my fingers touch his hand.

'This should keep you going for a while. I'll find a way to send you money every month, so you won't need to ask again.'

He resisted the temptation to count the coins in front

of me, but he couldn't stop himself fingering them, until he could get outside and check what he'd got for his five-day journey.

'Perhaps you'll come and see us some time?' he said.

'Perhaps.'

I couldn't have said which of us meant it less.

That afternoon, I sat by the window, looking out but not really seeing anything. I was thinking of my mother. I thought about the winter afternoons when she'd tell us stories by the fire, and the way she'd scolded us all the way home from the fair that day, and even the stew she used to make that still, in my memory, tasted better than anything on the king's table. Three years she'd been gone, and I didn't even know. I hadn't asked my father if she'd spoken about me in her last days, because I couldn't stand to hear if she hadn't, and I couldn't stand to hear if she had, and I wasn't there.

The queen noticed I was quiet, and called me over to ask if I was all right. I didn't want to tell the story and admit how stupid I'd been to think my father had any reason but money for coming, so I said I had a toothache.

As I lay in my chamber that night, I thought about that small kindness. With all the worries swirling round in the queen's mind, she'd still noticed I seemed out of sorts; compare that to the man who didn't think to tell me my mother was dead until he wanted money from me, and then pretended he'd come for my sake. So in the end the answer to Jeremiah's question was obvious. My mother was gone. My father cared no more for me than he'd done for his dogs; quite possibly less. Sam had his wife and child – since I'd broken my promise to him, I couldn't blame him if he never gave a thought to me. And to Annie, after all these years, I'd just be a name.

If I had a family at all now, it was there at court. I wasn't convinced the king was right in his fight with Parliament, not then nor later. But it didn't matter. I wasn't going to lose a second family like I lost the first one. So wherever they were going, I'd go with them.

Chapter Twenty-four

We made a sorry sight when we eventually fled. Jeremiah was right: it wasn't like the times we left for a summer at Hampton Court or Windsor. Back then, the entire court travelled in a parade of carriages, all of us dressed in our best, the horses' coats polished until they gleamed, and behind us wagons piled high with trunks and boxes containing everything from the queen's summer wardrobe to their favourite cups and plates. But on that cold, grey afternoon ten days into the new year of 1642, there were only half a dozen coaches, flanked by thirty or so guards, the rest of them left behind; there was no money to feed them or their horses. Ordinary carters had been hired to carry the baggage, and the queen insisted no one bring more than the necessaries. What she didn't say, but everyone knew, was that room was required for the other things they were taking with them: the crown jewels and every piece of silver and gold plate in the palace.

They'd clung on in London for longer than I expected. To no one's surprise, the peace the king had negotiated with the Scots hadn't held, and to fund an army to fight them, he'd had to recall Parliament. Knowing they had him where they wanted him, they demanded changes in return for the cash; a bit more power for them, quite a bit less for him. Over the months, he handled the situation like an idiot buying a pig: first battling with them, then attempting to appease them, then stamping his foot again at just the wrong moment. London had become so jittery that ordinary people were arming themselves, and the palace came to feel less like a sanctuary, and more like a prison. The king had a guard tower built at the outer gate, but instead of making us feel safer, it reminded us we'd never needed one before.

And suddenly there was no money in the kitty. Parliament had the purse strings pulled tight, and the king was running out of other places to go. And he had a lot of mouths to feed. Jeremiah worked it out one day: there were over a thousand of us at Whitehall, and by then the king had given the queen Denmark House, just down the river, where her chapel was, so there were a whole load more courtiers and servants there. Still, that problem was beginning to solve itself: servants who were fed up not getting their wages joined the ones who'd left because they were just plain frightened, and courtiers melted away too – they'd come to court with advancement in mind, and there was none to be had from a king who couldn't even pay his own bills.

I'd thought Jeremiah would stick it out, but his new love, Sukie from the kitchens, had other ideas. She was younger than him but older than me and, though I never mentioned this to Jeremiah, she reminded me of a goose, with that same bossy walk, a sharp way of speaking and a general air of being able to give you a nasty bite should she choose to. She kept him dangling for a week after he asked her to marry him, and then issued a list of her conditions: they were to leave London for Kent, Jeremiah was to ask for a proper cottage on the estate – 'No one knows horses like you do, but if you don't ask for what you're worth, be sure they won't offer it' – and he must promise always to take his boots off before he stepped across the threshold 'because your nose might not notice the smell of horses' doings, Jeremiah Hobley, but mine very definitely does.' But when they turned to walk down the aisle as Mr and Mrs Hobley, she smiled up at him as though he was the best thing she'd ever seen, and I thought, yes, he'll be all right with her.

When they left, I missed his company badly. By then, the queen spent most of the day ensconced with the king and his advisors – she told me they spoke to her as though she was a particularly simple four-year-old, but he valued her advice and insisted she was there. So I passed much of my time just wandering in the gardens, wondering how long it would be before I'd have to leave the place I'd come to call home, and what would happen to us then.

For months, the king and queen stayed put, convinced they could ride the situation out. When we eventually left, it was because they had no choice. That autumn, rebellion had broken out in Ireland, led by the Catholics, and of course people said the queen had stirred it up, as a sop to the pope for failing to turn England Catholic. Rumours began to swirl around that Parliament thought the same – and that they might even believe it well enough to accuse her of treason. When the king heard that, he decided enough was enough and marched into Parliament, with four hundred soldiers, to arrest the ringleaders. They'd been warned and fled, but the damage was done; with his usual knack for doing the wrong thing at the wrong time, he'd not so much stepped on Parliament's toes as trampled all over their feet, and they weren't going to stand for it.

A few days later, we were sitting in the chamber, the queen, three or four of her ladies, and me – it was cold, I remember, she'd told the maids to make the firewood last. The doors crashed open and the king walked in, his face livid red.

'What is it?' said the queen. 'What's happened?'

Shaking with anger and struggling to force out his words, he said Parliament had invoked a law allowing citizens to band together to keep the peace, and when they returned to Westminster the following day, to discuss the treason proceedings, they'd be accompanied by an army.

'They s-s-say twenty thousand will come, armed and h-h-horsed. And a th-th-thousand sailors on the river.'

The queen shrank back into her seat, her hands gripping the arms as though someone might appear there and then to tear her out of it. Westminster Hall, where the MPs and their army would be heading, was a step away from the palace. If they decided to take her into custody, the few hundred men the king could command at short notice would be powerless to stop them.

'They are coming for me,' she whispered, her eyes wide. 'Charles, they are coming for me.'

'The pretext is that it is to protect themselves,' said the king. 'But I would sooner trust the word of a snake. And if they think we will sit and take this boldness, they think wrongly.'

She was trembling by then, and he took her hand.

'We leave tonight, for Hampton Court,' he said. 'And I will make them regret this barbarous action, I promise.'

We spent just two nights at Hampton Court, the first most uncomfortably; we'd arrived in such a hurry that no beds were prepared. The king and queen and the children huddled together in one chamber, and the rest of us did as best we could with cloaks and rugs. Next morning daylight revealed what, in the panic of leaving, no one had thought of: Hampton Court, open to the river and surrounded by parkland, was no easier to defend than Whitehall. The queen started at every unexpected sound, her eyes straying constantly to the windows, and when, during dinner, a crash was heard from the kitchens, half the company, me included, jumped up, ready to flee. So everything that had been unpacked was packed again, and we headed for Windsor Castle, with its high walls and lookout towers. And there, the king and queen prepared for war.

Chapter Twenty-five

During those weeks at Windsor, the queen was the one who wanted war, more than the king. Still convinced – against all the evidence to the contrary – that he was the wiliest of leaders, he thought he could outsmart the other side by clever negotiation. But safe behind the thick walls of the castle, her fears had been replaced by fury, and she wanted them taught a lesson.

'How dare they!' she spat, as Parliament sent daily demands: the king must agree not to take political or religious advice from his wife; she must swear an oath not to meddle in such affairs; her Catholic servants and priests must be dismissed. 'These people don't deserve their king. They are ungrateful children who turn against their own father. And we are going to show them their father will not tolerate it.'

I understood why she was so set on a fight. Once, back in Oakham, a little cat wandered into our dog shed. Before I had a chance to grab it, the dogs had attacked, but there was a second when I saw it realise it couldn't escape. The same look was in the queen's eyes that day at Whitehall when she thought they were coming for her. And I'd seen for myself how it felt to be helpless at the hands of a mob, and how it makes you long to be powerful and strong, and take revenge on every single one of them. As I've said before, I wasn't convinced the king had right on his side, but by then I wanted to fight them too, for frightening her, and for driving us all out of a home, and a life, that I'd grown to love.

As arms and ammunition began arriving from the Tower and the arsenal at Woolwich, and all the talk was of war, I envied the soldiers who could go into battle and fight like men. Sometimes I'd imagine how it would feel to ride onto a battlefield, with flags flying and the crash of drums filling the air, knowing all that stood between you and death was your strength and your skill. But I'd never be allowed to fight. All those years of lessons at the palace meant that by then I could ride and shoot as well as any cavalryman, but what commander would allow me into his troop, and give the other side something to mock them for? I wasn't going to humiliate myself by suggesting it, but still, as the preparations for war went on all around me, I wished I was part of it, like any other man.

Now that it was clear the king and queen were going to fight, they needed money. Before we left Whitehall, back when life still seemed quite tranquil, Princess Mary, their eldest daughter, had been married off to a Dutch prince, but as she was only nine, and he twelve, once the contract was made, she stayed at home and he returned to Holland. Now the queen came up with the idea to take the princess to join her boy husband, and bring with her gold, silver and jewellery to sell to the merchants there. I was to go too, along with her priest

Father Philip, her chamberlain Henry Jermyn, and two of her ladies: Susan, a cheerful, practical sort, and Elizabeth, who was quieter but prone to uncontrollable giggles if something amused her. And the dog, Bonbon, who still went everywhere with the queen.

'We will appear to be nothing more than a happy little band, taking Mary to her new home,' she said. 'No one will suspect what else we carry with us.'

While it wasn't any great honour to be chosen because I didn't look like someone you'd pick to protect the crown jewels, I was excited at the thought of travelling across the sea. I thought it would be a wonderful adventure.

I changed my mind about that during our first evening on the ship, as I sat with my head in a bucket, being reunited with my dinner. We'd set sail on a bright winter day, but as we lost sight of land, the sky darkened and a vicious wind blew up, churning the waves into foam and making the sails twist and crack. As fat drops of rain pelted onto the deck, we scuttled below, thinking to make ourselves cosy until the storm blew over. What we didn't know was that it had no intention of blowing over. Not for another nine days.

As darkness fell, the wind grew stronger. We attempted to sit and eat dinner, but every few minutes the ship tilted and we had to grab our plates to stop them sliding to the floor. Susan just managed to catch a dish of kidneys before it landed in her lap. She held it up in triumph, to cheers from the company, only to miss the plate of cutlets that followed behind, sending Elizabeth into such a fit of giggling that it turned into hiccups and Susan had to pinch her nose to stop them.

But as the bucking and rolling grew wilder, the conversation died away and the faces round the table turned white and sweaty. Father Philip was the first to excuse himself from the room, but he didn't make it far along the passageway, and the sound and smell of him retching up his venison proved the final straw for the rest of us.

For a week and two days, the ship was tossed around like a bean in a box. At night, the crew tied us into our bunks, like so many swaddled babies; by day, all we could do was sit with buckets close at hand and try not to close our eyes, which for some reason made the churning in our bellies worse.

I shared a cabin with Henry Jermyn, the queen's chamberlain. He'd been at court as long as I had, but he was a few years older than me and spent most of his time flirting with the queen's ladies, so I'd never got to know him well. But if two people spend nine days confined in a cabin together, vomiting regularly and wondering if they'll ever stand on dry land again, they'll either conceive a lasting hatred for each other or become the best of friends. With Henry and I, it was the latter.

'It's not for me to wonder why the queen chose you for this mission, Nat, but it wasn't for your skilful aim,' he said one morning, when I missed the bucket and spattered the toes of his boots with sick.

'If we survive, I'll buy you a better pair,' I said. 'And anyway, that's good, coming from you. At least I haven't puked on your head.'

'Was it my fault you leaned out of your bunk just when I leaned out of mine? You're lucky my aim's as good as it is, from up there. Whereas you, you're right there – that damn bucket's nearly as tall as you are, and you still miss it.'

Holding on to the wall as the ship rolled again, he stepped over to the bundle of rags the crew had left for wiping our faces, dipped one into the pitcher of water beside them, and wiped his boots, then dampened another and passed it to me, before climbing back up to his bunk and lying down with a groan.

'What's it like though?' he asked, after a minute or so.

'What?'

'You know. Being so small.'

No one had ever asked me that. People often asked *why* I was so small, and offered their own theories as to the reason, usually involving my mother and witches, though on one occasion I was assured she must have had relations with a tomcat. People had mocked me for being small, and some had even celebrated me for it. But Henry was the first person who ever asked me what it felt like.

'It's hard to say. I don't know what it's like not to be.'

That wasn't really true though. I didn't *know* what it was like not to be small, but I'd imagined it often enough. And though I hadn't thought about it for years, I found myself telling Henry about that day at the fair, when I thought the faerie could make me grow.

'So then you just never got any bigger?' he said, when I'd finished the story.

'No. I tried a few different things, but nothing worked.'

'You do all right though, don't you? I still remember when you beat that Crofts boy in the race. Incredible.'

Thrilled at his praise, I leaned out of my bunk, eager to

prompt him into sharing his recollections of my triumph. As I did, the ship pitched, and I tumbled head first into the sick bucket.

'Nasty,' said Henry, peering over the side of his bunk. 'I'd stick to horses if I was you, Nat. I don't think swimming is your sport.'

Chapter Twenty-six

We reached Holland two days after the storm abated, thankful to stand on ground that didn't pitch and roll beneath our feet, and travelled to the capital, where we were to stay in the palace that would become Princess Mary's home. The royal family were lined up to greet us, and her new father-in-law, Prince Frederik, stepped forward, his arms open.

'Welcome, welcome,' he said, in a strange accent that sounded as though he had hot stew in his mouth. 'We are so pleased to have our new princess with us here at last.'

He leaned down to kiss Princess Mary on both cheeks, then nudged his son towards her. Prince William had grown a little since the wedding, but he was still only thirteen, and he blushed as he stepped forward and enfolded Mary in an awkward embrace.

'A perfect match,' said his father. 'They will be very happy together.'

I was idly wondering how the queen must feel to be giving Princess Mary away like this, knowing how difficult the early years of her own marriage had been, when I realised Prince Frederik was talking to me.

'And this must be the little prince,' he said, smiling fondly. In the same instant that I understood his eyesight wasn't the best, and he'd mistaken me for the queen's three-year-old son, I realised he was about to lean down to kiss me too. Unsure whether it was better to risk insulting him by jumping back, or embarrassing both of us by letting it happen, I stood, frozen.

'Your majesty!'

Everybody jumped as Henry leaned forward and swatted at the prince's head.

'I beg your pardon, your majesty, but there was a bee,' said Henry. 'I thought it would enter your ear.'

'Thank you,' said the prince, looking somewhat taken aback.

'Henry Jermyn, your majesty,' said Henry, bowing. 'The queen's chamberlain.'

Before the prince could resume his advance on me, I took my cue and bowed too.

'Nathaniel Davy, your majesty. The queen's dwarf.'

'A bee?' I said to Henry later, as we sat at dinner. 'In February?'

He laughed.

'Shut up, you ungrateful little toad, or next time a prince wants to give you a nice big kiss, I'll let him.'

He turned to his neighbour, a very pretty young woman with blue eyes and white-blonde hair, who'd previously introduced herself as one of the ladies in waiting to Prince Frederik's wife, Princess Amalia.

'My friend and I were just discussing how it is that all the women in Holland are so beautiful,' he said. 'I told him, they put something special in the cheese.'

It was a terrible line, but he said it with a twinkle in his eye, and she laughed.

'But sir,' she said. 'In that case, our Dutch men must be the handsomest in Europe.'

He looked around the table, letting his eye rest on one or two of the less well-favoured gentlemen, and smiled.

'Clearly,' he replied, 'you ladies are keeping the cheese for yourselves.'

She pretended to scold him, but her eyes were sparkling, and in a matter of minutes, they were talking as though there was no one else in the room. And I saw, over the next few days and nights, that that was how it always went with Henry. He was a born flirt, and quite indiscriminate in his attentions: within days, half the serving maids were twinkling at him, and even Princess Amalia, who was very serious and given to long and pompous pronouncements about art, was seen to blush and smile at something he whispered into her ear one evening after dinner.

I didn't disapprove; I was envious. I never said so though. Henry was tactful enough to simply ignore the fact that I would never have a woman look at me the way he did, and I didn't want to disturb our easy friendship by drawing attention to the difference between us. All the same, I often wished I could walk in his shoes.

I'd assumed, when the queen formed the plan of selling her jewels, that someone would simply take them all away and arrange the business for her, but it turned out that wasn't what she had in mind at all. Once we were settled at the palace, she sent invitations to the city's merchants, and two days later, the first one turned up, glancing with practised eyes round the room where we'd laid out the treasure. I had no idea she'd brought so much: strings of pearls, gold collars studded with sapphires and rubies, handfuls of rings and bracelets, coronets glittering with diamonds, even a set of pearl buttons she'd given the king as a present. Surprise flickered across her face as the merchant stood there staring at her, not bowing or even removing his hat, but she smiled sweetly, and led him over to the tables.

She showed him a necklace of fat pearls, holding it up against her throat, then put on a diamond bracelet, twisting her wrist so the stones sparkled. Jewels that she loved, and not just for their beauty; both of those were presents from the king. Yet here she was, not just accepting their loss, but hawking them herself, like the pedlars who used to knock on our door in Oakham with a basket of ribbons and trinkets. It was as unlikely as her picking up a broom and sweeping the floor, and it showed me how badly she wanted to help the king fight.

The merchant held a pair of earrings up to the light, as though he suspected the Queen of England might be trying to sell him baubles made of glass. He said something, and her face fell. Curious, I moved closer.

'But the value of the stones alone ...' she was saying. 'Surely if—'

'My final offer,' he said, shrugging his shoulders. 'You can take it or not.'

'Let me show you some other pieces.'

She picked up a coronet.

'No.' He pointed to the coronet, and the other big pieces, and shook his head. 'These are not your property. Your Parliament sent notices, they belong to the Crown.'

He was practically calling her a thief. She flushed red, and I expected her to remind him who he was talking to. But she took a deep breath and said:

'I can assure you these jewels are mine.'

He shrugged again.

'I will take the earrings, at the price I offered. Do you say yes or no?'

She bit her lip, and nodded.

It was the same story all week. No one would touch the bigger pieces, and the smaller ones sold at a third of their value. But she wouldn't give up. When she'd seen every merchant in The Hague, we travelled to Amsterdam and sold there. Still at terrible prices, but money was trickling in. She met moneylenders in Amsterdam too, securing loans from them, and sat for hours with the Dutch prince's commanders, questioning them about what she should buy, so when she met the arms merchants, she'd know what she was talking about.

I watched her one evening, almost knocking over a wine glass as she listed on her fingers the muskets, pikes and armour she'd bought, and I remembered the girl of fifteen who'd happily while away an afternoon teaching the monkeys tricks. That girl had long since disappeared, and in her place now was a woman who was enjoying being useful, who didn't care what she did or how she was humiliated, as long as she got the money the king needed. But her face was grey with tiredness. She and the king wrote to each other almost every day, even though the weather at sea meant messages could take anything from days to weeks to arrive. They put the letters into code in case they fell into the wrong hands, and she sat up late every night deciphering his and replying, as well as writing to anyone she could think of who might provide money, soldiers or weapons. She rubbed her tired eyes, and glanced at Bonbon, curled up asleep on a cushion in the corner. By the look on her face, she was wishing she could swap places with the dog.

A few nights later, I woke in the early hours and couldn't slip back into sleep. Thinking to read a while, I opened the door to the day chamber. The queen was asleep at a table, her head lying on a mess of papers. The creak of the door woke her and she sat up, her hair all awry, and started rummaging about, picking up sheets of paper, then throwing them down.

'Where is that transcript? I had it in my hand, and now it's gone.'

I picked up a paper from the floor.

'Is this it?'

'Yes…' She read through it, then shook her head. 'But it doesn't make any sense. I've gone wrong with the code again. If my eyes weren't so sore…'

She rested her head in her hands, rubbing at her temples.

'Your majesty, why don't I fetch Susan so she can put you to bed?'

'No, I have to read this letter, so I can send the reply. I have to make him see… but this cipher is so difficult.'

'Can I help? My eyes are good, and I'm wide awake.'

She looked at me.

'It's not many words, I think we could do it quite quickly,' I said. 'If you trust me…'

* * *

From then on it became my job to code and decode their letters, a responsibility I accepted with pride; at least now I could do something to help, though in my heart I knew it didn't compare to what other men would have to do on the battlefield. From the letters I learned that it wasn't just the difficulty of raising money that was clouding the queen's face with worry. The king was dithering and backtracking with Parliament, still certain he was clever enough to talk them round, when it was obvious to a fool and the fool's sister they were set on having their way. So I wasn't very surprised when, about five months into our stay, a letter arrived saying that a big store of arms in Hull, which the queen had warned him to secure, had been removed to London by order of Parliament.

As I started to decode it, she read my face.

'I knew it,' she said, taking the transcript and reading the first few lines. 'I told him this would happen.' She paced up and down, the letter in her hand, making the candles flicker as she passed them. 'Here I am,' she said, as much to herself as to me, 'turning myself into a pedlar, meeting every kind of ruffian, men who don't even raise their hats to me, all to make sure we have the arms we need.'

She turned to me.

'All he had to do was keep hold of what we already had. If he'd acted quickly, it was easily done. But no, he insisted on talking to those louts as though they were reasonable people. And look what that has cost us.'

She threw the paper down.

'He'll give in to them. They'll tell him he can't win when they are so much better armed, and he'll give them everything they want, until we're king and queen in name only. And then they will ruin England with their barbarous ideas.'

I thought she was right, at least about the king, but I didn't say so.

'If I was with him, I could make him stand firm,' she said. 'But from here, it's impossible.'

'Should we go back?'

'We can't. I'd be a weapon for them – if they took me, they could make him agree to anything. We can't go back until he defeats those scoundrels.'

I looked at her, a thought taking shape in my head.

'What?' she said. 'You've given me good advice before, Nathaniel, let me hear it.'

'You said, you'd be a weapon for them. So use that weapon yourself. Tell him that if he doesn't beat them, you can never go back to England.'

'He must realise that.'

It didn't seem to me that he realised that or very much else. I chose my words carefully.

'You said yourself, his majesty believes he can persuade them to be reasonable. It's a worthy aim and, given time, perhaps they will be swayed on some questions. But they will never be reasonable when it comes to you. That's what you need to tell him.'

It was four in the morning before the letter was finished. The queen had a tendency to make wildly dramatic statements, but I was sure it would strike home more directly if she spelt out simply and plainly that she could never again live in England if the Parliamentarians were allowed the kind of powers they wanted. So we drafted and redrafted it, and finally, I put it into the code. As I handed it to her to seal, the candle on the table burned to its end, and flickered out.

For four weeks, stormy weather stopped letters from England. Every day the shadows under the queen's eyes grew darker, and the worry made her so irritable that even Bonbon took to keeping out of her way. As August slid into September, we were tallying up ammunition orders when Susan came in, holding a letter from the king. The queen stood over me as I deciphered it. The first three lines held the news that must have been swirling around England for weeks. The king had issued a proclamation, asking his loyal subjects to fight alongside him. The war had begun.

Chapter Twenty-seven

We spent the early hours of our first night back in England cowering in a ditch outside the village of Bridlington, and before we'd even passed a night on English soil, I watched a man die.

It was six months since the king's proclamation; by the time the queen had bought all the arms she could afford, winter had closed in, and we had to wait out the worst of it before we could sail. News from home was scarce, but it was clear that the hoped-for quick victory wasn't going to happen. The entire country was split: the north and west were loyal to the king, but the Parliamentarian army held London – no surprise to me after that day at the Exchange – and the south-east all the way down to the coast, as well as a belt of towns across the Midlands. Yet when we stepped onto the quay that bitterly cold afternoon, the scene was peaceful. A thin blanket of snow lay on the ground, and a few flakes were still drifting down from a pure white sky. Soldiers had been sent to protect us, but in truth, I couldn't see what from.

A little knot of villagers had gathered on the snowy quay-side, and as the queen picked her way across the slippery cobbles, a fat man stepped forward, swiping the woollen hat off his head and bowing low.

'Welcome, your majesty,' he said. 'We're honoured to have you here. We're for the king in Bridlington, and so's everyone else in these parts.'

He ducked back, blushing, as she thanked him, then she laughed as a little girl peering from behind her mother's legs said in a loud whisper:

'Where's her crown then?'

'I never wear it in the snow,' said the queen. 'It doesn't do to let it get wet.'

They made us welcome, each of the cottages along the harbour front finding room for three or four of us to sleep. There'd obviously been competition for the honour of hosting the queen; we were to eat dinner with the fat man and his family, but sleep in a cottage a few doors along.

It was a long time since I'd seen her as happy as that night. We shared a simple meal with the family, their three little boys' wide-eyed stares divided between me and the queen. The wife apologised that there was only salted fish, but the queen said she'd rarely eaten a nicer dish, which made the woman blush to the tips of her ears. On a chest in the corner, there was a box made of beautifully polished wood, the lid covered with seashells, and the queen commented on how pretty it was.

'Jem made that,' said the wife, beaming at her husband.

'It's just something to do in the winter, on days we can't take the boats out,' said the man, his cheeks flushing.

He looked questioningly at his wife, and when she gave a little nod, he said, 'I have another, almost finished, your majesty. I could finish it tonight, and I'd be honoured if you'd have it. As a memento, you might say, of your time here.'

She protested that she didn't want to put him to any trouble, but he wouldn't be swayed, and when she accepted the offer, the man and his wife went so red I was afraid their heads might burst.

The family we were to stay with were equally welcoming, insisting the queen, Susan and Elizabeth take their bedroom, and Henry and I the little chamber where their children usually slept. Before we retired, the queen insisted on writing to tell the king she'd arrived safely.

'Do you remember how it was all those years ago?' she said, as I sat translating her letter into code. 'How I missed France, and my family?'

'Of course I do.'

'I never thought England would feel like home. But when I stepped onto that quayside today, I felt it in my bones. This is my country. And with God's help, we can save it from those barbarians. They can't win, not when good people like these support us.'

The first cannonball hit the cottage next door, at about three in the morning. Before I knew if I was awake or dreaming, an even louder bang shook our cottage, and the roof fell in, showering down shards of wood and clouds of dust and soot.

On the stairs, Susan was hurriedly wrapping a cloak around the queen. A soldier appeared at the door.

'Your majesty, we need to get you away. They've got ships in the harbour, they know you're here.'

People were spilling out of the houses, dragging screaming children as they fled from the seafront.

'Tell us where to go,' she said.

'The edge of the village,' said the soldier. 'There's a natural shelter, we'll take you there.'

'No, we can find it. Get everyone away. Henry, help them, we'll be fine.'

As we ran, following the villagers, shots thundered through the air and the quayside filled with smoke. I'm not ashamed to say I was terrified; none of us had expected an attack like that.

'Bonbon!' said the queen, stopping suddenly. 'I left her behind!'

She darted back towards the cottage. Susan shouted after her, but there was no point. Not when it came to that wretched dog. We ran to catch her, but with all the villagers fleeing in the opposite direction, Susan couldn't dodge through them as easily as I could. By the time I reached the house, the queen was already running upstairs, shouting Bonbon's name.

Just as she bent to yank the covers off the bed, a shot blasted clean through the wall, whistling above her head. We threw ourselves to the floor as bits of stone and mortar spattered the room, and there, under the bed, huddled against the far wall, was Bonbon. I squeezed underneath and wormed my way across, only for the blasted animal to bare her teeth and snarl at me.

'You bite me, and I'll leave you to die,' I said.

She gave a huffy little growl, but let me drag her out. The queen took her from me and we ran. Shots were still flying as the soldiers hustled the last few people out of their houses. The queen was faster than me, so she was well ahead when a shot whistled behind us. I turned: the fat man was hurrying out of his cottage, clutching a box with seashells on the lid. One minute he was there and the next he was blown apart. The shell box fell to the ground, quite unharmed. For a second my legs wouldn't move and I stood there as the snow turned red with blood. Then another shot blasted out and I ran.

The natural shelter the soldier had told us to head for was a ditch, with walls twenty feet high, that ran along the edge of the village, built as some sort of defence centuries before. For three bitterly cold hours, we huddled there, as shots boomed out into the night. Not until dawn, when the tide forced the ships to withdraw, could we finally emerge.

'How lucky this place was here,' said the queen brightly, as we clambered out, limbs stiff from the cold. 'You see, God is on our side.'

With my ears still ringing from the shots, and my nose clogged with dust and soot, I stared at her. Did she really understand what was happening? If God was on our side, how had the Parliamentarian ships been able to sneak up on us, and all the defenceless villagers, in the middle of the night? Then she looked at me, and I saw in her eyes that she'd been as frightened as I was. She just didn't want anyone else to see.

I didn't tell her the man with the shell box had died going back to fetch his present for her. But I couldn't stop thinking it might have been her blood, or mine, staining the snow red that night.

Chapter Twenty-eight

We knew now what we'd returned into: they'd stop at nothing to kill or capture the queen, and anyone associated with her. But she was determined to get the arms and the troops she'd brought to the king. He'd made his headquarters in Oxford, but between Yorkshire and Oxfordshire there was a solid belt of Parliamentary territory, and we'd be rats in a trap travelling through it. So it was decided that we'd go to York, and wait there until the king's forces cleared the route ahead.

As we rode through a reassuringly large and solid city gate, the horses' hooves clattering on the cobbles, a great roar went up. Even though it was a bitterly cold day, hundreds of people had turned out to welcome the queen, and they were packed into the narrow streets within the walls, cheering and waving makeshift pennants.

'Well, we should be safe from being shot in our beds tonight,' said Henry. He glanced up and tipped his hat to a buxom young woman who was leaning out of the window above an apothecary's shop. 'And don't take offence but, since we're clearly very popular with the locals, I might find better company than yours to share mine with while we're here.'

'Go ahead,' I said. 'I had enough of your snoring last night.'

'Seriously though, I'm glad of this.' He nodded at the queen, who was riding ahead of us. 'Bridlington was a lucky escape. If the king's got any sense, he'll tell her to send the arms and the men on, and stay here, where she's safe.'

The king didn't tell her to do that, and she wouldn't have listened anyway. After all those months she'd spent gathering arms and men for him, and learning about tactics and strategies as she did it, she wanted to play her part – not least because she didn't trust him to stand firm on his own. There was a letter waiting for her when we arrived at the house near the Minster where we were to stay. Impatient for news, she read over my shoulder as I decoded it. He was negotiating with Parliament, he said, but only so that no one could claim he was the one prolonging the fight. She threw up her hands.

'Negotiating, he says. With traitors?'

His letter finished with loving words about how much he missed her, but I hadn't even written those down before she started dictating her reply:

If you make peace with these people, it has all been for nothing...

Any agreement, she told him, would leave him worse off than he was before. The current Parliament had to be defeated and disbanded, and if he accepted anything less than that, she would go straight back to France, rather than risk falling into their hands.

* * *

We were staying in the home of the Ingram family, who owned quite a lot of Yorkshire. The house had been newly built from the ruins of the old archbishop's palace, sparing no expense, as its owner, Sir Thomas, insisted on telling us, in more detail than anyone required, over dinner that first night.

'We're honoured to have you here, your majesty,' he said, when he'd finished explaining exactly which part of Florence the wall hangings had come from. 'Of course this is the smaller of our homes, but I think you'll find it comfortable. And Lady Frances...' He nodded at his young wife, who hadn't yet opened her mouth and looked petrified at the thought that she might now be expected to, '...will be pleased to arrange your entertainment. We were thinking, perhaps a ball, nothing too extravagant, just local families.'

'Oh no,' said the queen. 'Please don't trouble yourself, our time here will be fully taken up. But of course I would be happy to receive those from the locality who support the king.'

If he thought she meant to meet them for polite conversation, he was soon disabused of that idea. Within days, she'd persuaded three local landowners to give money and men, and when the Ingrams ran out of wealthy friends to call on, she wrote to the governor of Scarborough, who was for Parliament but was rumoured to be considering switching sides, suggesting 'friendly talks'. That resulted in him defecting to the king, and bringing with him not just a useful port but a ship laden with arms, previously destined for Parliament's army.

It wasn't long before word of her successes reached them, of course. Realising she was now very much part of the fight, they wrote to invite her to London, to talk about their proposals for peace – but warned that if she refused, she could expect their forces to do all they could to stop her delivering the arms to Oxford. She kept them hanging for a week or so, but they must have known she'd never agree and, two months into our stay in York, came the news that told us they'd given up all pretence of making an agreement with her.

She was dictating a letter to the king when Henry brought in the newsbook that had reached York's streets that morning. He started to explain but she took it from him and read the words herself.

'Impeached,' she said, when she'd finished. 'You know, after all these years, I still find English so strange. Such a pretty word for such a nasty thing.'

I thought back to that day in Whitehall, when we'd first heard that they might accuse her of treason. She'd been so afraid, shrinking back into her chair, but now she hardly seemed to care.

'At least now they're honest: it's a fight to the death, between me and them,' she said. 'But we all know, it's been that for a long time.'

We finally set out from York on a fine summer's day, three months after we'd arrived. The troops were in high spirits now we were finally on our way: over the clip-clop of the cavalry horses we caught snatches of singing from the hundreds of foot soldiers bringing up the rear, the queen pretending not to hear the bawdier choruses. Determined not to show fear, she'd refused to travel in a coach and instead rode at the head of the train, laughingly calling herself their 'she-generalissima', but deadly serious as she discussed tactics with the troops' commander Lord Newcastle, a florid Yorkshireman who very much enjoyed the sound of his own voice. Before we left, there'd been days of discussions about the route we should take; although the Royalist forces had won strongholds we could aim for, out in open countryside we'd still be vulnerable to attack. During one such conversation, I'd ventured to make a suggestion and Lord Newcastle had looked at me with much the same expression he might have worn if Bonbon had suddenly pointed out a weakness in his argument. Then he laughed, and said, 'Comical little chap! But leave the fighting to the men, eh?' A few minutes later Henry, who hadn't been listening, put forward the same idea, and Lord Newcastle nodded and said, 'Exactly what I was thinking.' After much the same thing happened twice more, I kept my thoughts to myself.

Late that first afternoon, Lord Newcastle was delivering a long anecdote that was clearly going to culminate in yet another example of his remarkable military acumen, when a rider appeared in the distance, pelting towards us and shouting something we couldn't hear. He halted the troops and the great procession clattered to a stop.

The rider was a young woman. As she pulled up on the fine-boned white horse, the hood of her soft woollen cloak slipped back, releasing long red curls.

'Thank goodness,' she said. 'Mother thought you'd come this way, but I wasn't sure, and I know I'm supposed to curtsey, your majesty, but there isn't much time, if I don't get back soon they'll realise I've gone and—'

'Stop,' said the queen. 'Get your breath back.'

The girl took a deep breath.

'There's a plot,' she said. 'They're going to kidnap you.'

The queen's face went white, all bravado gone. We'd heard enough news of ambushes over the months to know that in the confusion of a surprise attack, anything could happen. Even surrounded by soldiers, she wasn't safe.

The girl, Arabella, spoke quickly and to the point: her family were Catholics, and for the king, but their home, Denham Hall, had been invaded by Parliamentarian troops a few nights before. Her father and brothers were with the king's army in Oxford, leaving only her, her mother and a handful of servants; there'd been nothing they could do when the soldiers took over the place. They'd been forbidden to leave, and ordered to turn any visitors away with the excuse that there was sickness in the house.

'They said if we disobeyed, they'd kill us. Our steward argued with them and the main man, Major Sarenbrant, he lifted his pistol and shot him. Just like that. He was sixty, Peter, he couldn't have harmed a fly. But he shot him dead.' She closed her eyes for a second, as if she was trying to clear the picture. 'I heard them talking, and we knew we had to warn you.'

'Do you know how they plan to do it?' asked Lord Newcastle.

She shook her head, the red curls tumbling round her face.

'No. I was just taking ale to the ones in charge – our best ale, of course, they don't stint themselves – and they stopped talking when I came in. I heard them say they had to get you before you reached Doncaster, that's all.'

'How many soldiers are there?' asked Lord Newcastle.

'About as many as you've got, I'd say. They're camped in

our fields. Major Sarenbrant comes and goes, but when he's there, he sleeps in the house. And there's always half a dozen of them around the house, guarding us.'

'If we strike by night, we can take them,' Lord Newcastle said to the queen. 'We'll work out where best to attack from and—'

'Wait,' said Arabella. She looked from the queen to Lord Newcastle. 'What do you mean, attack? You can't attack our house.'

'Young lady,' said Lord Newcastle. 'You don't—'

'If they see so much as one soldier, they'll kill everyone. You won't be able to stop them. I've already put us in danger, riding here to tell you. I thought you'd just turn back.'

Lord Newcastle shook his head.

'It's clear they know where we are. If we turn back, they could still come after her majesty – and we won't know where or when.'

'Could you get everyone out of the house?' asked the queen.

Arabella shook her head.

'I only managed to get out because Major Sarenbrant went off somewhere last night – the guards get lazy when he's not there, and Mother distracted them by letting all the pigs out. But tonight he'll be back – and I told you, he said if we tried to escape he'd kill us.'

The queen turned to Lord Newcastle.

'Is there really no other way?'

'If we knew where and when they planned to attack, we could ambush them on the road,' he said. 'But without that information, I'm afraid attacking the house is the only feasible strategy.'

'I'm sorry, Arabella, we don't have a choice,' said the queen. She turned to Lord Newcastle again. 'But we need to work out how best to protect the household. Get your best men together and we'll plan this properly. Quickly, there's no time to lose.'

She couldn't have done otherwise, I knew that. And it wasn't just fear for herself; if the Parliamentarians captured her, they could make the king do anything, and she couldn't let that happen. But the queen I'd known back in the Whitehall days wouldn't have made that decision so easily. The war had changed her, even by then.

I went to go with them, but Lord Newcastle held up a hand to stop me.

'I think the young lady's horse would appreciate some water,' he said. 'Perhaps you could show her where to find it?'

So now I was the stable boy.

I slid down from the saddle and stomped towards the water carrier; Arabella caught me up.

'I can't let them do this,' she said. 'You could speak to the queen, couldn't you? Make her understand—'

I gestured to the bucket of water I was filling.

'Does it look like she's waiting to hear what I think?'

'Whoa, no need to be so prickly. I just thought, because you were riding with her ...'

'She wouldn't listen to me. Not about that kind of thing.'

'Well, if you can't help, can you hurry up with that water? I've got to get back and warn everyone. Perhaps we can hide, somehow, though I can't see ...' She threw up her hands. 'Why didn't I find out more? That man said, didn't he, if they knew where it was going to happen, they could attack there instead?'

'But you didn't hear any details?'

'No, not a thing. I could find out tonight, I could listen from the priest hole – but once Major Sarenbrant's back, I won't be able to get out again.'

Of course; there was always a priest hole in Catholic houses. I'd seen one, once; the queen had been moved to tears at the thought of a priest trapped in the tiny, dark space, listening to the sounds of the house being searched and knowing his fate if they found him.

Arabella couldn't get out again with the information, because they were watching her – but what if someone else could? Someone they didn't know was there in the first place?

'The priest hole,' I said. 'Could you definitely hear them from it?'

'Yes, it's right above the hall. We used to eavesdrop on our parents when we were children – you can hear everything.'

'Could you get me in? And out?'

Lord Newcastle shook his head when I explained the plan.

'This is no time for jokes, little man.' He wagged a finger at me. 'The threat to her majesty is serious, and—'

'It's not a joke,' I said. 'It's the only way we're going to find out what they're planning. And if there's anyone who can get in and out of that house without being seen it's me.'

'We've worked it out,' said Arabella. I'd expected her to laugh when I told her my idea, but straight away, she'd started figuring out how we could do it. 'I can smuggle him in and hide him. And once Major Sarenbrant's asleep, he can slip away.'

'I can be back here by dawn,' I said. 'Major Sarenbrant's

not expected until very late, so they won't be attacking tonight.'

'Simply not possible,' said Lord Newcastle. 'Now, your majesty, we really should—'

He gestured for the queen to walk with him, but Arabella caught her arm.

'Just give us one night,' she said.

'You owe her that,' I said. 'She took a big risk coming here.'

Lord Newcastle's eyebrows shot up, and he looked at the queen. But she nodded; ever since the days when we'd stood in front of Mr Van Dyck's easel, she'd trusted me to speak plainly to her when others wouldn't. She held up her hand as Lord Newcastle started blustering about how they were wasting time and needed to get on with planning the attack, and turned to me.

'What if you can't get out again?' she said.

'Then you do what you have to do,' I said.

'This is quite ridiculous,' said Lord Newcastle. 'Your majesty, I must—'

'It isn't,' said the queen. 'It's a good plan.' She shook her head. 'But it's dangerous. If you're caught…'

'Your majesty,' I said. 'You once told me you knew what it was like to be treated as a child when you were no longer one. Well, I'm not a child. I'm a man. And I can do this.'

We looked at each other for a long moment, then Arabella spoke up.

'I don't want to be rude, but I can't wait any longer. Is he coming or not?'

The queen nodded.

'Yes. He's coming.'

* * *

At last, I had my chance to do something braver than sitting at a desk and transcribing letters. But I hadn't envisaged that service to involve being smuggled into a Parliamentarian stronghold in a potato sack. I'd been hidden under Arabella's cloak on the ride to the house, and we'd managed to get through a side entrance to the parkland and down to the stables without being seen. But between there and the house, there'd be guards. The vegetable store was by the stables and the sack was the best idea either of us could come up with. She fetched a barrow and I climbed inside the sack and curled into a ball, with potatoes piled on top of me. The light was fading by then; if I kept perfectly still, surely the guards wouldn't look too closely? But for all my longing to be a hero, I kept remembering Jeremiah's words. *You'll be a trophy. If they get their hands on you, they won't let you go.* And now it wasn't just my own life I was risking; if they found me, what would they do to Arabella?

'I'm going to wheel you up to the back door, but there'll be two guards before we get there,' she said. 'Don't move, don't make a sound, until I tell you it's safe.'

A blast of cold air and the crunch of gravel told me we were outside. A moment later footsteps walked towards us.

'What are you doing out here?' asked a voice. 'You were told to stay inside the house.'

I held my breath.

'We need potatoes for the major's dinner,' she said, her voice perfectly steady. She went to walk on, then gasped as the barrow jerked back; one of the soldiers must have caught hold of her arm.

'Perhaps she fancied some male company,' another voice said. 'You wouldn't be the first to be hot for a soldier, sweetheart. When it comes down to it, you've got the same between your legs as any dairymaid, haven't you?'

My stomach turned to ice. I couldn't let them touch her.

And how are you going to stop them?

'Let me pass,' she said. Her voice didn't waver, but as she leaned forward and adjusted the opening of the sack, making sure I was covered, her hands were shaking.

'Too good for us, is that it? Why don't we see about that?'

'Take your hands off me,' she said. Her voice trembled a little but then she said more steadily: 'Unless you want the major to hear about this.'

'Leave off, Dan,' said the other soldier. 'If she goes telling tales, there'll be trouble, you know what he's like. We'll get another bloody soldiers of Christ lecture.'

'You'd think there'd be some benefits to being in God's army,' grumbled the first soldier, but the resignation in his voice told me he'd stepped back.

Arabella lifted the handles of the barrow.

'Wait a minute,' said the second soldier. 'That's a lot of potatoes, just for the major's dinner and yours.'

My blood froze. A hand grasped the top of the sack.

'We could do with a few spuds ourselves,' he said. 'You won't miss one or two—'

'Is something wrong?'

The woman's voice came from the back door of the house.

'I was just coming, Mother,' said Arabella. 'With the potatoes.'

She jerked the barrow up and strode towards the door, muttering 'Don't run, don't run' under her breath.

'What happened?' said her mother. 'Did they—'

'Not now! Let's get inside. You won't believe what's in this sack.'

Chapter Twenty-nine

The priest hole stank. It was a shallow space between the ceiling of the main hall and the floor of a bedroom, the narrow trap door hidden under a heavy wooden chest. The previous inhabitants must have been rats, and they weren't long departed; the smell they left behind was nearly as bad as the prospect of their company if they decided to return.

'Hurry!' said Arabella's mother, standing guard at the bedroom door. 'If the guards come...'

Lady Denham hadn't been best pleased to discover what was in the potato sack – I think her exact words to Arabella were, 'Child, are you stark raving mad?' She'd insisted they hide me straight away, so even the servants wouldn't know I was there.

Major Sarenbrant had sent word that he expected to arrive after ten, and they should have food ready for him.

'He's a pig,' Arabella said. 'Sits there like he owns the place. He's as thin as a pin, like a skeleton with skin on it, but he eats enough for three men. Mind you, he gets more than he bargains for. I spit in every dish I take in.'

Lying in the dark, I thought about the priests who'd

hidden there, listening to the house being searched. Perhaps the darkness made me fanciful but I swear I smelt fear; it seeped out of the walls, mingling with the sweet stench of rats' piss. And I was in the same position as those priests. If they discovered me, at best, they'd keep me as a hostage, but they might just as easily kill me. We'd passed a rough grave on the way to the stables; the poor steward hadn't even had a Christian burial. And I'd be as much of a trophy dead as alive.

My big chance to be a hero, and suddenly the whole idea was ridiculously foolish. We couldn't even be sure I'd hear anything useful, let alone that I could escape with the information. I thought of the queen's face, pinched with fear when she heard about the plot. She was counting on me, and my excitement at getting the chance to be useful had turned into a heavy dread that I might fail her. But there was nothing to do except wait and hope.

At last, footsteps sounded below. A door opened and closed, chairs scraped back, and a voice said:

'Right, Owen, let's see that map.'

From the commanding tone, I guessed he was Major Sarenbrant, the skeleton-faced man Arabella had described, but his accent was a shock. I hadn't heard it in a while but I'd have known it anywhere: he was from Rutland, or at least thereabouts. A moment's thought told me it made sense. I knew my home county was in the hands of the other side – I'd heard they'd even commandeered the duke's old house as their headquarters – and from here, they'd be the nearest Parliamentarian forces. I just wasn't expecting that the man plotting to kill the queen might be someone I could have passed by at the Oakham fair, or stood beside in the market-place.

There was a pause, I guessed while the man called Owen was unfolding the map, and then he said, 'This is the place we'll do it. Just outside Mark's Cross.'

'You're sure they'll go that way?' said Major Sarenbrant.

I couldn't have heard them more clearly if I'd been sitting at the table with them. Which meant if I made the slightest move, they'd hear me too.

'It's the best road, and those guns are heavy – they won't risk getting stuck in the mud on another route,' said Owen. 'They're travelling slowly, they won't reach this spot till around four. If we leave at first light, we can be waiting for them, and we'll attack just before this fork, see, where there's plenty of cover. That bridge is narrow, it'll stop them turning back.'

The door opened, and I recognised Arabella's light footsteps.

'About time,' said Major Sarenbrant. 'I hope the meat is better cooked than last time.'

She didn't reply, and I smiled in the darkness. *I spit in every dish I take in.*

They ate without talking, the silence broken only by the clink of knives on pewter. I pictured the place they'd described. *Near Mark's Cross, a narrow bridge, plenty of cover* – the road must go through woodland then. *A fork in the road.* If I saw a map, I'd be able to find it.

I was concentrating so hard that when something brushed my hand, I instinctively flinched. My arm nudged the purse at my waist, and the coins clinked.

'What was that?' said Owen. I sat, frozen. 'That girl – I bet she's eavesdropping.'

'You're imagining things,' said Major Sarenbrant. 'She couldn't hear anything through that great thick door anyway. Sit down and finish your dinner.'

Something brushed my hand again; the bravest of the rats had decided to reclaim their billet. Its claws made only the faintest of scratching sounds on the floor, but the slightest move from me would send it scrabbling noisily away. Major Sarenbrant must know the Denhams were Catholic; it wouldn't take much to work out there was a priest hole above him. I sat rigid as the rat got bolder, running across my legs and chewing at my breeches, and steeled myself not to flinch if it bit me.

When the meal was finished, the map must have been got out again; Owen was talking about the woods on either side of the road.

'They'll move to protect her as soon as they see us,' said the major.

'Of course. But I've assigned men to pick off the guards around her straight away – one to one. It'll be chaos, and Crabbe and his men will grab her and get her away before the troops behind even realise what's happening. Whatever damage we can do then will be a bonus.'

'Get her down to London and hand her over as fast as you can. We don't want to risk them trying to get her back.'

'I'm keeping men and horses back for that,' said Owen. 'And it's a full moon tomorrow, so they won't need to wait till morning.'

'Good. The sooner she's in the Tower, the better. If this works, it changes everything. He'll do exactly what he's told once he knows we've got her.'

'And her?'

'We all know this country's never going to be safe with a papist queen. They'll get what they want from him and once it's all signed and sealed, they'll give her what she deserves. This country's dealt with treasonous queens before. If we have to, we'll do it again.'

He was talking about killing her, as though it was nothing. And it would be a brutal death; you'll know as well as I do how Queen Anne and Queen Katherine died. I was desperate then, to get out and take back the information about the ambush, but there'd be no chance until they went to bed.

After a while they called for more ale. This time Arabella's mother brought it.

'We've made up the blue room for you, Major,' she said. 'And I've put hot bricks in your beds, with it being such a cold night.'

'No,' said Major Sarenbrant. 'I don't want that room again, it's draughty. The chamber above here must be warmer, give me that one.'

'That's my son's room, it's not made up, with them being away, and—'

'Well, get it made up. We leave at dawn, and I want to get to bed.'

Major Sarenbrant's heavy footsteps strode across to the bed, and his boots dropped to the floor. *Keep calm; don't lose your nerve. You can still make this work.* I'd have to wait out the night, but if he left at dawn, I could get the information back to the queen in time. *If they don't find you first.*

The fire downstairs had sent up some warmth, but as the

night drew on the chill from the floor seeped through my clothes. Major Sarenbrant had either overdone the ale, or had problems with his bladder; he got up and pissed in the pot at least five times. After so many hours, you might imagine the effect that had on me, and there was nothing to do but answer the call of nature where I sat, adding wet, cold breeches to my troubles.

In the darkness, my eyelids sagged. Afraid that if I fell asleep I might move or make a sound, I dug my fingernails into my palms and mouthed the words of every song I could think of. But it was no use. As my head fell forward, I jolted awake, heard a grunt of surprise and realised it had come from me.

Moments passed. *He didn't hear. He's still asleep.* Then the bed creaked. My heart hammering, I strained my ears for the splash of water in the pot. It didn't come. He stood still. *He's listening.* Then he walked across to the chest. The floorboards creaked as he shifted his weight; testing them, listening for the hollow sound that would tell him what he'd found.

Wood scraped on wood. *He's moving the chest.*

I closed my eyes, waiting for the sound of the trap door lifting. The thought struck me suddenly that he was probably weighing up whether to open the trap door himself, or fetch reinforcements. He didn't know who was inside, or what weapons they might have. The scraping sound again confirmed it; he must be moving the chest back.

But he didn't go to the door and open it. He walked back to the bed, there was the splash of piss in the pot, and then, unmistakably, the creak of him lying down again. It took me a few panicked moments to see: when you hear a rat trap snap in the night, you don't get up and deal with the captive then and there. You wait till morning and dispose of it at your leisure.

Chapter Thirty

I waited through the long hours of darkness, imagining the moment when the trap door would open above me. I remembered what Arabella had said about Major Sarenbrant shooting the steward without a thought. But they wouldn't do that to me, not straight away. They'd want to know what I knew first, and I didn't want to think about what they might do to make me tell them. *Or what they'll do to the people who hid you here.*

It was almost a relief when at last he rose and left the room. I listened for boots running up the stairs. They were going to get a surprise when they saw me, and I hoped that if nothing else, I'd make the major look foolish for seeking reinforcements. I was just beginning a prayer that I'd be strong enough to withstand whatever they did to me, when his voice came from below.

'We've no time to eat now. Pack up some provisions for us to take. We leave in ten minutes.'

It was Arabella who worked it out.

'Shh,' she said, putting a finger to her lips as she opened

the trap door. 'The major's gone, but there are guards downstairs.'

In a whisper, I told her what had happened in the night.

'He moved the chest?'

'Yes. I heard it, scraping on the floor.'

She glanced across at the bed, then bent down.

'Like this?' she said, struggling to pull out a drawer in the chest. It was stiff, and I recognised the noise immediately. She pointed to the bed, where a thick red rug lay pulled aside. 'He went looking for extra covers. I should have thought, he's always complaining of the cold. Christ's blood, if he'd moved the chest...'

We were both silent for a moment.

'Right,' she said. 'Let's get you out of here.' She beckoned me over to the window. 'There are two guards just below. Mother's going to ride down the drive, as though she means to leave. They'll try to stop her, and while they're busy with that, you can sneak out the same way we came in.'

'She can't do that. You don't know what they might do.'

'Yes we do. But we don't have much choice, do we? If they find you here, we're all dead anyway.'

Lady Denham came out of the stables on a chestnut mare, looking neither right nor left as she set off at a brisk trot. It took a moment for the guards to realise what was happening, and by the time they ran after her, shouting, she was a good way ahead.

We ran across to the stables, where an elderly donkey was hitched to a cart.

'Fitch is old, but he can still go at a clip and he knows the way to the village,' said Arabella. 'Take the road beside the church, that'll get you back to where they were going to set camp. You can leave the cart anywhere, but find a grassy field for Fitch – I don't know when I'll be able to fetch him.'

The cart step was high off the ground; as if the potato sack hadn't been humiliating enough, now I was going to have to get her to lift me onto the seat. But before I could ask, she went to the back of the stables and came back with a stool for me to step up on. I was about to thank her for being so thoughtful, but I stopped myself in time. *Don't be stupid: she just doesn't want to touch you.* I remembered how people in Oakham had been like that sometimes, as if they thought my misfortune might somehow rub off on them.

Foolishly, I'd been flattered when she assumed I had some influence with the queen, pleased that she hadn't taken one look at me and dismissed me as of no importance. But if she turned out to be just a silly, superstitious country girl after all, what was that to me? Turning my back on her, I climbed up. There was a basket on the seat.

'Bread and cheese,' she said. 'I thought you might be hungry.'

'Thank you.'

She looked at me, with her head on one side, as if she was about to say something, but she didn't. I flicked the reins, and the donkey moved off.

Chapter Thirty-one

With what I'd overheard, it was easy to pinpoint where the Parliamentarians intended to attack. While the queen's party stayed, well guarded, in camp, Lord Newcastle took a contingent of our troops to ambush theirs at the very place they'd expected to ambush us. They came back whooping and hollering in triumph: they'd caught the other side completely by surprise, thanks to the same dense woodlands Sarenbrant's men had been planning to hide in. The soldiers Sarenbrant had expected to pick off the queen's guards one by one had got picked off themselves, and they'd got a good proportion of the ones that came behind them too.

'To our secret weapon,' said Lord Newcastle, the old hypocrite, as he raised his tankard to me that night. As always, the queen insisted we eat outside, sitting round a fire just as the soldiers did. Extra rations of ale had been given out to celebrate the victory, and through the haze of woodsmoke came periodic cheers, as the circles of men round their fires recounted the events of the day.

'They must be cursing now, trying to work out how we knew,' said Henry. 'Here's to Nat Davy, the queen's spy.'

When dinner was over, the queen said she had an announcement to make. Henry nudged me: 'Wait till you hear this.'

Thanks to me, she said, we'd been able not just to foil the kidnap plot, but do some real damage to the other side.

'You showed true courage, Nathaniel, and it deserves to be recognised.'

Lord Newcastle nodded.

'Very well deserved,' he said.

My heart thumped. They'd realised I could be useful. I didn't dare hope I'd be assigned to a troop, but even if they let me ride along on a skirmish, that would...

'I am appointing you Honorary Captain of Horse,' she said. 'With my thanks.'

It took me a moment to recognise the words. Honorary Captain of Horse. The same title the king had given their eldest son, nine-year-old Prince Charles, when the war began. I thanked her, of course, but as I looked around at the real soldiers who'd fought that day, I couldn't feel proud of a made-up honour fit only for a child who would never see the field of battle. Other men proved themselves with strength and skill, but the only talent I'd shown was being small enough to fit into a potato sack. The soldiers cheered, but they weren't cheering me as one of their own.

As we sat on into the night, celebrating the victory, I drank my share of the ale and sang my share of the songs, so the queen wouldn't think I was ungrateful. But disappointment sat in my guts like a stone. And I kept thinking about the girl, Arabella. If anyone had shown courage it was her, and her mother: they'd seen what Major Sarenbrant was willing to do to anyone who so much as argued with him, yet they'd taken the risk, to save the queen. And we'd left them to it. Ever since I'd driven away from the house in the cart, I'd been telling myself they'd be fine, no one had seen me there, there was nothing they could be blamed for. But all the same, I wished I knew for sure. She might be just a silly, superstitious country girl who thought she could catch bad luck from touching me, but I didn't want anything bad to happen to her.

Next morning, we were stamping out the last of the fires when she arrived, riding the same white horse. This time the red hair didn't tumble loose from her hood; it had been cut in ragged tufts to just below her ears, and a bruise marked her cheek, staining the pale skin violet and blue. My stomach turned over: what had we done?

'They made my mother tell them,' she said. 'And then they killed her.'

As Susan dabbed witch hazel on the bruise, Arabella explained that her mother had managed to talk her way out of trouble with the guards, pretending she hadn't realised she wasn't even allowed to go into the village. But Major Sarenbrant was already suspicious about our ambush, and when one of the guards mentioned the commotion with Lady Denham, he realised something had been going on at the house. He lined the whole household up and threatened to kill Arabella unless someone told him what had happened.

'He held a knife against my throat. I told her not to tell. I said they were going to kill us anyway, so why help them?' She put a hand up to her ragged hair. 'That's when he did this.

With the knife. He said if she didn't say, he'd do the same to my neck, and he couldn't promise that would be a clean cut either.'

'Jesu,' said the queen. 'You poor child.'

'So she told them. Except she didn't say it was me that sneaked Nat in, she said it was her. But they didn't believe her.' She looked down for a moment and took a deep breath. 'He told two of the soldiers to take her outside and shoot her. I tried to stop them but he had hold of me. I bit him though.' She pointed to the bruise. 'That's what got me this. But it was worth it. I bit his finger to the bone and I didn't let go till he hit me. He screamed like the pig he is.'

She stared out through the door of the tent, as though she was seeing it all again in her head.

'She didn't struggle or anything,' she said. 'She was so dignified.'

I thought of the night before, when the camp had caroused into the early hours, celebrating our victory, and I'd been awarded my pretend honour. We'd won this round, but Arabella and her family had paid the price, just like the man with the shell box.

The queen took her hands.

'I'm so sorry, Arabella. But we'll get revenge for this.' She turned to me. 'Fetch Lord Newcastle. We'll attack today, this very morning.'

'No,' said Arabella. 'They're gone. They smashed up the house, destroyed everything they couldn't steal, and then they went.'

'How did you escape?' asked Henry.

'I didn't, the pig let me go.' She looked at me. 'He told me to ride here and give you a message from him. He said he knew who you were, and to tell you you're a traitor to the county of Rutland, and to England. And if you ever cross his sight, you'll die a traitor's death.'

Chapter Thirty-two

With her home destroyed and no family nearby, Arabella was alone. The queen wanted to send her, with a guard of soldiers, back to the Ingrams in York.

'They're good people,' she said. 'They'll take care of you until your father and brothers come home – which, God willing, will be soon.'

'No,' said Arabella. 'I'm coming with you. I want to see you beat the people who killed my mother, and I think I've earned the right to.'

The queen did her best to dissuade her, but even by then I'd realised that once Arabella decided to do something, God himself would have a difficult time talking her out of it. A mere queen didn't stand a chance. So when we set off again, she came with us.

From the first morning, she rode with Henry and me, a little behind the queen and Lord Newcastle. And I wasn't pleased. It wasn't that I didn't like her, not at all. But Henry and me, we'd got used to each other: we could ride for miles in a companionable silence, or just as easily pass the time making childish jokes, becoming sillier and sillier until our bellies ached from laughing. But if a woman was around, he couldn't stop himself from flirting – even an old crone we passed on the road would get a twinkle and a tip of his hat, and more often than not, he'd receive a gummy smile in return. And since Arabella had attached herself to us, I concluded she'd fallen for him just like all the others, and I didn't fancy spending my days as a gooseberry while they made cow eyes at each other.

So I got into the habit of dropping back and staying out of their conversation, or riding ahead with the queen and Lord Newcastle, even though his endless stream of stories beginning 'Speaking from my extensive experience ...' made me want to slice my own ears off. That made the miles very long, and it also threw me into a melancholy cast of mind. Ever since my father's visit, my thoughts had often turned to Sam and his wife and daughter. I was happy for him, but it brought back our childhood days, when I watched him grow and become able to do things I couldn't do. Now he had something I'd never have. Jeremiah did too, and then the two lovebirds riding along in front of me became another reminder of what I lacked. I thought I'd become resigned to it, but a part of me couldn't quite accept the truth; can anybody ever accept that they're impossible to love? So no matter how much I told myself to forget about what I couldn't have and be glad for the life I'd got, I still dreamed of a wife to love, who would love me back.

One afternoon on the road, I'd been deep in such thoughts, and by the time we stopped to make camp I was feeling thoroughly sorry for myself. Wrapped up in my brooding, I wasn't concentrating and, instead of sliding down from Shadow's back, holding on to the strap as I usually did, I got my foot caught in the stirrup. Arabella saw my plight.

'Wait,' she said, as I wriggled my foot, cursing. 'Let me help.'

'There's no need, I'm fine.'

I didn't want to see the disgust on her face if she had to touch me.

'You're obviously not,' she said, her hands on her hips. 'But if you'd rather struggle, and make a show of yourself, go ahead.'

'I can do it. You don't need to stay.'

'You'll be sorry you said that if I go and you fall on your head and die.'

'I am not going to fall on my head and die.'

I tugged my foot but the stirrup had twisted and I couldn't get it free. My face flushed red under Arabella's steady gaze; why didn't she just go away?

'This is silly,' she said. 'What if I just untangle your foot? That's all, I won't lift you down.'

Shadow skittered to the side, annoyed at the feeling of me hanging so awkwardly. She'd be tired and hot from the long ride; it wasn't fair of me to keep her from food and water.

'All right,' I said.

Ignoring my grudging tone, Arabella untwisted the strap and eased my foot out. I slid down and bent to brush off my breeches, hoping to hide my embarrassment.

'Thank you,' I said, without looking at her. 'I would have been able to get down anyway, but—'

'Oh, for goodness' sake, what is the matter with you?' I looked up. She folded her arms, and glared down at me. 'What have I done? Come on, tell me. What have I done?'

'I don't—'

'Every time I open my mouth, you make yourself scarce. Going on ahead, or hanging back on your own. So I know there's something.'

'No, it's not—'

'I'm too blunt sometimes, I know that. But I don't think I've said anything to offend you, and if I have, you ought to be a man and tell me what it is, not sulk like a silly little boy.'

'I don't sulk. I just get bored listening to you and Henry flirting with each other like two pigeons in the spring.'

'Flirting?' She made it sound like I'd accused her of walking down the street naked. 'When have you heard me flirting with Henry? Tell me. When?'

'I make it my business not to listen.'

'You just said you got bored listening to us.'

'Well anyway, it's no skin off my nose if you two want to be alone together.'

She rolled her eyes.

'We don't. You've got it wrong.' A blush crept across her cheeks as she spoke. 'Henry's a nice man, but he's not the kind of man I like. In that way, I mean.'

I didn't believe her; that blush told its own story. *You hope I'll tell Henry what you said and make him keener on you.* He always liked the ones who played hard to get best.

'So there's no need for you to ride by yourself,' she said. 'Not on my account, anyway.'

'Well, sometimes I like to, as it happens.'

'Fine,' she said, throwing up her hands, and turning to stalk away. 'Do what you like. It makes no difference to me.'

Chapter Thirty-three

I thought about that conversation later, and I wasn't very proud of myself. I shouldn't have been so rude about accepting her help and I needn't have brushed her off when she said that about me riding with them. She'd only been trying to be friendly, and even if I didn't believe her when she said she wasn't sweet on Henry, what was that to me? I was tired of riding by myself too; it was boring and lonely and it caused me to dwell on things that made me sad. So the next morning I joined them as we set off. Arabella raised an eyebrow, but she said nothing about our encounter the day before, and nor did I.

Wanting to atone for my churlishness, I thought I ought to make conversation with her, so I asked if she was looking forward to seeing her father and brothers again when we got to Oxford.

'Well, I'm *hoping* to see them. If Matt and Edward haven't shot their own heads off by then.'

Henry laughed.

'Arabella doesn't think too highly of her brothers.'

'That's not true,' she protested. 'I love them. But I wouldn't trust them to find the right end of a broom, let alone a gun.'

'Tell Nat about the lessons,' said Henry.

'He doesn't want to hear about that.'

'He does, it's funny. Go on.'

'Well, they had tutors, before they went away to school, but they hate book learning and my father kept getting rid of the tutors because the boys couldn't hold the simplest things in their heads – especially Ed, he's hopeless. When it got to the fourth tutor in a year, Father said he'd set them a test after a month, and if they couldn't pass, they'd get a whipping.'

'Guess what she did?' said Henry. 'She charged her brother sixpence, put on his breeches, and pretended to be him. Every morning for a month.'

'We were very alike when we were small,' said Arabella.

'And she got full marks in the test.'

'Did your father ever find out?' I asked.

'He realised something was amiss as soon as he heard Ed had got such good marks. Then when the tutor said he was very attentive and keen, he worked it out – my father's quite clever, we don't really understand why he has such stupid sons. I had to give Ed his sixpence back; it was only fair when he got a whipping after all. But I got what I wanted.'

'What did you want?' I asked.

'My father let me go to lessons, after that. That's why I did it, to show him it wasn't a waste for a girl.' She narrowed her eyes at me. 'I suppose you thought I meant a new dress. Or a pair of satin slippers.'

'No, I thought probably a kitten with a pretty ribbon round its neck.'

She laughed.

'Very funny. So, have you got brothers, Nat? Or sisters?'

I found myself telling her about Sam and Annie, then Henry joined in with a story about his brother getting his head caught down a rabbit hole and, all in all, the miles passed quickly that morning. And I had to admit, I didn't see her do anything that you could describe as flirting – no doe-eyed looks, no secret smiles, and when Henry commented that green eyes had always been his favourite, she told him tartly that green eyes were no better or worse for seeing with than any other kind, and since she didn't need them for anything else, their colour made no difference to her.

She didn't fool me – she'd fallen for him, like all the others. But to her credit, she didn't make it obvious, and before long, I became as comfortable with the two of them as I'd once been with Henry alone, and it was hard to remember a time when Arabella hadn't ridden between us every day, regaling us with anecdotes about the unfortunate Matt and Ed, or setting us tests on Latin, or Greek, or mathematics, to prove a theory she had that girls, once taught, were cleverer than boys. She beat us nearly every time and I came to feel quite sorry for the hapless brothers, not to mention the tutor.

And then one day – and I'm well aware you have a knowing smile on your face as you read this – I woke up and realised the first thought in my head was a thought of her. Somewhere between Bridlington and Newark I had fallen in love, and now I started each day looking forward to seeing her face, and went to sleep smiling about a joke we'd shared, or a sarcastic comment she'd made. You saw it coming, I'm sure. But it crept up on me so quietly that I didn't have a chance to protect myself.

You'll be thinking me stupid, and deluded. Let me put you straight: however stupid you think me, I thought myself more so, but I wasn't deluded. There was no way on earth she would ever look at me, and day after day, I told myself to pull back, to stop hoping for the impossible. But if you've ever been in love yourself, you'll know you might as well tell water to flow upwards.

Sometimes, on the road, she'd go quiet. Henry never seemed to notice, but by then there was no sound I liked better than her voice. I'd glance up and see that same distant look in her eyes she'd had when she was telling us what happened to her mother; she was seeing it all over again. But she didn't speak about it until one night when we sat round the fire after dinner. Henry was talking about his parents and she asked how long it was since he'd seen them. He was trying to remember, when she said:

'You should have said goodbye to them, properly, before all this started. How are they going to feel if you get killed and you didn't say goodbye?'

Henry said he wasn't planning to be killed, but she wasn't listening.

'I quarrelled with my mother that day, you know,' she said. 'Just before the soldiers came back.' She laced her fingers together in her lap, and unlaced them again. 'She said to be careful what I said, because they'd be angry, and I told her she was letting our family name down by bowing and scraping to them. And I said ... I said my father would be ashamed if he could see her.'

She looked down, as though she'd only just noticed what her fingers were doing.

'She told me to go to my chamber, and I was still up there

when they got back. Then it all blew up, and we didn't have a chance to talk again. So she died thinking that's what I thought of her. And I didn't even mean it, not really.'

She thought for a minute, looking out into the twilight. The glow from the fire lit up her shorn red curls, and ice ran down my spine at the thought of that knife at her throat.

'No, that's a lie,' she said. 'I did mean it. I hated seeing their smug faces when she asked what they'd like for dinner, and if the ale was to their liking. But I know she did it to protect us and I wish I'd said so before it was too late. So that's what I mean – you should have said goodbye properly.' She turned to me. 'It's different for you, obviously.'

'Why?'

'Your family sold you, didn't they? When you were ten, the queen said – that's terrible.'

'Why does it make things different for me?'

'Well, they won't really care if you die, will they? And they don't deserve for you to bother saying goodbye to them.'

'This is a gloomy subject,' said Henry. 'How about we talk about something other than our impending deaths? That white mare of yours – have you ever bred from her?'

Henry could talk for ever about horses and so could Arabella, but I didn't join in. I was thinking about what she'd said. Was it true no one in my family would care if I died? I thought of my father, almost twitching in his eagerness to get away and count the money I'd given him. He'd be missing the monthly sums I hadn't been able to send since the war broke out, but I didn't think my death would touch him for any other reason. My mother was gone, and Annie was just a baby when I left: I doubted she even had any memory of me.

But surely Sam hadn't forgotten me? Not that he wouldn't have been justified if he had; I'd had no trouble forgetting my promise to find him a place at court. But he wouldn't, not Sam. I pictured him, telling his curly-haired little girl about the uncle who'd gone to London to live with the queen. I wondered if he'd told her about the day I nearly got my head sliced off in the wheatfield, or the time we'd tried to stretch me and I'd fainted and he'd thought I was dead.

I thought about Bridlington, and the man with the shell box. Henry might joke that we weren't planning to die any time soon, but that man hadn't been planning it either. If it had been my blood turning the snow red that night, Sam would never know that I hadn't forgotten him, not really.

'You're quiet,' said Henry. 'What's the matter?'

'I think,' I said, 'there's something I've got to do.'

Our next stop was Newark; from there it was only forty miles to Oakham, but forty miles through Parliamentarian territory. And just outside Oakham itself, Major Sarenbrant, headquartered up at the duke's old house on the hill. The queen didn't want me to go but she understood why I had to; she had her own brothers and sisters who she might never see again. She offered me a guard of soldiers, but Lord Newcastle pointed out that was asking for trouble. What I needed was a way to slip in and out of the town without attracting attention, and it was Henry who came up with the plan.

'How do I look?' he asked as we got ready to leave, jamming a battered straw hat on his head.

'No worse than usual,' I said.

He was wearing a dirty smock and a worn pair of breeches he'd bought from a very surprised farmer on the road to Newark, along with a cart and a load of hay. One of our older horses was hitched to it, her coat rubbed with dust to disguise her quality. Who was going to notice a farmer taking hay to market? And no one would suspect I was hiding in the hay.

The sun had barely come up, and only the night guards were awake, but just as we were ready to go Arabella came running from the tent she shared with Susan, still in her nightgown, tufts of hair sticking up at the back of her head.

'I didn't want you to go without saying goodbye,' she said.

Henry looked baffled but I understood. She wanted to tell him she loved him, just in case. The stupid idiot couldn't see it; he had no idea how lucky he was. Trying to ignore the hard clump of jealousy in my stomach, I walked to the front of the cart and pretended to check the horse was properly hitched, humming to myself so I couldn't hear what they were saying. They didn't speak for long – Arabella wouldn't be one for flouncy words – and after a couple of minutes, she walked round to me.

'Nat,' she said. 'I know why you want to go. Probably better than most. But if you changed your mind, no one would blame you. Not even Sam, if he knew.'

I couldn't blame her for trying to talk me out of it. I was putting Henry in danger too; of course she wouldn't want that.

'I didn't persuade Henry to come,' I said. 'He insisted.'

'I know that,' she said, her brow furrowing into a frown. 'Anyway... I just wanted to say, be careful.'

I sat on the edge of the cart as we pulled away. She stood watching, worry clouding her lovely face; she must be wondering if this was the last time she'd ever see Henry. Perhaps she'd even hoped he might declare himself before he went, which he obviously hadn't. When she disappeared from sight, I dug myself into the hay, lay on my back and closed my eyes. But I still saw her face, and it was many miles before I stopped wondering what it must be like to see a look like that and know it was for you.

Chapter Thirty-four

We'd only been travelling a couple of hours when we passed the first patrol. I lay rigid under the straw, hardly daring to breathe. From the moment Henry murmured 'Soldiers up ahead', Major Sarenbrant's threat rang in my ears, and as the hooves of their horses slowed, I was certain we'd been caught. But Henry wished them a cheery good morning, and the horses clip-clopped on, then picked up speed as they passed us.

By the time we reached Oakham, we'd passed three lots of Parliamentarian soldiers on the road, without attracting any notice, and I'd relaxed enough to make a little tunnel through the straw to see out. The town had hardly changed at all and as we trundled along familiar streets, I was ten again, walking to the bakery, making sure I had a retort ready if I came across Jack Edgecombe and his friends.

Henry stopped to ask someone where Sam lived. I was pleased to hear it wasn't at our old house; I didn't want to see the place without my mother in it, and I definitely didn't want to run into my father. But I so much wanted to see Sam again. I shouldn't have left it so long, but now I could make amends.

* * *

My brother's wife turned out to be a plain girl, in every sense of the word. In fact if you wanted someone to demonstrate what plain meant, Sarah would be the one for the job. I don't mean she was ugly: her features were neat and in proportion, her skin was neither ruddy nor dark and she was neither bony nor overly plump. But there was a fearsome tidiness about the way her mouse-coloured hair was scraped back into a knot, and the look on her face when she opened the door, though not unfriendly, said she wouldn't be going as far as a smile until she was sure the occasion warranted that sort of display.

She didn't see me at first.

'Yes?' she said to Henry. 'Can I help you?' He looked down at me, and she followed his gaze. She looked puzzled for a second, then clapped a hand to her mouth. 'Oh! Are you... is it... Nat?'

I nodded.

'I'm sorry to come unannounced...' I said, forgetting that everyone in Oakham came unannounced. 'I was hoping to see Sam.'

'But he's not here.'

Of course: Sam would be at work in the fields. He'd hardly be sitting at home in the middle of the morning. She must be thinking I was daft. As she started to say something, a couple of women came round the corner. Sarah stepped back, opening the door.

'You'd better come in,' she said. 'Quickly now.'

The cottage was very like our old one, just the one room, though a little bigger than ours, with a table and two stools, and a pallet neatly tucked against the wall. Perched on one of the stools was a little girl with curly hair, gazing at me with my mother's brown eyes.

'Hello,' she said. 'I'm helping Mama.'

She pointed to a tangle of yarn in her lap, one end haphazardly wrapped around her right hand, and I remembered all the winter afternoons I'd done the same with my mother.

'She's not as helpful as she thinks, our Lucy,' said Sarah, ruffling the little girl's curls and smiling for the first time. 'But she does her best.'

'Did you name her after our mother?' I asked. 'She looks a lot like her.'

'People often say that, though I never met her so I can't say. But yes, that's where we took the name from. It was Sam's wish, what with her dying just before we met, and I had no complaint with it. It's a nice enough name, not too fancy.'

I had the impression 'not too fancy' might be the highest form of praise for Sarah. I wondered what she'd have made of me if she'd seen me at court, dressed in velvet and lace.

The little girl slid down from the stool, carefully placing the yarn on the seat. She looked at me with a little frown creasing her brow.

'How old are you?' she asked.

'I'm twenty-seven,' I said.

'No you're not!'

She giggled, putting her hands in front of her mouth.

'Lucy, this is your uncle Nat,' said Sarah. 'Remember, Father told you all about him?'

Lucy's eyes widened.

'Father tried to make you big,' she said. 'And then you went to live with the queen.'

Sam hadn't forgotten me. Suddenly, more than anything, I wanted to see his dear old face.

'So which farm is Sam working on?' I asked. 'Is it Whitefields? Or Arrowhill?'

'You can't see him,' said Sarah.

'I won't disturb him while he's working – I'll wait till they take a break.'

'You don't understand. Sam's not working the land anymore. He's a soldier.'

My soft, gentle brother, a soldier? I must have looked as though I hadn't understood; she repeated it.

'So where is he?' I looked up at Henry. 'Just our luck if we've come all this way and he's already at Oxford with the king.'

Henry gave a little shake of his head. For a second, I still didn't understand, and then, so slowly I could almost feel wheels turning in my brain, the pieces slotted into place. Rutland was for Parliament.

'He's fighting on the other side?'

'There's only one side round here,' said Sarah. 'They pressed most of the men in Oakham, not long after it all started.'

Of course. That was why she'd had hustled us inside when she saw her neighbours coming. People in Oakham knew who I was and they'd know whose side I was on.

'If you're seen here now, they'll say Sam's a spy,' said Sarah. 'And you'll no doubt remember, Sam's not a quick thinker. If they confuse him with questions, he'll end up admitting it. And from what I've heard of Major Sarenbrant, he's not one to show mercy to spies.'

That much I already knew.

'Does he know I'm Sam's brother?'

'I shouldn't think so, there's hundreds of them quartered up at the big house. Sam's just a pikeman. I don't suppose Major Sarenbrant even knows his name.'

That was something. And I had to keep it that way.

'Will you tell Sam I came?' I said. 'And tell him...'

What could I say? I'm sorry I forgot about you for all these years? Come and see me when we're back in Whitehall, if you're in the area? My glance fell on Lucy who, after her initial burst of bravery, was peeping out from behind her mother's skirt.

'Tell him he has a lovely family. And I hope we'll see each other again when this is all over.'

After making sure there was no one in the street outside, Henry stuck the battered hat back on his head and I burrowed into the pile of hay. As we rumbled away from the town, I thought about what I'd heard. Sam, a soldier? I pictured him in the stiff leather tunic and metal helmet of a pikeman. I'd never seen pikemen on a battlefield, but I'd watched ours practising, the sharp steel ripping through sacks of sawdust that stood for the bellies of the other side, the men roaring as their blades hit home. I couldn't imagine Sam doing that, let alone going into battle with the intention of killing. But he wouldn't have had much choice, any more than the hundreds of men pressed into the king's army had. And it turned my stomach to think that all the times I'd cheered a victory by our side, I could have been celebrating my own brother's death, and I'd never even have known.

* * *

We turned onto the road to Ashby, where we were to rejoin the queen. Henry wished the driver of another cart good morning, and I watched it pass by from inside my hiding place. Just a simple farmer and a load of hay; the perfect disguise. And it very nearly worked.

Chapter Thirty-five

We were a couple of miles out of Oakham when the wheel came off. Our lives at the palace hadn't furnished either of us with practical skills, and it took us two hours and a great deal of cursing to fix it. When it finally slotted back on, we were so busy congratulating ourselves that we forgot to listen for hooves on the road; by the time we heard the soldiers coming, they were already visible in the distance.

There were four of them: a routine patrol like the ones we'd seen on the way. Henry shoved me under the hay, and I lay perfectly still as they rode up and clattered to a stop.

'Having trouble?' said one.

They didn't see me. We'll be on our way again in a minute.

'No, no, just a little problem with the wheel,' said Henry. 'It's fixed now.'

The cart shifted as he climbed back into the seat.

'Where are you headed?' said the same voice.

'Just back to my farm.'

'Where's that?'

Henry didn't know the area at all. I closed my eyes and prayed he wouldn't say something daft.

'Not far,' he said. 'Now I must get along.'

He clicked his tongue at the horse but she didn't move. *They're blocking the way.* I told myself they were just showing a hapless farmer who was in charge; I'd seen our soldiers behave the same way on the march south.

'Where?' asked the soldier again. 'You don't sound local.'

Say Ashwell. Say Edmondthorpe. Or Pickwell, even.

'Over near Bennington,' he said.

Henry, you bloody idiot. He must have seen the name on a signpost.

'Bringing that hay back from market, are you?' said the soldier.

'That's right.'

Henry didn't know why he was asking that. But I did. Bennington was miles away, over on the other side of the county. I closed my eyes and waited.

'From Oakham market?'

'Yes. Now, if you don't mind—'

'Special, is it, the hay in Oakham?'

Henry didn't answer. He was sharp enough to know we were caught, even if he didn't know why.

'Only, I'm wondering why you wouldn't buy your hay at Grantham market,' said the soldier. 'Instead of coming all this way.'

'Look,' said Henry. 'I've done nothing wrong and, with your permission, I'd like to get home to my wife and children.'

'Well, you see, there's another thing I'm wondering,' said the soldier. 'And that's what you were so keen to hide in that hay when you saw us coming.'

Of course. They were making sport of us all along. And now the game was up.

You'll die a traitor's death.

'I wasn't hiding anything,' said Henry. 'I was just fixing my wheel.'

The soldier laughed.

'You're lying. We saw you. Now do you want to tell me what's in there or shall we look for ourselves?'

My heart was hammering in my chest. But Henry wasn't giving up.

'All right,' he said, with a deep sigh. 'It's my son. He's a bit simple, and stunted in his growth, and he's afraid of soldiers. I didn't want him to see you and be frightened.'

I held my breath. Could it work?

'Perhaps you're a father yourself, sir?' said Henry.

'I am.'

'Then you'll understand, I need to get him home to his mother. And there'll be no end of trouble for me if he's in a state when she sees him.'

There was a pause.

'I can't let you go without checking. Lads, see what's in there, but go gently.'

My turn now. Eyes down, mouth shut. *You can pass for a child, of course you can.*

'Yes sir,' said another voice. A voice I recognised. It took a moment to place it, and then I knew I was done for.

I wasn't going to let him drag me from my hiding place like an old rag doll. I pushed my way out of the hay, and stood. He stopped, halfway down from his horse, his stupid mouth open like a fish just popped from the hook.

'That's Nat Davy,' said Jack Edgecombe. 'That's the queen's dwarf.'

Chapter Thirty-six

Almost seventeen years from the day when I stood at the door and heard eleven shillings chink into my father's hand, I was back at the big house on the hill. The lawn in front was a sea of tents and inside, the marble floor was barely visible under a layer of mud and dirt, patterned with the prints of soldiers' boots. What, I wondered, would the duke say if he saw his fine home now?

Major Sarenbrant was sitting behind a big table. Arabella was right: he did look like a skeleton with skin. His face was long and thin, with hollow cheeks and dark shadows under his eyes, and the hands that held the documents he'd been reading were bony.

He peered at me as though I was an insect on the ground.

'The queen's little doll-man – so you really are as small as they say. I see now why it was so easy for the girl to smuggle you in.'

'Where's the man who drove the cart?' I said. 'He has nothing to do with anything, he's just a farmer. You should let him go.'

Major Sarenbrant stretched his thin lips into a smile.

'A good try. And loyalty to a friend is always to be admired. But we know who your companion is.' He walked round to stand in front of the desk, and stared down at me. 'I sent a message. With the girl.'

A traitor's death. A part of me wanted to plead for my life, to say whatever I could to save myself, but there was nothing to say that would make any difference, and the better part of me was glad of that. If I was going to die, at least I'd try to do it bravely.

'You know, I suppose, what happens to traitors?' he said.

I took a breath to steady my voice.

'I know you kill innocent women. Lady Denham had done nothing.'

'She harboured a spy. She asked for what she got.' He leaned against the desk, his bony arms folded. 'But if you think that's what you've got coming – a nice clean shot to the head – I'm afraid you can think again. I promised you a traitor's death, and a traitor's death is what you deserve.'

I already knew what he meant, and he knew I knew. But he was going to spell it out anyway.

'Hanging is never a nice death,' he said. 'Too many variables. Miscalculate the drop, or tie the noose badly, and they dangle like puppets, slowly suffocating.'

He waggled his long, skinny fingers, to demonstrate the movement, but there was no need. As you know, I'd seen plenty of hangings. When they went wrong, the way he'd said, the only hope was to have friends in the crowd who'd pull on your legs to break your neck and put an end to the agony. There'd be nobody there to do that for me.

He put his head on one side, as though a thought had just occurred to him.

'And of course, with you being so very small, and light, that makes the calculations very difficult indeed.' He shrugged. 'Even a professional hangman might struggle to get it right. And we don't have a professional hangman here. But I'm sure my men will do their best to make sure it doesn't go on too long.'

I once saw a man who took forty-five minutes to die, his fingers clawing at the rope, his eyes bulging and his face turning blue. How long would it take for my scant weight to pull the rope tight around my neck?

'I promised you a traitor's death, and I'm a man who likes to keep his promises,' Major Sarenbrant said. 'But in your case, there are other considerations.'

Hope flickered. *Don't show it.* He was playing with me and I wasn't going to give him the satisfaction of seeing it work.

'You are, I understand, very precious to the queen,' he said. 'So I'm going to make her an offer. We'll release you, and Mr Jermyn, if she agrees to come before Parliament and listen to our proposals for peace.'

'Agree to be your prisoner, you mean. I heard you, remember? You want to capture her so you can make the king surrender.'

'And thanks to you, we have another chance.'

'She won't agree,' I said. 'She's not stupid.'

'We'll see. But at the very least she'll be distracted. And if that gives her less opportunity to encourage the king in his obstinance, it can only further the cause of peace. And who knows, perhaps you'll be saved from the noose.'

'I don't want to buy my freedom that way. If you're going to kill me, then kill me.'

'You mistake my meaning, I'm afraid. I wasn't offering you

the choice. The choice will be hers.' He waved a hand at the soldiers standing behind me. 'Take him away – and watch him. He's craftier than he looks.'

As we reached the door, he spoke again. 'What were you doing here, in Rutland?'

'I wanted to see my father, but I couldn't find out where he's living now.'

'Ah,' he said. 'Just your father?'

'My mother died some years ago.'

'And what about your brother?'

I didn't answer.

'Samuel, isn't it? You thought I didn't know. And I wouldn't have – we're a large company here, I don't make the acquaintance of every pikeman.' His lips stretched into that thin smile again. 'But your brother came to see me, as soon as he heard you'd been taken. To plead for you.'

Sam must have had to pluck up all his courage to face a man like Major Sarenbrant, and not only admit to being my brother, but ask for mercy for me, the enemy. I pictured him, a grown-up version of the boy I remembered, beetroot-red, stumbling over his words, but determined to say what he'd come to say. The good, loyal brother, who I'd forgotten about when my life took me somewhere more exciting.

'Don't take it out on him,' I said. 'Please. If he's on your side, he's loyal, I can promise you that. Nothing I've done has anything to do with him.'

'Oh, I realise that. Your brother didn't exactly strike me as a master spy.'

He smirked, and I wanted to punch him in the eye so badly that my fists clenched of their own accord.

'No, I won't be punishing him,' he said. 'In fact, I have him in mind for a special mission. Who better to take my message to the queen? If he wants to plead for your life, he can plead to her.'

There was nothing to lose now.

'Can I see him?' I asked. 'Before he goes?'

He thought for a moment, then shrugged.

'Why not? I'm sure a reunion will strengthen his resolve to persuade the queen – and your life is in her hands now.'

They locked me in a room upstairs. It was almost empty of furniture, just one chair standing by the window, but there was something familiar about it. After a while I realised: it was the room where the seamstresses used to work. Where they'd put me in the blue clothes with the gold lace, and I'd looked at my reflection in the window and seen the boy I was to become.

I sat on the floor. The wooden panelling on the wall pressed against my back and the floor was cold beneath me, yet I struggled to grasp the fact that it was all real. That very soon, I would be dead. I feared the agonising death ahead of me, and I mourned the loss of the future I hoped for, when the war was over and we could all live at court again. But worse, much worse than that, was the moment when I realised I had already seen Arabella for the last time. Never again would I hear her voice, snappy with irritation, or bubbling with laughter; never watch triumph sparkle in her eyes when she beat me or Henry in one of her endless quizzes.

How would she feel when she heard I was dead? Though she could never love me as a man, I believed she was fond of me, as she might be of a brother. I hoped that if I took a long time to die, if my eyes bulged and my face turned blue, she wouldn't hear about it. I didn't want her to think of me like that. But perhaps she wouldn't think of me at all; if they killed Henry too, the loss of me would be nothing to her, and if they let him go, the joy of that would be what filled her head, not thoughts of me.

Either way, I hoped she'd get to know that I didn't betray the queen. When Major Sarenbrant explained his proposal, I'd been certain she wouldn't think of doing what he asked. But then I remembered Bridlington. With cannonballs screaming through the sky, she'd risked her life to save her dog. Faced with my brother, begging her to save my life, could I be sure she'd say no? That she wouldn't convince herself she could talk them round, tell herself they wouldn't dare harm her?

I didn't want to die. But I couldn't let her risk her life for me. She had children, she had a husband who loved her. I had lived for twenty-seven years, and there was no one whose heart would be broken if I didn't live another one. So what choice was there? I had to convince Sam she mustn't be allowed to give herself up, and I'd have to rely on him to convince her.

Chapter Thirty-seven

My brother looked just as I'd pictured him: same curly hair, same face, with its slightly puzzled expression, but tall now, and broad, like our father used to be. His feet, in their soldier's boots, were enormous.

'Nat,' he said, his face breaking into the slow smile I remembered so well. His thick leather tunic creaked as he knelt down and hugged me so hard I was afraid he might crack my ribs.

'It's good to see you,' he said, when he finally released me and we sat down on the floor. He must have been thinking about what was going to happen to me, and so was I, but suddenly I wanted to put off the moment when one of us had to say it.

'I should have come before,' I said, as though we'd just bumped into each other in the street. 'I always meant to.'

'I used to think you'd come back,' he said. 'For good, I mean. I thought, Nat won't like it there, he'll miss Oakham. I used to go and stand on the Stamford road sometimes, and see if I could see you coming.'

All through those first months at Whitehall, when I'd

pined for home, I'd never thought about how lonely he'd be without me.

'But Mother said I wasn't to think that way,' he said. 'She said it was a big chance for you, and I should be pleased you'd taken it. And then when we heard they were writing poems about you and all that, well, we were so proud, I can't tell you.' He laughed. 'And you won't believe this, Nat – Jack Edgecombe started going around saying he was a friend of yours. Till I punched him on the nose.'

That I'd have liked to see.

'You know it was Jack that brought me in?' I said.

He nodded.

'Full of it, he was. That's how I found out. I couldn't believe it when I heard you were here.'

'We went to your house and—'

'You met Sarah then? And my little Lucy?'

I nodded.

'She looks so much like Mother,' I said.

'I know, you should see her when she's cross. She's the spit of Mother then. Scares me sometimes.' He smiled, and nudged me in the ribs. 'Bet you never thought I'd marry as fine a woman as Sarah.' Luckily he didn't wait for an answer. 'And she's not just pretty – clever as a cat, Sarah is. Lucy's got her brains too. She can do little sums on her fingers already – remember how long it took me to learn adding up?'

'Except when it came to getting your fair share of the dumplings. You always counted them well enough.'

'Ah, well, in that she is like me. Loves her food, does Lucy.'

I started telling him about the food at Whitehall, me babbling on about fricassees and cutlets and syllabubs, and him shaking his head in disbelief, and now and then saying, 'What did that taste like?' But all the while I was talking, I was thinking, this will be the last time I see him. And then he asked me something about the kitchens at Whitehall, and I started to answer, but I couldn't carry on, and the words just came out.

'They're going to hang me, Sam.'

He flinched, and shook his head.

'No. I won't let it happen, Nat, I promise. You've got to tell me what to say, what will make the queen agree to come.'

'She can't. If she lets them take her, they'll charge her with treason and they'll kill her.'

'No, that's not what Major Sarenbrant said. They just want to make her understand it's not right for the king not to listen. And I've got to make her see she's got to say yes so they'll let you go.'

'No. I don't want you to persuade her. I don't even want you to try.'

'But—'

'I want you to tell her I'm already dead. It's the only way.'

It took me a long time to convince Sam, but I always could talk him round in the end. We said our goodbyes, as best we could, and I made him promise to send Major Sarenbrant a message saying the queen refused to meet them, rather than bringing the news himself. That way, I hoped, the deed might be done before he got back. I didn't want him there to see it.

I spent the next four days in that same little room. During daylight hours, I kept myself calm by thinking over my memories. What a strange and unexpected life I'd had: from our little house in Oakham and the tiny world I knew there, to the splendour of the court and the adventures of the past few months. But most of all I thought about Arabella. For the first time, I let myself wallow in loving her, and think about how it would be if she loved me back. There was no harm in it now, was there? I imagined the life we could have together when the war was over; I even pictured us old and grey, sitting in front of our own fire somewhere, and watching our grandchildren play.

But as the shadows lengthened towards evening, my thoughts weren't strong enough to keep the fear away. All the hangings I'd ever seen played themselves out in my mind, though I couldn't tell if they were really memory, or terrified imagination. Men pissed themselves with fear as they were led to the gallows, and screamed for someone to pull on their legs and end their agony. Eyes bulged from livid red faces, and necks cracked; the lucky ones.

When at last I slept, in my dreams the rope was stiff around my neck. I stood on the cart beneath the gallows, as a crowd of leather-tunicked soldiers laughed and mocked me; in one dream someone called out, 'Who'll be the smallest man in England now?' The cart moved beneath my feet as the horses fidgeted at the noise, and I struggled to keep my footing, to give myself a few more seconds of life. And then, as Major Sarenbrant gave the order to pull the cart away, I would wake up, soused with sweat, and panting with fear. For a second, relief flooded through me as I realised it was just a dream, before I remembered the truth, and dread filled my body and made my bones feel light as air.

Chapter Thirty-eight

The message came on the evening of the fourth day. I was at the window as the lad slipped down from his horse, and patted his satchel to check it was still there.

'So you were right,' Major Sarenbrant said. 'A pity. We could have brought this war to an end, and begun to get the country back to peace again. But the queen doesn't want peace. She wants power.'

And your side don't?

'What did she say?' I asked.

'Read it for yourself.'

The message was the one I'd dictated to Sam. That meant he'd told her I was dead, as we'd agreed. It was just as I'd planned, and yet I realised as I stood there that until that moment, I'd been keeping alive a tiny hope that something – I had no idea what – might happen to save me.

'You can't seriously have thought she'd come?' I said, trying to keep my voice steady. 'She'd just as well have signed her own death warrant.'

'Instead she signed yours.' He leaned against the edge of

the table, his arms folded, and looked down at me. 'Tell me –
do they really believe they can win?'

'They're certain of it.'

He sighed and shook his head.

'We can't let that happen. We can't go back to living under
a king who treats us like children, who must do as he says
because it's he who says it.'

I didn't reply. I'd seen as well as anyone that the king was
a good man but a poor ruler, made more so by his belief that
everything he did or thought or said was right because it
came from him. But that didn't make the other side right. I
remembered Bridlington and the ships looming up out of the
night, intending to kill us in our beds, along with the villagers
who'd done nothing to anyone. And Lady Denham, shot like
a dog. Both sides were certain God was with them, but if that
was true then why had so many people on both sides died?
The major's voice broke through my thoughts.

'So I'm afraid the likes of you pay the price. It will be the
day after tomorrow, at noon. If I were you I would use the
time wisely, to make your peace with God.'

Of course, they wouldn't let me see a priest, but I accepted
the offer to pray with a minister. Though I'd never have said
so to the queen, it always seemed to me that a loving God
wouldn't consign anyone to hell for the way they prayed, or
who they did their praying with. So we prayed for my soul,
and I offered up a silent prayer to God to watch over Arabella
and give her a happy life. I couldn't bring myself to ask for
that life to include a husband, so I left that for God to make
up his own mind about.

After the minister left, I watched from the window as soldiers built the gallows to hang me on. I kept telling myself to turn away, but my legs wouldn't move. Two soldiers quarrelled over the length of the timbers, one of them indicating with his hands how tall I was, the other shaking his head as if to say that that wasn't relevant to the measurements they were taking. One shook the upright to test its solidity, and nodded, satisfied, and then they pulled up the cart and positioned it underneath the cross-timber. Only when one of them left and came back with a thick rope did I climb down from the chair and sit on the floor. *Lord, let me able to bear it bravely. And please, make it quick.*

I doubted I would sleep that night but I must have done; weak sunlight was just breaking the darkness when I woke to shouting outside and feet thundering down the stairs. Still half asleep, I stumbled to the window. The camp was alive with activity: soldiers were spilling out of the tents, some still shrugging on their tunics, horses were being saddled, weapons made ready.

I listened at the door. At first there was just a babble of noise, men rushing about, shouts I couldn't make out. Then Major Sarenbrant's voice.

'I want the men out in ten minutes,' he said. 'They think they can surprise us into a siege, but we'll be waiting for them on the road.'

'Is she with them?' asked another man.

'The lookouts said not. She'll have done what she did up north, keep plenty back to protect her. But if we can do some damage to what she's sent, that'll be something.'

'How many shall we leave to guard the house, sir?'

'A couple will do. I want every man we can get on the road. We're going to teach them a lesson this time.'

That was when I realised that either Sam hadn't delivered my message, or she hadn't believed it. And even though we were in the middle of Parliamentarian territory, she was going to try to rescue me. For all my praying for a dignified, brave death, I can't deny that relief and hope flooded through me. But the plan had obviously been to attack the house and its encampment, and now, just as we'd ambushed their troops in the north, they were going to do the same to ours.

Within minutes, the house was as quiet as a stone; outside the only movement was the flapping of a tent side that had come adrift in the breeze. I paced the room, climbed onto the chair and strained my eyes for any movement on the road in the distance, climbed down, knelt and prayed, paced the room again.

Hours passed before I glimpsed something moving, far off on the road. Was it just a trick of the light? No: there it was again, sunshine glinting on a helmet. A soldier – but from which side? There was only a short stretch of road visible beyond the trees at the bottom of the hill, and I pressed my face against the glass to see better before he disappeared, but I couldn't tell. I held my breath and watched the drive up to the house.

He was one of theirs. As he galloped up, the two guards who'd been left behind rushed out. Struggling to get his breath back, he slid down from his horse before he spoke, but when he looked up, his face told me what I needed to know: things had not gone their way. I sent up a quick prayer of thanks – God must have heard more from me in those few hours than he usually did in a fortnight – and watched as they argued about something. One of the soldiers turned and pointed up at my window. The rider's eyes widened, but he shrugged, then led his horse off towards the stables, while the other two ran inside.

The queen's forces had won, or were winning, that much was clear. The messenger must have brought orders for us to be taken somewhere else, before we could be rescued. I'd have to do whatever I could to stop them moving us; the queen's men couldn't be far away, even minutes might make a difference.

I pressed my ear to the door. The soldiers were rushing about and, after about twenty minutes, the big front door slammed. I ran to the window. They were sprinting towards the stables, and then all three rode past the front of the house and down the drive. My heart lifted: they must know the queen's forces were on their way, and they were escaping while they could.

Then I smelt the smoke.

Chapter Thirty-nine

They'd set the house on fire, with me and Henry in it. The orders must have been to burn it down rather than let it fall into Royalist hands. I pressed my face to the glass and looked down; wisps of grey smoke were seeping out from under the door below. If they'd set the fire in the front hall, it wouldn't be long before the wooden staircase and the panelling on the walls caught light. The window of the room I was in didn't open, and even if I could smash the glass, the lead bars between the lights wouldn't let me escape.

Was that a voice? I put my ear to the door; there it was, louder this time:

'Nat! Where are you?'

Henry. From somewhere on the same floor, but not close.

'At the front. Where are you?'

'Room at the back. Furthest from the stairs. I can smell smoke.'

'They've set the place alight. Can you break the door down?'

'I could if I wasn't tied to a chair.'

The smell of smoke was stronger now; it was drifting up past the window. I tried to pick up the chair, thinking I could use it to smash the door, but it was heavy and I couldn't lift it high enough. I ran at the door then, as hard as I could, but it held fast, as I'd known it would. I kicked at it, hurting my foot more than I did the door, and slumped to the floor, my head in my hands. It couldn't end like this. The queen was trying to rescue us, I had to hold on. But smoke was seeping up through the floor now, catching in my throat. As it filled the room, I was suddenly sleepy; all I wanted to do was lie down and close my eyes. Fight it, I told myself. *Fight it.* But my eyes were too heavy to keep open.

'Nat! Nat!'

The voice calling my name came from far away. Someone was shaking me, but I wanted to sleep.

'Wake up! Nat!'

The face looking down at me was familiar, but I couldn't place it. My head was foggy and it hurt to breathe. It was hot, but not hot like summer, and there was a noise, a roaring noise…

Fire.

Then it came back to me, the house was on fire and I was trapped, and Henry was tied to a chair but we had to get out… I sat up and my head swam. I started to cough and I couldn't stop, and then I vomited until I thought my body would turn itself inside out. But I was vomiting onto grass.

I'm outside.

'You had me worried there, I thought you'd never wake up,' said the voice, and I recognised it as one I never thought to hear again: Sam's.

I looked up. The fire had taken hold of the house. Flames

poured from the windows, licking hungrily at the roof, and the air in front of it shimmered. There were a dozen or so soldiers with us, standing watching the flames.

'We got you out just in time,' said Sam.

'Henry,' I said. 'Henry's still in there—'

'Oh, now you remember,' said a voice beside me, and I turned too quickly; my head swam again and I puked up what was left of my stomach.

'Just like old times,' said Henry. His voice was croaky, and he had to take a rattly breath to speak again. 'At least you missed my foot this time.'

'Had you fooled, didn't I?' said Sam. 'You really thought I was going to do what you said.'

We'd left as soon as Henry and I could stand; Major Sarenbrant's troops had taken a battering from ours and the survivors had scattered, but we were still in Parliamentarian territory. The soldiers found a cart from somewhere and bundled us into it, and we were headed for Stratford, where the queen's forces had made camp.

'You were always the clever one, Nat, but I thought you'd lost your head entirely that day,' Sam went on. 'As if I'd have let you get yourself killed.'

'So what did you do?'

'I just told the queen the truth. You said she was clever and like a soldier herself now, so I thought she'd know what to do. And she did.'

Major Sarenbrant's decision to meet the queen's troops on the road rather than risk a siege of the house hadn't helped him at all; the lie of the landscape meant her forces had seen them coming from a good way away, so they were ready to fight. And what neither I nor Major Sarenbrant had known was that the queen had negotiated to collect new forces at Newark. The rest of our troops were tired from the long march down from Bridlington, but these men were fresh and Major Sarenbrant's soldiers couldn't match them. Nor could they protect their commander; he'd been killed in the fight, and I sincerely hoped it hadn't been quick.

We learned as we rode that Sam had climbed a ladder and gone into the burning house to rescue us.

'You're a brave man, Sam,' said Henry.

Sam blushed and shook his head.

'Not me. I was scared of our ma coming back to haunt me if I let anything happen to this one, that's what it was.'

'She'd have been proud of you,' I said. 'But what are you going to do now? They'll have you down as a traitor for helping us.'

'I'll come over to your side. There's plenty have done that already.'

I thought of the queen, steeling herself to sell her jewels like a pedlar because she was so sure they had to win the war, that it was the only way to save the country. And Major Sarenbrant, so certain it was wrong for the country to go back to the way it was. Did they have any idea how many of the men they commanded didn't care one way or the other? The troops the queen had picked up in Newark had been on the other side before; now they were fighting for her because their general had decided he'd backed the wrong horse. Ordinary soldiers changed allegiance of their own accord too, and in either direction, for better money, for convenience, or just because the war in their area was going against them. Even I'd chosen my side from loyalty, not because I was certain they were right.

'What about Sarah?' I asked. 'And Lucy? They can't stay in Oakham, can they?'

'I'll ride with you as far as the Oakham turn, then go and fetch them,' said Sam. 'I don't say Sarah'll take kindly to the idea, she loves our little cottage, but plenty of women and children follow along, she'll soon settle in. She'll want to be where I am, that's the main thing.'

The camp celebrated that night, not just because we'd beaten the Parliamentarians and Henry and I had returned safely, but because we were close to Oxford and the long journey was almost over. Arabella was wearing the same dark-green dress I'd first seen her in, the copper lights in her hair bright against it. On the journey back, my stupid mind had kept drifting to the thoughts I'd had when I was locked in that little room, of the life we could have together, of how it would feel to know she loved me back. She liked me, didn't she? Only as a friend so far, but couldn't that change? Look at the way the king and queen were in the beginning: they'd hated each other, yet in time they became as devoted as any two people could be. Surely then it could happen if one person already loved the other and there was only half as much to change? I wouldn't even mind if she didn't love me as much as I loved her, as long as she loved me enough to want to be with me. And then we got back, and I looked at her, and knew my brain must have been addled by the smoke. She would never want me.

I kept thinking of how she'd laugh if she knew what had been in my head, and I was afraid she might just look at me with her sharp green eyes and see. So before long I left the circle round the fire to their songs and reminiscences, and went back to my tent. I was sitting there, lost in thought, when Sam came over.

'You all right?' he said.

I mumbled something about being tired. He came in and sat beside me.

'That Arabella was asking where you'd got to.'

'Was she?' I said, doing my best to sound uninterested. But my face gave me away.

'I knew it,' said Sam, slapping his knee and laughing. 'I saw the way you looked at her when we got here. Well, you're a dark horse. How long has that been going on?'

My first thought was to deny it, but suddenly all I wanted was to talk about it with the one person in the world who wouldn't laugh at me.

'It's not going on,' I said. 'She's not interested in me.'

'Looked to me like she was.'

'Don't be stupid. Why would she want someone like me? Women want a man who's tall and strong.'

'Well, I didn't just see the way you looked at her, I saw how she looked at you,' he said. 'She looked like you were something precious she'd lost and never thought to see again.'

'This was when we arrived back at camp, wasn't it?'

'Yes, and she—'

'I was sitting next to Henry,' I said. 'He's the one she was looking at.'

'He wasn't the one she was asking for just now.'

'She probably just wants to tell me off for putting him in danger. Sam, there's no way Arabella would want me.'

'Yes but, see, I thought that about Sarah,' he said. 'Her being so pretty and quick and clever – I was sure she'd never look at a clot like me. But I liked her so much, I couldn't get her out of my thoughts. So I thought what I'll do is, I'll get work on Whiteladies Farm – that's where she was a dairymaid – and then I can see her every day, and that'll have to be enough.'

'What changed your mind? What made you get up the courage?'

'Oh, I didn't. I was that sure she wouldn't want me, I never said more than good morning to her. No, it was Sarah – she came up to me one day and said did I want to take her to the fair or not, because if not, she'd go with Toby Averson, the cowman. It was as much as I could do to get the word out, but I said yes, and that was the beginning of it.'

He smiled at the memory.

'If I can get a wife like Sarah, I don't see why you're so sure Arabella wouldn't love you. They're funny things, women, and they don't always do what you think they'll do.'

He was wrong. He might think himself lucky to have got Sarah for a wife, but if ever there was a case of love being blind, it was that one. The match was at least as lucky for her as it was for him, and nothing like the situation between me and Arabella. There was no chance for me with her, and I would just have to live with that.

Chapter Forty

Arriving in Oxford was like stepping back in time. The king and the two eldest princes rode to meet us, and as our procession came through the gates, bells rang out and people were hanging out of windows, cheering. In the fifteen months we'd been away, Oxford had become the new capital of England, as far as our side was concerned, and it was bursting at the seams with soldiers, courtiers, court officials and their servants.

After all we'd experienced since we set foot back on English soil, it was the strangest of summers. Soldiers were drilled in the college courtyards, ammunition was stored in the grand halls, and the great quadrangle of Christ Church echoed with the bellowing of cows penned up to feed all the extra mouths. Every night, our troops went out to strike at the Parliamentary forces in the towns around, and every day news came of battles up and down the country. But for us, life went back to the golden days at Whitehall. There were dinners and dancing, poetry and plays; the king and queen strolled arm in arm through the cloisters, and courtiers picked up their old squabbles and flirtations as though the months in between had never happened. And me? I spent that summer trying to bring about a marriage between my best friend and the woman I loved.

Sam had given me the idea when he told me about finding work on the same farm as Sarah. 'Then I could see her every day,' he'd said, 'and that would have to be enough.' Since I'd be foolish to hope for anything else, couldn't that be enough for me too? And if Henry married Arabella, I'd have it: they'd both stay at court, wherever court eventually turned out to be, and I'd see her all the time. Otherwise, before long she'd be wooed by some lord and whisked off to his country house after they married, and I'd be lucky to set eyes on her once a year.

Henry was ready to marry; on nights when we'd both taken too much ale, he'd often told me that when the war was over, he wanted to settle down and have a family. He wasn't in love with Arabella, but he'd always seen her as a challenge, and Henry liked a challenge. It wouldn't be difficult to put the idea into his head.

My chance came when the queen held a ball at Merton College, where we were staying. Henry and I were sharing a room, and as we got dressed for the evening, I said I had something to ask him.

'What is it?' he asked, bending down to adjust the buckle on his boot.

'Will you ask Arabella to dance with you?'

He looked up, laughing.

'And get my head snapped off? Why would I do that?'

'She asked me if I thought you would. It seemed to me she wanted you to.'

'Are you sure you didn't dream this, Nat? Arabella thinks I'm an idiot who can't tell tripe from treacle. You may recall she said as much the other day.'

It was true, she'd said exactly that, after Henry had ventured to suggest book learning was overrated, and parents would do better to let their sons spend more time hunting and riding. But that was just Arabella; she was like that with everyone, and if she was more so with Henry, that must be to cover up the fact that she was sweet on him.

'Perhaps I've got it wrong,' I said. 'Forget I mentioned it.'

'But did it seem as though she wanted me to ask?'

'I thought so, yes. But I probably shouldn't have said. Don't mention it to her, will you?'

Of course it worked. As soon as we entered the room, Henry scanned the crowd, looking for her. But I saw her first. She had her back to us and someone had done something clever with her hair, twisting it up at the back of her head so it looked as though it was long again. There were pearls threaded through it and she was wearing a dress of pale cream satin. She must have borrowed it from Susan, who was about her height but plumper; the neckline was a bit loose and it hung down a little, exposing the pure white skin at the top of her back. When she turned and saw us, I realised I'd been holding my breath.

Henry was clever. He didn't try to flirt, the way he usually would with a woman he was interested in. He knew that wouldn't get him anywhere with her. But he was attentive – he fetched her drinks, pointed out foods she might like on the table, opened a window when she said she was too warm. She made a face at me then, as if to ask what he was up to, but I looked away.

When he asked her to dance, she shook her head and said she was a bad dancer. But he took her hand and she let him lead her onto the floor. I didn't want to see, but I couldn't look away.

At first she was awkward, biting her lip as she concentrated on the steps. But Henry was one of the best dancers at Whitehall and he hadn't lost his skills; with him guiding her she began to find her confidence, and by the end of the dance she was laughing with pleasure, her cheeks flushed and her eyes shining. They danced three times more, and by the third, I'd seen enough. I was sitting by myself in an anteroom, working my way through a jug of claret, when she came and flopped down beside me.

'There you are,' she said. 'I've been looking everywhere for you.'

I ignored the way my heart flipped over when she said that. *It doesn't mean what you want it to mean.*

'I thought you were dancing,' I said.

'Was I terrible?' she asked.

'No. Not at all.'

'I had no idea it could be so much fun. At home, the men were such clodhoppers. But it's different when your partner knows what they're doing – it feels like flying.'

'You dance very well together, you and Henry.'

'Well, Henry dances well – I just followed as best I could.' She nudged me and smiled. 'Don't tell him I said that though, he's conceited enough already.'

I poured myself another cup of claret and took a deep gulp

to give myself a reason not to answer. It was starting to go to my head, but I didn't care.

'Are you all right, Nat?' she said. 'You're very quiet.'

'I'm fine.'

'Do you ... I mean, it can't be very nice, watching everyone else dance and not being able to join in.'

She was sorry for me. If I'd been miserable watching Arabella and Henry together, it was nothing to hearing those words. I wanted her to love me, not pity me.

I slammed down the cup and stood. The room reeled around me.

'Who says I can't join in?'

I marched into the hall and looked around. In the far corner, Bonbon was perched on a cushion. Making sure people saw me, I stalked across, bowed deeply, and said:

'Would you allow me this dance?'

There were giggles behind me as I picked her up. She gave an irritable growl but let me carry her onto the floor. I joined onto the end of the row of dancers; they were all watching now, some looking puzzled, others already laughing. Holding Bonbon under her front paws, I skipped up the line, whirled her round and skipped back again, holding my head high and keeping a straight face, to make people laugh all the more. By the time the dance finished and I placed my partner on the floor and bowed to her, the entire room was looking on and laughing.

'Bravo, Nathaniel,' said the queen, wiping tears from her eyes. 'And Bonbon, where did you learn to dance so well?'

As I left the room, people were saying how comical I was and how I used to make the court laugh back in the

Whitehall days. But Arabella wasn't laughing; she looked at me as though she'd never seen me before. I'd wanted to make her see she needn't feel sorry for me, but all I'd done was show her I was a little clown, there to entertain like any other freak.

My head was spinning – the claret and the whirling around hadn't been a good combination – and I had to squint one eye to see properly. Arabella called my name but I ignored her and made for the door. Outside, I took a deep breath of the cool night air to try to steady my head, but it was too late. I puked the evening's drink onto the grass, splashing my boots with blackcurrant-coloured liquid.

'Nat Davy, Honorary Captain of Horse,' I said quietly. 'Just look at you now.'

The next morning my head was throbbing, and to try and clear it, I went for a walk along the river. Sunlight glittered on the water and trees threw dappled shade across the path. The turquoise flash of a kingfisher skimmed the air, and I sat down to watch it catching its breakfast. I'd been trying to block out the memory of the night before, but as I sat there watching the river flow past, I couldn't stop the thoughts any longer. I'd been an idiot. I'd set out to get Henry and Arabella together, but when I saw them, I lost control and acted like a fool. Because, in my heart, I hadn't really accepted that to keep her, I had to lose her.

Well, I told myself, it's time to make up your mind: risk her disappearing from your life for ever, or get used to seeing her as another man's wife. I tried to imagine life without her and what I saw was a long, dusty road, with no destination in sight and nothing to see along the way. A life without any colour in it.

It would hurt to see her with Henry; I was in no doubt about that now. But I'd take that over the thought of never seeing her at all.

Chapter Forty-one

All that summer, it looked as though things were going to go the king's way. The men and arms we'd brought with us injected new spirit into his forces, and shortly after we arrived, they took the city of Bristol, snatching the valuable port right out of the other side's hands. Exeter, Bath and Dartmouth fell to our army too, and when I went to see Sam at his barracks, he told me they barely had room for all the new recruits who'd abandoned Parliament and come over to what looked like the winning side.

'Looks like I swapped just in time,' he said. 'Everyone says the tide's turning our way now.'

'Let's hope so.'

'I reckon you'll be back in London by Christmas,' he said. 'So if you stop dragging your feet and get things settled with that Arabella, you could be married in the spring. Give us a cousin for Lucy.'

'I've told you before, she's not interested in me. As a matter of fact, I think there's a good chance she'll marry Henry.'

His eyes widened as I explained my plan.

'You say I gave you this idea?'

'Yes – you said you got work on the farm where Sarah was, so you could see her.'

'But I didn't try and get her to marry someone else, did I? I always thought you were the clever one, Nat, but that's got to be the stupidest thing anyone's ever done.'

I don't know why I even told him; I should have known he wouldn't understand. Arabella marrying Henry was the only way I could be sure of not losing her completely, so as the summer rolled on, I did everything I could to push them together. After the ball I continued to drop hints to Henry that Arabella was keen on him; a remark she'd made, a look I'd seen. He was intrigued, as I'd known he would be. Henry was used to women falling for him and making no secret of it. The idea that Arabella had been hiding her true feelings all along fascinated him, and he was determined to charm her into showing them. Then I started hinting that others were paying court to her. Henry loved a competition, and the prospect of a rival or two only increased his interest.

And yet, if Arabella noticed, it didn't show. She continued to tease him as she'd always done and snap at him if he said something stupid, and any attempts at compliments were dealt with just as they'd been when we were on the road, with a roll of her eyes and a sarcastic reply. I wasn't looking forward to the day when she did show her feelings for him, but at the same time, I was puzzled. I'd always been sure she hid those feelings because she didn't think they were returned, but couldn't she see that now was her chance? If she didn't give him some encouragement soon, Henry might get fed up and the whole plan would fall to pieces.

In the end, I asked her. It had been a rainy week and we'd all been cooped up inside the college. When the sun finally came out one afternoon, she asked me to go with her to collect some fabric from the shops, and I made up my mind to do it then.

Over the months, we'd had long conversations on all kinds of subjects, but this time, I struggled to get round to what I wanted to say. We talked about the war, about another ball the queen was planning, and about Arabella's father and brothers, who she'd visited that morning – the hapless Ed had just become engaged to the sister of a fellow soldier, and though Arabella was pleased for him, the pleasure was bittersweet, because her mother wasn't there to see it. But by the time we reached the shops, I still hadn't found a subtle way to broach the subject of her and Henry. So I decided to do what she always did when she wanted to know something: just ask.

'If Henry asked you to marry him, would you say yes?' I said.

'What?'

She stopped and looked down at me.

'Henry. Would you marry him?'

'What are you talking about?'

'I think Henry's in love with you.'

'Don't be silly, Nat. Henry flirts with everyone.'

'I'm serious. You must have seen it.'

She rolled her eyes, and sighed.

'All right, yes, he's been acting oddly lately. But that's just because things are different here. You know, court manners or whatever they call it.'

'It isn't that. I know him and—'

'Well, I don't think so, but anyway, no.'

'What?'

'No, I wouldn't marry Henry if he asked me. I've told you before, I'm not interested in him in that way.'

'I don't believe you.'

I hadn't meant to say that; her reply just took me by surprise. As soon as the words came out of my mouth, her face told me it would have been better if they hadn't.

'Oh, you don't?' she said. 'I suppose you think I should just accept any offer and be glad of it, in case I don't get another one?'

'No, of course not. But you could do a lot worse than Henry. And I thought ... well, I've always thought you were keen on him.'

'And I told you I wasn't. I told you plain as day, ages ago, and I've just told you again. You might be the smallest man in England, Nat, but sometimes I think you're the biggest idiot. Now, if you don't mind, I think I'll do my errands by myself.'

She stalked into the shop, and slammed the door behind her.

After that, she started acting differently with Henry. Where once she'd have cut him off with a scathing remark if he told too many boring hunting stories, now she listened patiently. She laughed at his jokes, even the feeble ones, and complimented him when he wore a new pair of boots, instead of calling him vain like she used to. The conversation had done what I intended it to, and I supposed she really hadn't believed Henry was doing more than flirting before. What I couldn't understand was why she was so cross that I'd guessed her secret; she barely talked to me in the days after that conversation, and nothing I did made her laugh anymore. One day, she noticed me watching as she bent forward to pluck a piece of fluff from his coat, and gave a funny little shrug, as if to say, 'So what? Now you know.'

It wasn't long before Henry confided in me that he was thinking about asking Arabella to marry him. The funny thing was that he'd become less infatuated with her since she'd begun responding to his advances – Henry always did enjoy the thrill of the chase – but instead, he'd come to see this new, strangely compliant Arabella as exactly what he wanted in a wife.

'She was always a bit argumentative for my taste,' he said. 'But perhaps she'd just been overindulged at home – all that business with the lessons, and dressing up like a boy. I think she's realised now, it's not the way to carry on.'

I didn't think that at all. I didn't believe she'd really changed; she was just playing a game, like other women did. It surprised me, but then, I knew as well as anyone, people did strange things for love.

Chapter Forty-two

For the king and queen, that would be the last golden summer. By autumn, the Parliamentarian army had a new leader, an East Anglian general called Cromwell, and while at first our side laughed at stories of his bluff way of speaking, and called him 'potato face', it was soon clear that under his leadership their forces had gained a backbone of steel. Through the winter, our strongholds around the country fell one after the other, and by spring, the mood at court was fearful. If the Parliamentarians marched on Oxford, it was by no means clear that our forces could keep them out, and if they got in, there would be no mercy – not for the king and queen, and not for anyone who'd been on their side.

By then, the king and queen's reunion had produced its natural result: she was expecting another child. This time the pregnancy was difficult, and made more so because she'd been ill for months, with terrible rheumatic pains in her arms and legs. So when the other side began to close in, the king insisted she had to leave Oxford, to keep herself and their baby safe. It went without saying that we'd go with her, and Henry decided to wait no longer.

'I'm going to see Arabella's father today,' he told me at breakfast one morning. 'If he gives permission, I'll ask her tonight.'

I spent that morning wandering round the city on my own. I couldn't tell you what I saw or heard; I'm not sure I'd have noticed if the entire Parliamentarian army had marched in and seized the place. I kept squashing down a small and stupid hope that Arabella's father would refuse his permission, though there was no reason for him to, and if he had, he'd have prevented the very thing I'd been scheming to bring about.

Of course he didn't refuse. He said the match was a good one but the decision was Arabella's. Henry planned to ask her to walk in the college gardens after dinner, and I didn't even let myself hope she'd say no. I left the hall as early as I could – Henry's uncharacteristic nervousness was making me want to hit him – and went to my room.

I'd been lying on my bed, listening to rats scratching in the roof, for about an hour, when there was a knock on the door. Henry, come to share his triumph. Pretending to be asleep would only put off the moment, so I sat up, but before I even got off the bed, there was another knock. It sounded tentative for Henry, who usually rapped on doors as though he was trying to make a hole in them. The thought – all right, the hope – flickered through my mind that perhaps she'd said no, and that was why he was less ebullient than usual. I got up to open the door.

'Can I come in?' said Arabella.

I was so surprised that I couldn't think of a word to say. She sat down on the bed and I stood in front of her, not really sure what else to do.

'I wanted to talk to you,' she said, not looking at me. She fiddled with her gloves for a bit, half taking one off, then putting it back on again, and then she looked up. 'You know... I expect you know... Henry's asked me to marry him?'

'I knew that was his plan, yes.'

She took both gloves off again, and folded them in her lap. It seemed to take her a long time to be satisfied that they were folded quite right.

'This is very difficult,' she said eventually. 'I think I'd better start again. What I meant to say first was I'm sorry I haven't been very nice to you lately. It was just... I don't know, I think I might have misunderstood when you asked me if I'd marry Henry.'

There was a question in her voice, but I wasn't sure what the question was.

'I didn't mean to upset you when I asked,' I said. 'I just... I knew he liked you and I wanted to know if you felt the same.'

'Why?' she asked.

'What?'

'Why did you want to know?'

Because I wanted you to marry him, because you'd never marry me, and that was the only way to keep a little bit of you, I wanted to say.

'Henry's my friend,' I said. 'I didn't want him to get his hopes up if there was no chance.'

'I see.'

'Are you going to marry him?'

'I don't know. I've asked him to give me a few days to decide.'

I hadn't expected that. She smiled a thin little smile.

'Of course, he thinks I'm just exercising my womanly wiles. Keeping him guessing.'

I smiled too, as though that was ridiculous, when it was exactly what I'd have told Henry if he'd asked me.

'Right,' she said. She took a deep breath and held it for a second, with her lips pressed together. 'I'm just going to ask what I came to ask. Do you ... that is ... is there any reason why I shouldn't marry Henry?'

What did she mean, any reason?

'Why are you asking me that?' I said.

She looked at me, her head on one side.

'You don't know why I'm asking?'

I shook my head.

'You really don't?' she said.

'No.'

Then a thought struck me.

'Do you mean ... I know Henry has a reputation, I know he's been a ladies' man. But he'll be a good husband, I'm sure of that.'

She looked down at her hands, and pulled on her gloves again.

'Right,' she said, standing up. 'Well, you've answered my question, Nat. Thank you.'

She walked to the door, and left.

She didn't wait the few days she'd asked for. The next morning, she accepted Henry's proposal. I'd steeled myself to look happy for them when word got round and everyone began congratulating them, but as it turned out their news was overshadowed by bigger events. That same morning, word came that Parliamentarian troops planned to march on Oxford within days. It was time to go.

I made a quick visit to Sam's barracks to say goodbye, only to find him setting off on his way to me.

'I had a letter,' he said. 'From Annie. Father's dead.'

It wasn't a shock; my father was a good age by then, and I knew from Sam he'd had trouble with his chest in recent years. I couldn't find it in myself to be sad either, not for a man who'd cared less for me than he did for his dogs, and he hadn't cared that much for them. And yet as I stood there, what I thought was that, no matter what I did, I could never make him proud of me now.

When we left the next day, the queen's party was almost the same one that had landed at Bridlington so many eventful months before: Henry, me, Susan and Elizabeth, Father Philip, a few servants, and now Arabella too. The queen had been so happy to be on home ground again that day, standing there on the snowy harbour, joking with the fishermen and their families. The woman who sat opposite me in the coach now looked like a different person. The parting with the king and her children had been tearful and her eyes were still red. In pain from her rheumatism and exhausted by her pregnancy, she was hunched over like a woman twice her age, and as the coach rumbled along she winced at every bump and rut.

Our destination, Exeter, was still held by our side. Safe in the home of a family who supported the king, the queen took to her bed, attended by Susan, Elizabeth and Arabella, so Henry and I were left to our own devices. He'd been unusually subdued since we left Oxford, and one morning, when we were out for a walk, he turned to me and said:

'Does Arabella seem happy to you?'

'What do you mean?'

'It's just – well, shouldn't a girl be a bit more cheerful about getting engaged?'

I'd seen it too. She'd been quiet throughout the journey and there were dark shadows under her eyes, as though she wasn't sleeping well. But I'd put that down to her being worried for the queen, as we all were, and to the anxiety of being on the road again after feeling safe in Oxford.

'I don't think anyone's feeling very cheerful at the moment,' I said.

'No, I suppose not. And perhaps she's upset we can't get married sooner – this isn't the time for a wedding, that's for certain.'

I didn't ask when he thought the time would be right. Seeing Arabella walk out of a church as Henry's wife was what I had to do to keep her in my life, but that didn't mean I was looking forward to it. As far as I was concerned, they could wait for ever.

We stayed in Exeter for three months, and in June, the queen gave birth to a baby girl. It was a difficult labour and we were all afraid neither she nor the baby would survive. But though the child was small and sickly and the queen was in more pain than ever, they lived. For a brief couple of days, it seemed a hopeful sign – and then came the news that Parliamentary forces were heading for Exeter. The queen wrote personally to Cromwell, asking for safe passage to Bath, where she could take the waters and recover her health. I was with her when his reply arrived, refusing her request, and suggesting she'd get more benefit from the air in London.

'For as long as they allowed me to breathe it,' she said, throwing the message into the fire. 'And God knows, that would not be long.' She stared into the flames for a moment, then turned to me. 'Fetch the cipher. I need to write to the king.'

She dictated the letter, and I set it into code. She wouldn't take the chance of being captured, she said, knowing his love for her would make him do anything his opponents asked. So we were fleeing to France.

If I'd known what would happen there, I'd have stayed and taken my chances in Exeter, but I didn't, and so began a chapter of my life that I remember with no happiness at all.

Chapter Forty-three

I expected to be away a few months, until the king's forces rallied and it was safe to come home again. But as the news from across the sea became more and more bleak, it was clear we'd be living in exile for much longer. Not long after we arrived, I had a letter from Jeremiah – he'd never been much for correspondence, but I didn't want to lose touch, so I'd written to let him know where we were. Kent, he wrote, was under Parliamentary control, and his master's estate had been sequestered – seized because he was a Royalist, and sold to someone else, to bring in money for the Parliamentarian army.

'*The new master's a merchant, down from London,*' Jeremiah wrote. '*Doesn't understand country ways, but he's very well in with the county committee, and they're the ones running things now. I tell you, Nat, we're living in a nest of snakes. You've only to let a wrong word slip, and your own neighbours will turn you in, the better to show they're on the right side. Luckily my Sukie saw the way the wind was blowing – right back when we moved here, she said to me, we shouldn't say too much about where we've come from, and we didn't. We keep our heads down, and pray for better times, but I'm very much afraid I don't see them coming.*'

* * *

The queen's family made her welcome, giving us apartments in a palace beside the river in Paris, where the tall windows let sunlight flood in onto the rich tapestries and paintings that lined the walls. The beds were hung with silk and velvet and she had a household of servants waiting on her once again. But she scarcely noticed any of it. Still plagued with pain night and day, she spent all her time writing to anyone who might supply money or troops, and I was kept busy putting her daily letters to the king into code. I didn't mind; it distracted me from thinking about Arabella and Henry. Though – to my relief – the two of them weren't exactly turtle doves, and no date had been set for the wedding, seeing his hand touching her shoulder or resting for a second on her waist was torture to me.

So, when old faces from the Whitehall days began appearing in Paris, at first I was pleased. Over the next eighteen months, as the Parliamentarians captured swathes of Royalist territory, more and more of those who'd allied themselves with the king found England an uncomfortable place to be and headed for France. A bigger group meant I was thrown together less with Henry and Arabella, which could only be a good thing, I thought. Until someone arrived who I'd sincerely hoped never to see again.

There were four of them, in thick cloaks and riding boots; the tallest walked in front and the others fell into step behind. People turned to look as their heels clicked across the floor. Henry was standing talking to the queen, so he saw their faces. Long ago, after one too many glasses of claret, he'd prised out of me the reason why I came to race Charles Crofts, and when he realised who the taller man was, he looked round for me. But I already knew. I'd have recognised that strutting walk anywhere.

It must have been fifteen years since I last set eyes on Crofts. After he left Whitehall, he'd been back a few times to visit his father, but since neither of us was eager for the other's company, we managed never to cross paths. Now here he was, a grown man. He'd been tall for his age back then, and now he stood a clear couple of inches over most of the men in the room. He bowed deeply to the queen and announced himself to be at her service, as did his companions, cousins of his from Northumberland.

I listened as he gave the latest news from England. The north was entirely in Parliamentarian hands now; his uncle's family had been forced to leave their estate. Letters were coming very erratically at that time and the queen hadn't had a message from the king in weeks, so she was eager to hear everything he had to tell. They talked for some time before she dismissed him, thanking him for the news and telling him he was very welcome at the palace.

At the door, I stepped forward and put out my hand. We were men now; Crofts was probably nothing like the boy who'd taunted me all those years ago.

'Remember me?' I said.

He looked down, and smirked.

'Pie boy,' he said. 'Still hanging around then. And still a little runt.'

Chapter Forty-four

I told myself it didn't matter. Things were different now. I wasn't the little boy who'd capered about in costumes. I was the one who'd saved the queen from the kidnap plot. I'd been beside her when we came under attack in Bridlington and she trusted me, and only me, to code her letters to the king. What was Crofts? A cocky young blade who'd ridden in the odd skirmish, then made his exit when things got a bit too dangerous. And now he was just a hanger-on, here because he had nowhere else to go. I wouldn't be seeking out his company, but I was determined not to change my habits to avoid him either.

For a while it worked. The queen was having problems with her eyes by then, and asked me to draft her letters as well as putting them into code. The war at home was going badly, and with very little territory left to defend, the king was trying to be clever. By then, his opponents had split into factions – Cromwell and the army wanted things to go one way, and the Members of Parliament another, and on top of that there were the Scots, dangling the idea that they might help him out if he saw fit to come over to their way in the matter of religion, and get rid of bishops. So he'd started negotiating with all three, boasting in his letters to the queen that he could play one against the other to get what he wanted. Well, as I've mentioned before, the king's high opinion of his own negotiating skills was not shared by me, and by then, it wasn't shared by her either. She was sure he'd end up giving way to one or other of them, and sent increasingly furious messages telling him to stand firm. So between them, their letters kept me busy and that meant I rarely saw anything of Crofts. If our paths did happen to cross, he invariably made some comment about pies – there'd never been much variety to his wit – but I shrugged that off well enough.

Over the following months though, more exiles arrived, mostly of the same stamp: young men who'd treated the war as a game, and then made themselves scarce when they realised it wasn't. At home, the king's influence had imposed a certain seriousness on court life. But in France, with the queen distracted by her efforts to secure support for the war and stop the king doing anything stupid, her new court became a place where too many people had nothing better to do than drink, play cards, set each other dares and make sport of those who weren't in their company. The queen's priest, Father Philip, was mimicked for his stooped posture and the tremor that had come with age; Lord Drage, who'd been injured in battle, was the subject of a crude little poem comparing him to a donkey with three legs. And of course, I didn't escape.

They took care never to do it in front of the queen, and at first they left me alone when I was with Henry and Arabella too. I didn't mention it to her or to them. Not just because I didn't want anyone else to fight my battles for me, though I didn't. It was more that I didn't want them to see me through Crofts' eyes, even for a second. But keeping it a secret made me feel so alone, the way only people who are different feel alone. There's an invisible wall between us and the rest of the world, which even the people who love us are on the other side of. Sometimes, you can forget it's there, but every time I saw Crofts' mocking face, it reminded me what people – even people who were my friends – must see when they looked at me.

I hoped in time they'd get bored, but of course they didn't; there was so little else to do. They invented a game where they'd take turns to suggest how a wife might be found for me: recruiting a magician to bring a doll to life, carving a face onto a turnip, dressing Susan's poodle up as a woman. It caused so much hilarity that before long they were playing it at the dinner table every evening. I could tell just by the smirks directed at me but, because they usually sat some distance away, it was a while before Henry happened to overhear. His face darkened and he turned towards Crofts.

'Don't,' I said. 'He's just an idiot. It doesn't bother me.'

'Well, it bothers me and—'

'What's going on?' said Arabella, who'd been talking to someone else. She hadn't heard what Crofts said, and I didn't want her to.

'Nothing. Henry was just saying he thought the meat was tough tonight.'

When she'd gone to bed, I asked Henry not to tell her what we'd been talking about.

'I don't want a big fuss made about it. It's better to ignore him.'

'I'd happily thump him for you, but I know you don't want that,' he said. 'But I don't understand why you're letting him get away with it. You're never short of a smart remark, you could show him up for the clod he is with half a dozen words. Get people laughing at him and he'll soon leave you alone.'

How could I explain to Henry – tall, strong, normal Henry – it wasn't as easy as that? It was true, I could have made Crofts look stupid with a few words – but he'd only have to mention 'Mrs Turnipina Davy', or whistle over the damned poodle and ask if it would have me as its wedded husband, and the company would dissolve into laughter. And when that happens, when they're all looking down at you, picturing you marrying a turnip on a stick and laughing till their sides ache, you can make all the smart remarks you like, but you're just pissing in the wind.

Would things have been different if Crofts hadn't seen me at the window that day? I don't know. But that was when it all changed. The window was at the turn of a staircase and as I glanced out, Arabella was walking Bonbon in the garden. The dog was in her last months then and very smelly, with rheumy eyes and patchy fur. She could barely shuffle along on her bandy little legs, but she still liked to take a turn round the garden, nosing at bushes and lifting her face to smell the air.

I leaned against the window. Arabella – who normally walked as though there wasn't a second to be lost – matched the dog's painfully slow pace, looking down and speaking encouragingly to her. Now and then she'd stop to let Bonbon sniff something interesting, then lean down to give her a little pat before they moved on.

I didn't hear him come up the stairs behind me. Normally, Crofts' confident steps were hard to miss, but I suspect he'd seen me and crept up to find out what I was looking at.

'So that's how it is, pie boy,' he said. 'Well, well.'

I turned, startled. He grinned and wagged a finger at me.

'All our efforts to find you a wife, and you had one in mind already. She's a bit tall for you though. Oh, and promised to someone else.'

There was no point in denying it; anything I said would only give him more sport. My face burned and, not wanting him to see, I turned to walk on up the stairs.

'I wonder if she knows?' he called after me. 'Or have I found out your little secret?'

I pictured him walking up to Arabella at the dinner table and telling her, in front of everyone. How they'd all laugh: there I was, the court freak, thinking to throw my heart at the most beautiful girl in the place. It was as comical as anything they'd have seen at the theatre, back in the Whitehall days. He wouldn't even care that Henry was sitting there. If I'd been an ordinary man, it would have been something to whisper in corners. Did she love me back, people would ask; was Henry being cuckolded even before he was married? With me, it was a safe joke; Henry could laugh along with everyone else, though I knew he wouldn't.

But the worst was that Arabella would know. Once, I'd worried that if she realised I loved her, she'd laugh at me. But I knew her better now. She wouldn't laugh; she'd look at me with pity in her eyes, and that I could not bear.

That evening I sat, as usual, with Henry and Arabella.

Crofts and his friends were sniggering, now and then looking over at us. The room was full. Were there more faces round the table than usual, or had I just not noticed before how big the company had grown? I listened to Arabella and Henry talk without hearing a word they said, swallowed food I didn't taste, and waited.

The food came and went, and still Crofts hadn't moved. I looked down the table and he happened to glance up at the same moment. He looked across to Arabella, then pushed back his chair and sauntered over.

I stared at my plate, not wanting to see their faces when he spoke.

'Henry,' he said. 'Just wanted to let you know about something.'

'Yes?'

'It's quite important.'

Laughter bubbled behind his words.

'Well, tell me then,' said Henry.

Crofts bent down.

'Hello, Nat,' he said. 'Didn't see you there. Then again, you're easy to miss.'

He sniggered, and glanced back towards his friends.

'What did you want to say?' said Henry.

'Oh, yes. Message from the stables. That grey you wanted to take out hunting tomorrow, she's lame. You'll need to choose another mount.' He murmured into my ear. 'What did you think I was going to say, pie boy?'

When he got back to his seat, he said something to his friends and they all fell about laughing.

'What did he say to you?' asked Arabella.

'Nothing,' I said. 'Just one of his stupid remarks. He's an idiot.'

I should have known Crofts wouldn't have his fun all at once, not when he'd found such an entertaining game to play. At dinner, he'd sometimes stroll up to our end of the table, seem to hesitate, then walk on to speak to someone else. Once he came up to Arabella and pretended he had something important to tell her, then apologised and said no, he had the wrong person. And if he passed us on the stairs or in the gardens – which he did very often now – he'd be humming this or that song about a disappointed suitor, or a secret love, and smiling to himself.

Every day, I woke up thinking, 'Will it be today?' But he would choose the time and place, and all I could do was wait.

Chapter Forty-five

He chose the night of my thirtieth birthday. Henry had gone with the queen to see a financier in Arras, so neither of them were at dinner. That should have made me wary but Crofts had been leaving me alone lately, and I foolishly hoped he'd tired of the game. At dinner, a toast was drunk to my health and as the cheers died away, Crofts said:

'Thirty years old. About time you were married, I'd say, Nat.' He glanced round at his friends, all smirking like fools. 'Perhaps there's a lady you have your eye on?'

I'd already decided that when it happened, I'd go along with the joke. Arabella would see through it but if I could maintain some dignity in front of everyone else, I'd at least cheat Crofts out of some of his fun and perhaps make it less embarrassing for her too.

'Why do you want to know?' I asked. 'Are you worried I'll be so popular there'll be no one left for you?'

It wasn't much of a joke but it didn't take much then. Laughter rang round the table and someone yelled out:

'Watch yourself, Crofts, you've got competition.'

'Let me reassure you,' I went on. 'That hairy-faced kitchen maid you're so keen on? I'll happily leave her to you.'

Everyone laughed and Crofts' cheeks reddened. So far I was winning but he held the best cards. He put his head on one side and grinned, then stood and strode towards me.

'I think we should find you a wife now,' he said, gesturing round at the table. 'Perhaps there's a lady here who'd like a husband she could dress up like a doll?'

With one quick movement he stepped forward and plucked me out of my seat. Stupidly, I hadn't expected it; it was years since anyone had done that to me. He held me in front of him, my legs dangling. Any attempt to get free would only make me look more comical, so I rolled my eyes as though this was a small inconvenience, held out my hands and said:

'Don't blame me if you're trampled in the rush. Miniatures are very fashionable this year.'

The faces round the table laughed.

'Good answer!' someone shouted.

'So,' said Crofts, 'let's see what we have here.' He took my right wrist between his finger and thumb and held out my arm. 'Full complement of limbs, somewhat small but in work-ing order.' He gestured towards my head. 'All his own teeth, plentiful hair. But here's the rub ...' He pointed at my breeches and laughed. 'Not so good in the— '

'Put him down,' said Arabella.

I couldn't look at her but her voice told me she was shaking with anger.

'Put him down,' she said again.

Crofts turned to her. *Now it'll come.* I closed my eyes so

I didn't have to see her pity. But before he could speak, she poked him hard on the shoulder.

'What is wrong with you? Nat is the queen's Honorary Captain of Horse. He saved her life when you were messing about, pretending to be a soldier and never getting near a battle. He nearly lost his life. He didn't run away when things got difficult, like you did. Now put him down.'

Crofts sniggered and glanced around but the laughing had died away, and people were looking down at the table or whispering among themselves. He set me on the table with a shove.

'As for the rest of you,' Arabella said, 'none of you, not one, has been as brave as Nat. He's a better man than most of you will ever be and you should be ashamed of yourselves for not showing him more respect.'

Crofts leaned down and muttered in my ear.

'Seems you have an admirer, pie boy. But I doubt she'd be so keen if she knew you and your tiny cock wanted to get into her bed.'

He stalked off, snatched out his chair and threw himself down in it. Arabella sat too, and people started to talk among themselves, as if they wanted to pretend nothing had happened.

'Why did you have to do that?' I said, my cheeks burning as I clambered down from the table.

'What?'

'Why did you have to humiliate me?'

'I humiliated you?' she said. 'What are you talking about?'

'I was all right. I was making a joke of it. I didn't need you to save me.'

She threw up her hands.

'I'm your friend, Nat, I'm not going to stand by and watch while—'

'You made me look stupid. Having to be rescued by a woman. It's just given them something else to laugh at me for. Next time just leave me alone.'

I regretted what I said even before I got to the door of the hall but I walked out anyway. I stomped back to my room and lay on the bed, my face hot with shame. If Arabella had said those words in any other situation, I would have been walking on the ceiling. She meant them too; Arabella didn't give fake praise. She usually didn't give praise at all, and I shouldn't have thrown it back in her face. But it wasn't how it was supposed to be. Men were supposed to rescue women, not the other way around. If I felt less of a man being dangled like a doll by Crofts, having her come to my rescue just made it worse. And he wouldn't let this go, I was certain of that. He'd be even more determined to humiliate me now.

It took a long time to fall asleep that night, and as I lay in my bed, reliving the evening over and over again, I made a decision. I wasn't going to wait for Crofts' next move. I'd taken him on before and I'd do it again. This time, though, it wouldn't be a horse race.

I was only halfway through telling Henry what I'd decided to do when he shook his head.

'I'm not letting you risk your life for that fool.'

'It's not for him, it's for me,' I said. 'And I wouldn't be risking my life. We'll fight to first blood, not to death. I'm a good shot and so is he; we both know where to aim. A flesh wound, that's all – and I don't intend it to me be that's wounded.'

'Even if you could guarantee that, which you can't, you know as well as I do what they think about duelling here. For God's sake, Nat, men have been executed for it.'

He was right. In the years before we'd arrived, duelling had become so common in France that people said you couldn't walk through the streets of Paris for an hour without seeing two men set on killing each other with pistols or swords. The government had responded with a string of decrees promising ever stronger penalties, and now if your opponent didn't kill you the law might instead. But only if you were caught.

'No one will find out,' I said. 'We'll do it at dawn, out in the forest.'

'This is madness, Nat. Why don't you just tell the queen about him baiting you? She could put a stop to it in an instant.'

'Is that what you'd do, if it was you?'

'No.'

'Then you know why I won't do it either. I know Crofts: if I can beat him, in front of his friends, like I did before, he'll leave me alone. So will you be my second, or not?'

He looked at me for a long while.

'All right,' he said. 'But I don't like this, Nat. I don't like it at all.'

Chapter Forty-six

The morning of the duel dawned crisp and cool; a haze of dew still covered the trees as we rode into the forest just outside the city. The appointed spot was a clearing not far in, flat and wide but hidden from the outside by a ring of fat oak trees.

Predictably, Crofts laughed when I issued my challenge. But when he realised I was serious, he liked the idea. Crofts was a born sportsman and this was his chance to get back at me for beating him all those years ago. We agreed to duel with pistols on horseback – the closest we could come to fighting as equals – and the contest would be won when one of us wounded the other.

Henry and I sat on a fallen log for fifteen minutes or so before they arrived, neither of us speaking. I ran through my strategy in my head. I had a bigger target to hit than Crofts, but the closer we got to each other, the smaller that advantage would be. So my best chance was to get in the first shot, as quickly as possible. I had no qualms about taking advantage of my size; Crofts' bigger, stronger hands helped him when it came to holding the pistol steady and I considered that made us even.

They came riding through the trees, Crofts and half a dozen of his friends, and they were all laughing together as they dismounted.

'I thought you'd chickened out,' I said. 'You took your time.'

'I'm ready,' he said, patting a bag that was slung over his shoulder. 'Got my weapon right here.'

'Better watch out, pie boy,' said one of the others. 'He's dangerous with that thing.'

They all laughed; I should have seen then that something was afoot.

Crofts' second and Henry had a quick conversation to make sure we were all agreed on the rules.

'Right,' said Henry, when they'd finished, 'I call the duellists forward to show their weapons.'

Crofts winked at his friends and walked forward. I took out my pistol and held it in front of me. He dipped his hand into the bag he was carrying, and it was only then that I realised. *Whatever's in there, it's too big to be a pistol.* The whole gang of them burst into gales of laughter, but for a moment I couldn't make out what he was holding. Then I saw it. A water squirt. They were kept in the stables in case of fire, but the stable boys played with them, soaking each other in mock battles. I'd challenged him to a duel and he'd brought a toy.

I stood there as Crofts wiped tears of laughter from his eyes. He waved the squirt around his head, shouting 'Bang, bang!', and one of his friends yelled out, 'Watch out, pie boy, you could drown if he shoots!'

Their laughter echoed round the clearing and hot anger rose through me. *You are not going to cheat me of this.*

'Are you turning down my challenge?' I said.

He looked down at me, a smirk playing around his mouth.

'Never could take a joke, could you, pie boy? You can't seriously think I'm going to fight you.'

'I beat you once,' I said. 'I can do it again. Someone here must have a pistol you can use, so are you going to accept my challenge or back out like a coward?'

He narrowed his eyes at me.

'You really want to do this?'

'I said so, didn't I?'

'Right. Let's do it.'

We faced each other, on horseback, pistols raised, waiting for the signal. I was so filled with anger and bitter humiliation I could barely think. *Calm down. Don't lose your advantage.* Henry raised his arm, then let it fall, and we charged forward. I lifted my pistol and aimed it at Crofts' shoulder. He had broad shoulders, Charles Crofts, plenty of room to graze the skin and do no real harm. I held my hand steady. *Get the first shot.* He pounded towards me, I squeezed the trigger and something – I never knew what, a bird flying out of a tree perhaps – distracted me. I lost my focus and my arm swung out. The recoil from the shot knocked me off balance, I fell and, as I hit the ground, everything went black.

Chapter Forty-seven

When I opened my eyes, I was lying in the damp grass. I tested my limbs; nothing broken. No bleeding either. Henry was crouching beside me, and I couldn't read the look on his face. Had I won or not?

'He missed me,' I said. 'Did I get him?'

Henry bit his lip and looked down. He started to speak, then someone shouted:

'No, wait for the doctor. You're wrong, he can't be ...'

Across the clearing, Crofts' friends were standing in a circle. One moved aside and there he was, on the ground. He was lying completely still, a cloak laid over his chest, and the cloak was soaked with blood, so much dark red blood I couldn't tell what colour it had once been. His cousin was kneeling beside him. He looked up at the man who'd shouted, and shook his head, then took the cloak and lifted it gently over Crofts' face.

I scrambled to my feet and shook off Henry's attempt to stop me going closer. One of Crofts' boots must have caught in the stirrup when he fell from his horse; it was half off, hanging crookedly from his foot. I wanted to put it back on for him. He always liked to look sharp, Crofts, he wouldn't want to lie there dishevelled. But when I moved towards him, my stomach churned and I had to walk away into the bushes, where I vomited, over and over.

I had hated him in life, but I'd never intended this. And I couldn't even find my hatred of him anymore. Why had it seemed so important? Now all I felt was pity for his poor broken body and hot, searing guilt for what I'd done. It had been my hand holding the gun. It had been me who'd suggested the duel and then insisted on going through with it when Crofts turned it into a joke. It was my fault. My stupid pride had caused a man's death.

Henry took charge, quietly and efficiently organising a messenger to fetch transport for Crofts' body, and asking Crofts' friends to stay quiet about what had happened so he could tell the queen first.

'What will happen now?' I asked him as we finally rode back to the palace.

'To be honest, Nat, I don't know. Everyone there knows you didn't mean to kill him. They all saw it, just as you said – something startled you and you missed your aim. It could just as easily have gone the other way. But—'

'But it didn't. I killed him. I've got to pay for that.'

'The queen will do her best for you, you know that. But I don't know if she can get you out of this one.'

She'd already heard what happened from Henry, but she listened patiently as I stood in front of her, too ashamed to look up, and gave my account. I didn't say why I'd challenged Crofts to the duel, only that there had been a disagreement between us.

'I swear, your majesty, I didn't mean to kill him,' I finished, 'but I know I deserve to be punished.'

'Oh, Nathaniel, how could you be so stupid?' I looked up. Tears glistened in her eyes; were they from sadness or anger? 'To risk everything for a stupid quarrel. I swear, to the end of my life, I will never understand men.'

'What will happen now?'

'I don't know. It's not up to me – I have no status here but what they choose to lend me. And you know the problems duelling has caused in France.' She sighed. 'You've been a good friend to me, Nathaniel. Almost a brother. And I believe you when you say this was a horrible accident. I'll do what I can for you. But please, don't hold your hopes too high. There will be a price to pay.'

For the next three days and nights, I stayed in my room, ashamed to face anyone. Whenever I closed my eyes, I saw it all again: Crofts riding towards me, so stupidly sure he was invincible, then lying dead on the ground, his face white against the garnet-red blood soaking his cloak. The second night, I dreamed it had all turned out differently, that I'd woken to see Crofts lying on the ground, but then he'd leapt up, laughing: 'Fooled you, pie boy! Did you really think you could hit me, you little runt?' And then I woke, and the truth came seeping back in like cold water running through my veins.

Arabella came and knocked on the door, I don't know how many times, but I told her to go away. If I hadn't been so stupid as to fall in love with her, when she could never love me, Crofts wouldn't be lying dead in the palace chapel. How could I let myself look at her, knowing that?

On the evening of the third day, Henry brought me the queen's answer.

'She's persuaded them to let her deal with the matter, but they've made it plain she's to punish you as seriously as they would.'

I'd expected that; I couldn't blame them.

'So she says you're to go.'

'Go?'

'Leave France. She'll give you a letter of introduction to her sister's court in Savoy, but you're to make it look as though you escaped. Then she can say she knew nothing about it.'

'No. I'm not running away.'

I was sitting on my bed; he bent to one knee and looked me in the eye.

'Nat, Crofts' death was a terrible thing, but it was an accident. You've done good things in your life and this doesn't cancel them out. You have to do what she says.'

'I can't. I did it, I'll take the punishment.'

'All right, look at it this way. You know what state the queen's in. She's still not well, and she's worried to death about what's going on at home. Would you really give her the pain of making her punish you? Or will you help her by making the problem disappear?'

He stood, and I looked up at him.

'When do I have to go?'

'At dawn, tomorrow.'

I took my leave of the queen later that night. I'd been so caught up with my own troubles lately, I hadn't noticed how thin and pale she'd become; her eyes were ringed with shadows and her once-rosy cheeks were hollow. But she insisted on sitting up with me until the candles burned down.

'In these times,' she said, 'I've learned to say my goodbyes properly. You never know when it might be for the last time.'

We talked about old times: the days when she and the king could hardly bear to be in the same room; the happy years at Whitehall, before all the troubles started; and our time on the road together.

'You've changed so little these past few years,' she said, 'and look at me, old and worn.' I started to deny it but she shook her head. 'No, it's true. The times we've been through have taken their toll on me. When I look in the mirror, I wonder if the king will even recognise me when we see each other again.'

She gave me the letter for her sister.

'Stay there until I send for you. I don't know how long it will be – perhaps a year or more – but this will be forgotten in time. And perhaps by then we'll all be home again.'

Did she really still believe that? The king was losing the war, we all knew it. And if the other side won, it would never be safe for her to go home.

'Let's hope so,' I said.

When I woke the next morning I found a letter poked under my door, with my name scrawled across the front in Arabella's handwriting. I wanted to break the seal and hear her voice once more, even though it was only saying goodbye. But that would just make leaving harder. I tucked it inside my coat, and made up my mind that I wouldn't read it until I was far away.

Henry came with me to the edge of the city. We rode mostly in silence, but I was glad of his company. And there was nothing we needed to say; just as we'd always been able to share a joke without saying a word, that day we didn't talk about the sadness of parting either.

'You never did buy me a new pair of boots,' he said, as the city gate came into sight. 'To replace the ones you puked on.'

'It was barely a spatter. You were as fussy as a girl in those days.'

As we slowed to a halt, he said, 'It's a long ride down to Turin. Where will you break the journey?'

All through the long, sleepless night before, I'd been thinking about the queen's letter, but it was only as I opened my mouth to answer Henry that I finally made my decision.

'I'm not going to Turin. Everyone there will know what I did, and I'm too much of a coward to face it.'

'My friend, if there's one thing you're not, it's a coward.'

I shrugged.

'Well, I can't do it.'

'Then where will you go?'

'I don't know. Somewhere no one knows me, somewhere I can get a position in a house and keep my head down.'

I did know, by then, where I was going. But if I told him, he'd try to persuade me out of it.

'How long will you stay away?' he asked.

'I don't know.'

'Can I tell the queen? She'll worry when she finds out you haven't arrived in Savoy.'

'Tell her I'll write, as soon as I'm settled. You know she thinks the next time we see each other, it'll be when we're all on our way home?'

He raised an eyebrow, but didn't answer.

'I suppose you'll be married by then,' I said.

He nodded.

'I've decided we should just do it quietly,' he said. 'The queen won't mind, we've waited long enough.'

I thought of the letter, tucked inside my cloak, the last words I'd ever hear from Arabella before she became another man's wife.

'Well then,' said Henry. 'This is it, old friend.'

I nodded.

'We'll meet again,' he said. 'When all this is over.'

'I hope so,' I said. 'Goodbye, Henry.'

The way to Savoy was south; I watched Henry ride out of sight, then turned north and headed for the coast. I had let the queen down so badly, just when she needed friends around her, and now there was only one thing I could do. I would go home to England, and fight for the king. No one would care, now, that I gave the other side a reason to mock; the fight was all but over anyway. Nor would I make any difference to the result, but I fully intended to die trying. It wouldn't atone for Crofts' death, nor the anguish I'd caused the queen, but it was all I could offer.

I boarded the first boat bound for Dover and watched France disappear. The wind buffeted the sails; we'd make good time if it continued. I felt inside my coat, pulled out the letter from Arabella, and looked at it. I wanted so badly to hear her voice again, but after the terrible thing I'd done, I didn't deserve the comfort it would give me. I reached up, the letter between my fingers, and let the wind take it.

Chapter Forty-eight

We didn't make good time: after a couple of hours, the wind dropped, and the ship was becalmed for a day. But that gave me a chance to think about what to do when I arrived. I planned to aim for Oxford, but how I was to get there was another matter. I didn't know if anyone would still recognise me – it had been a long time since the days of the newsbooks and poems proclaiming me the smallest man in England – but if they did, I'd be as much of a prize to the other side as I ever was. And from the start, I'd pass through territory where people would be only too pleased to turn me in. The whole of the south-east had been solid for Parliament from the start – in that one letter I'd had from Jeremiah, he said there'd barely even been any fighting in Kent. Once the army had taken control of the ports and the big towns, people had either genuinely sided with their cause, or decided it was safest to pretend they did, if necessary by denouncing a neighbour just to be sure everyone was convinced.

So before the cliffs of Dover came into sight, I used my pocket knife to cut my hair short, trampled my hat until it looked battered and worn, and scuffed my boots with sand from a fire bucket. My travelling clothes were simple, and I hoped that with the rest of my adjustments, no one would notice the fine cloth they were made from. I'd still stand out, there was nothing I could do about that, but as long as no one realised who I was, I had a chance of getting to Oxford.

I stood on deck as we approached, remembering the day we left for France, when we all thought we'd be home again in a few months. So much had happened since then, on both sides of the water, and none of it good. I was so lost in my thoughts that it wasn't until we were close to land that I saw the soldiers. The harbour was full of them, walking up and down in twos and threes, now and then stopping people and seemingly asking them questions. If they were checking travellers coming off the ships, I was in trouble. They'd know mine had come from France, and I stood out a mile from the few other passengers, merchants to a man. I looked around: could I hide somewhere, wait until everyone else got off? But the other passengers were gathering on deck now, and I couldn't do that without attracting attention.

There was nothing for it but to brazen it out and hope for the best. I wracked my brain for a reason I could give for being in France, that wouldn't associate me with the king's side. All I could come up with was a cock and bull story about delivering a special package for an uncle who traded in gems, which I could back up with a few convincing phrases dredged up from my memories of the queen selling her jewels in Amsterdam. It wouldn't withstand more than a moment's scrutiny, but it was all I had.

As the sailors lowered the gangplank, three soldiers

approached. Would they come on board, or wait to check us as we stepped off the ship? If it was the latter, I might just have a chance to run. My heart pounding, I watched as they walked briskly towards the ship. And then carried on past it.

As I walked away from the ship, hardly able to believe my luck, one of the sailors shouted down, asking a woman walking by what was going on.

'Never seen so many soldiers down here,' he said. 'What are they after?'

'You haven't heard the news?'

'Wouldn't be asking if I had, darlin', would I?'

'It's the king,' said the woman. 'He's chucked it all in. And they say he's running to France.'

The soldiers weren't checking passengers arriving; they were checking who was leaving. I got the full story – or at least as much as anyone knew then – by listening to the talk at a tavern near the end of the harbour. Before I left France, the last message from the king had news of yet another defeat, this time at Stow-on-the-Wold, dangerously close to Oxford. He was in low spirits, he'd written, but still sure he could either win round Parliament or swing the Scots to his side with his wily negotiations. Now I learned that since then, his last strongholds in the West Country had fallen. With next to nothing more to defend, he'd left Oxford – in disguise, so the tavern-keeper said – and nobody knew where he was. Some speculated that he'd fled to France, others to Princess Mary in Holland, but what was clear was that he'd given up the fight.

I sat at a table, staring at my mug of watery ale.

Where do I go now?

I couldn't fight for the king if the king wasn't fighting anymore, and I couldn't go back to France. Suddenly weary, I closed my eyes for a second, and as so often happened, my mind conjured up Crofts' white, lifeless face, and hot guilt washed over me again. I had to pay for what I'd done. I'd have liked to do it in a way that would have brought me some honour, but that option wasn't open to me now, and perhaps I hadn't deserved it anyway. So there was only one way left. I would give myself up. Pick any soldier on the harbour, tell them who I was, and put myself in line for the traitor's death I'd been promised by Major Sarenbrant, all that time ago. Traitor, murderer, what difference did it make?

Leaving my ale untouched, I walked out. A hundred yards away, a pair of soldiers were talking to a ship's captain. One wore the uniform of an officer; that would shorten the process, at least. I waited outside the tavern for the conversation to finish. After a couple of minutes, the sea captain shook his head in answer to what must have been a final question and walked off. The soldiers stood with their back to me, and as I walked towards them, I heard the officer say,

'Reckon the bird's flown, don't you?'

The other man nodded.

'Run off to his papist whore of a wife,' he said. 'And good riddance to the pair of them.'

I turned and walked away. I couldn't hand myself over to the people who'd tried to kill her in her bed, that night in Bridlington, and who'd plotted to snatch her and put her in the Tower. So I would have to find somewhere else to go. I didn't know where Sam was, or even if he was still alive; there'd been no way to get a letter to him while he was moving about with the army. There was only one other person I could think of to go to. Someone I knew would give me shelter, until I could work out what to do with myself.

It was three days until the next stage wagon left Dover; not wanting to hang around where there were so many soldiers, I decided to walk. It was more than twenty miles, a long way for my short legs, but I was in no hurry, knowing that once I arrived I'd have to confess why I was there.

I remembered Kent as a lush, green county, with orchards full of apple and cherry trees, and well-fed cattle in the pastures. Now I saw fields lying fallow and fruit trees chopped down, I guessed for firewood. Though there'd been little fighting in Kent, its men would have been pressed to fight elsewhere, and not all of them would come back to plough and plant. And the soldiers who'd held Kent for Parliament would have taken what they needed with scant concern for who owned it, just as I'd seen ours do in Oxford. It was a shock to see: if this was a county that had escaped the worst of the turmoil, what must it be like in the places that had been fought over so bitterly?

At night I slept under hedges, wary of entering an inn. Luckily the weather was kind, and the long road left me so tired that I slept almost as soon as I lay down, yet still Crofts' face haunted my dreams, and I would wake up before the dawn, sweating despite the morning chill.

At last, footsore and weary, I stood in front of a cottage that was surrounded by neat rows of carrots and cabbages, with four red hens pecking around in the dirt. I knocked on the door and, when it opened, there was Jeremiah's dear, kind face, just exactly as I remembered it.

What I didn't know was that while I made my way up from the coast, fresh news had come from the north. The king hadn't fled to France, or Holland; he'd surrendered to the Scots. The old fool thought he could come to terms with them but, within days, it was obvious he was their prisoner. The war was over, with us on the wrong side. And, wrapped up in my own misery and guilt, I hadn't stopped to consider that by turning up on their doorstep, I was putting Jeremiah and his family in danger too.

The battles might be over, but that didn't mean the fight had been forgotten. In the eyes of the other side, I was a traitor, and if Jeremiah and Sukie were found sheltering me, they'd be guilty of treason too. They had a son now, Michael, a happy little lad just past his first birthday, with tufty fair hair that made him look like a baby bird. It was to him that Sukie's sharp brown eyes darted when Jeremiah insisted I could stay as long as I needed to.

'We can hide him,' he said, in answer to her look. He turned to me. 'You'll promise not to step outside in daylight?'

I shook my head.

'I can't let you do this. I'll go.'

'No you won't.' He looked down at his feet. 'I didn't take my part in the fight, Nat. I don't say I regret it, not when I see women and children whose men went off to war and didn't come home. But the queen was good to me, and I didn't stand by her. So the least I can do is stand by you now, and I want no arguing about it.'

Part Three

Chapter Forty-nine

There was an apple tree outside the cottage; when I knocked on the door that day, after my long walk from Dover, it had been covered in pink blossom. One morning, as I glanced out of the window, I saw there were little apples hanging from the branches. I had been in hiding for four months, stepping outside the house only once darkness fell, for a quick walk to exercise my legs and get some fresh air.

Being so near to London, news reached Kent quickly, and at least once a week, Jeremiah or Sukie would walk into Canterbury and bring back the latest newsbook. Week after week, we read that the king was still negotiating with the Scots, and with Parliament, about how the country should be run, and who'd decide what prayerbook we used on a Sunday, and whether he could still appoint bishops to tell us all what to do. It was hard to see where it was all going, because one newsbook contradicted another, but I knew what he'd be doing: trying to play one side off against the other, congratulating himself on his cleverness. Still, after all that had happened, thinking he could get things back to the way they were.

But Parliament and their army were in charge of the country now, not him. Not long after I arrived, Sukie came back from Canterbury white-faced, with a story she'd heard. The local barber and the innkeeper had made a joke about Cromwell in front of some soldiers in the marketplace, and the soldiers had dragged them out of the crowd and taken them away. People had mumbled and murmured, she'd been told, but no one raised a finger to stop it. After about an hour the soldiers rode into the square, with the two men on another horse, tied back to back with nooses hanging round their necks. They took them all the way to the gallows, with the innkeeper's wife and daughter running behind, weeping and begging the soldiers to let the men go. Only at the last minute had the soldiers announced the thing to be a joke, but it had plainly seemed serious enough to their prisoners, one having pissed his pants in fear at the sight of the gibbet. None of us said it but I knew all three of us were thinking the same thing when Sukie told that story. They'd done that as punishment for a couple of silly remarks; what would they do if they caught hold of us?

And so I was stuck, and they were stuck with me, and none of us knew how long that might continue. The house had two rooms, a parlour and a bedroom, and there was a space under the thatch that Jeremiah made into a place for me to sleep, with a ladder I could shin up and pull in behind me if anyone came to the door during the day. There were no neighbours nearby, but now and then someone called wanting eggs from Sukie's chickens. If she was outside tending the plants, she'd see them coming and warn me, and when she was indoors, we kept a wary eye on the little window, so no one could take us unawares.

Jeremiah headed off to the stables at dawn and didn't come home till dusk, so during the day, it was just Sukie and me and little Michael in the cottage. Sukie, I discovered, wasn't a great talker – she rationed her words as though there might be limited supply and she wasn't going to be the foolish person caught short. But it didn't need words to tell me that she didn't want me there: I heard it in her irritated sigh as I came down the ladder each morning, and saw it in the pinched look on her face as she put a third plate on the table each evening. I understood perfectly well why. They'd made a nice life for themselves, and thanks to her foresight, they'd said little about where they'd come from when they arrived; it wasn't generally known that they'd ever had anything to do with the king and queen, only that they'd once worked in a big house in London. The new master who'd bought the estate when it was confiscated was very definitely on the other side – the word was that he was personally acquainted with Cromwell – but he seemed to think as highly of Jeremiah's skills as the old one had, and as Sukie said, it made no practical difference to them whether Jeremiah's wages came from a friend of the king or a friend of Mr Cromwell; a penny bought the same amount of bread, either way. And now here I was, a cuckoo in their happy little nest, and a dangerous one at that.

I'd told them why I had to leave France, that first day when I arrived. I couldn't bring myself to recount the whole story; I missed Arabella so badly that I couldn't let myself mention her name. But Jeremiah knew well enough how Crofts could be, so I didn't need to reveal the content of the taunts.

'He always did know how to get under your skin,' he said. 'If I'd have been there, I hope I'd have turned you away from the whole foolish idea. But I know you well enough to be sure you're telling the truth: you never meant for things to go the way they did. So let's have no more talk of murder, and punishment. It was an accident, and that's that.'

All the same, I knew that if I hadn't killed Crofts, I'd have been safe in France, and they'd be safe too. Which gave Sukie all the more reason to resent my presence, and the danger I brought with me.

She was one of those people who's perpetually in motion, no sooner finishing one task than she began another, and though the cottage was a good size, I always seemed to be sitting where she wanted to clean, playing with little Michael where she needed to sit and sew, and generally getting under her feet and on her nerves. At first I tried to make myself useful by helping with the household work, but I was cack-handed at most things, and Sukie's pursed lips when I got her spinning in a knot or dropped the butter on the floor told me I wasn't improving the situation. And if I attempted to chat, she'd answer, politely but very briefly, and then go back to whatever she was doing. I tried to tell her, more than once, how grateful I was to them, but each time she cut me off, saying:

'It's Jeremiah's wish, and that's good enough for me.'

A kind of unspoken agreement grew up between us though, that when Jeremiah came home, he would never hear anything to suggest we hadn't spent the day in perfect amity, and at night when he and I talked, she would sit with her sewing and join in now and then as though we were all old friends.

Being starved of conversation during the day, and having no contact with the outside world except for the odd startled rabbit on my brief evening walk, I was avid to hear just about anything Jeremiah had to tell, even though it was about people I'd never clapped eyes on. There was a stable boy who had a mysterious rash (Jeremiah had great forebodings about that, but it disappeared as suddenly as it came), an undergroom who was enjoying a dalliance with the blacksmith's wife and, from time to time, stories about the new master of the estate, Sir Peter, a wealthy merchant who lived alone with his son.

'His wife died having the boy, you see, and then both his daughters, they've married into old Kent families – happy enough to have his money, but not so keen to keep up the family connection,' Jeremiah explained. 'Tom the coachman told me even their servants laugh about him – over at Barden Hall, they call him Sir Peter Moneybags. But he's a decent enough master, treats us all fairly, so it makes no difference to me where his money comes from.'

'How old is the son?' I asked.

'Fourteen or fifteen, I'd say. Not a bad lad, for all that his father's spoilt him. He's high-handed in his manner, but as I said to you many years ago, you can tell what a person's like by the way they are with horses. He's one of those people who just understands them, and they understand him. To tell you the truth, I think he sometimes wishes he could work down there in the stables with us.'

'And earn a groom's wage, instead of raking in money in his father's business?' said Sukie.

'Money's not everything, my love,' said Jeremiah. 'Look at me, here, with the three people I love best in all the world, under the same roof. I'll grant you the circumstances aren't what I'd have chosen, but I'm better off than that lonely man counting his money up at the big house. That I'm sure of.'

Sukie didn't answer, but judging by the vicious way she stabbed her needle into the stockings she was mending, I think it was fair to say she wasn't convinced.

The only thing I was allowed to do to help around the house was to amuse Michael. While Sukie was scrubbing the table so hard I thought it might wear away, or slicing a mountain of cabbage to pickle for the winter, I would take him by the hand and walk him round and round the parlour, his bandy steps getting steadier all the time, or sing him songs and pull faces that made him laugh and try to copy me. He was a lovely child, always babbling happily – I wondered where that came from, given Sukie's parsimony with words and Jeremiah's tendency to see a lead-grey lining in every cloud – and I enjoyed spending time with him. But when, during the morning and afternoon, Sukie laid him in his crib to sleep, or on the days when she took him with her to market, I had nothing to do but sit and think, and my thoughts weren't happy ones.

Whatever Jeremiah said, it was my stupidity and pride that had caused Crofts' death, and the nightmares I still had about that morning in the forest often hung over me during the day. I thought about the queen too. She must be half mad with worry over the news from England, and I'd added to those anxieties; she'd be expecting to hear from me by now, and I knew she'd be worried that something had happened to me. Or worse, perhaps she'd believe I'd abandoned her just when she needed her friends. But there was no way to get a message to her; it would be dangerous even to try.

And of course I thought too of Arabella, even though I had no right to. If Henry had been true to his plan, they'd be married now, perhaps even with a child on the way. I didn't like the pictures that thought painted, but I couldn't keep them out of my head; it was like when you have a cracked tooth and you're driven to touch it, over and over again, even though it cuts your tongue.

Chapter Fifty

As autumn turned into winter, our forced companionship became even more uncomfortable, both for me and for Sukie. During the summer, with vegetables to tend in the garden, she could get away from me for a while, and I from her. But with the November winds whistling round the cottage, we were shut in together all day long, and the hours until Jeremiah came home seemed endless.

One such day, towards the end of the afternoon, I was sitting beside Michael's crib, amusing him with silly rhymes; normally he was asleep at that time, but he had the beginnings of a cold and it had made him fractious. Sukie was stirring a pot over the fire, and the set of her shoulders told me I was irritating her, so I stopped talking. She lifted the cooking pot from the hook and put it on the table next to me, but just then Michael realised the game was over, and let out a wail.

'Now see what you've done,' said Sukie, and as she gestured to Michael, her hand caught the handle of the pot and tipped it towards the crib. She screamed and I threw myself down, pushing the crib out of the way just as the steaming broth poured out onto the floor where it had been. It splashed my arm and even through my thick shirt, it was scalding hot.

Sukie grabbed at the overturned pot, dropping it with a yelp as the metal burned her hands. Michael was bawling in earnest now and she tried to pick him up but cried out as her hands touched his skin; I saw then that they were red and already blisters were forming. Remembering what my mother used to do for burns, I grabbed the bucket we used for washing. She was pale and shaking as I held her hands in the water.

'It could have killed him,' she kept saying, over and over. 'He's so little, it could have killed him.'

'Michael's fine,' I said. 'It didn't touch him.'

She wouldn't be reassured though, and the only way I could make her keep her hands in the water was to undress him and show her that every inch of his skin was unblemished.

Just as I was dabbing comfrey juice on her poor hands, Jeremiah came home.

'What's happened?' he said, his wide eyes taking in the two of us, the stew all over the floor, and Michael's red and tear-stained face. 'You're hurt—'

'I'm fine,' said Sukie, with an uncharacteristic wobble in her voice. 'And Michael's fine. Thanks to Nat.' She turned to me. 'You saved his life.' At that she burst into hysterical sobs, which set Michael off again. Jeremiah's face told me he'd never seen Sukie in this state and he wasn't quite sure what to do, but he took her in his arms and patted her back as though she was a horse, while I picked up Michael and tried to soothe him.

'What happened?' asked Jeremiah again, as Sukie sobbed into his ribs.

I told him only part of the story; he didn't need to know she'd been snapping at me when she knocked the pot over.

It was only then that she turned to me and said, 'I didn't even ask. Are you hurt?'

I rolled up my sleeve; there was a red patch the size of an apple, and I could feel it burning still.

'Make him a cold poultice,' she said to Jeremiah. 'Plenty of comfrey.'

By the time she'd finished supervising his clumsy positioning of the poultice, Sukie had regained her normal demeanour and before long, having realised she couldn't hold the broom, she was issuing instructions on cleaning up the stew from the floor:

'Don't leave any scraps trapped between the flagstones. And look there, Jeremiah, you've missed a bit.'

But as I went to climb the ladder to bed that night, she stopped me and said,

'I never thought I'd say this. But thank goodness you were here.'

Sukie's hands were slow to heal and for a good three weeks she couldn't pick anything up without pain. In the normal run of things, someone on the estate would have volunteered a daughter to help out for a while, but of course we couldn't have anyone in the house so, very much against her will, she had to let me take over some of her everyday tasks. I was a willing pupil – it was good to have something to do – but not an especially talented one.

'How did the good Lord make men's hands so clumsy?' she would say, as I hacked the peel off a turnip, nearly losing a finger in the process. My first attempt at making small beer met with the comment that we'd be as well to drink water straight from a ditch, and when I glanced up from scouring the cooking pot with sand – which I thought I was making quite a good job of – she rolled her eyes and said:

'It's just as well you weren't down in the kitchens at Whitehall. You'd have been out on your ear the first week.'

One afternoon, while I was chopping up carrots for a stew, she asked me how I'd come to be at the palace; she hadn't been there back then and it seemed Jeremiah had never told her that part of my story. The question took me aback; as I've mentioned, Sukie wasn't one for chatting and I couldn't remember her ever asking me anything that wasn't a strictly necessary question related to our daily life. But I think the rest of her was so unaccustomed to sitting still that her tongue just started going instead.

'My father sold me,' I said. 'To the Duke of Buckingham. You won't remember him, but he was very well in with the king.'

'He sold you? What do you mean?'

'Just what I say. He took eleven shillings for me.'

'Were your family very poor then?'

'We were fairly poor, yes, but that wasn't why. He wouldn't have sold my brother or my sister. He wanted rid of me, that's all.'

It was so long ago, and so much had happened since, but still, saying those words made me feel like that boy again, left at the door of the big house with a pat on the head.

'How old were you?'

'Ten. My mother tried to talk him out of it, but she couldn't.'

'I'm sorry to speak ill of your father, but that was a wicked thing to do.'

I didn't answer. She looked down at Michael, playing by her feet.

'I couldn't let this one go off and live with strangers like that.'

'Well, you won't have any reason to.'

She was quiet for a minute, watching Michael trace shapes on the floor with his finger.

'I worried when I was carrying him. That he might, you know... be like Jeremiah. Jeremiah worried about it too.'

She looked up.

'Don't misunderstand me – in my eyes, Jeremiah is the handsomest man in the land. But I know he had a hard time of it, being a bit different from other people. I suppose it was that way for you as well.'

'Sometimes it was.'

We both fell silent for a bit then, but for the first time, it wasn't an uncomfortable silence. And when we sat down to our dinner and the stew proved to be as salty as seawater, she never said a word.

Chapter Fifty-one

By the time Sukie's hands were healed, I'd improved my household skills, and once she was back in charge of her kitchen, I was allowed to help with a few tasks – 'the ones even a child couldn't do wrong'. It made the days pass more quickly, and helped to turn my thoughts away from all I'd left behind.

In the first weeks after I arrived, we'd all been jumpy; the slightest noise outside would send me up the ladder to the loft, and when we sat down to eat, Sukie never took her eyes off the window. But by the beginning of winter, we'd all grown more used to our strange situation, and though we were still careful always to keep an eye on the window during the day, once darkness fell there seemed no need to worry; the cottage was out on the edge of the estate and nobody ever came near at night. So when, one evening as we ate our dinner, we heard the thunder of horses' hooves approaching, it took us so much by surprise that for a moment we just looked at each other. Then the horse stopped right outside, and Sukie hissed, 'Hide! Now!'

I scrambled up the ladder and dragged it in behind me,

as there came a thumping on the door and a voice shouted, 'Jeremiah!'

'It's Sir Peter,' whispered Jeremiah. 'What shall I do?'

'Open up, man!' shouted the voice outside.

I looked around me in panic, even though I knew the tiny space contained only me, a straw mattress and some bedding. *Nowhere to hide.*

Fists bashed on the door again. Jeremiah's long legs crossed the floor in two paces, and the door opened.

'You're needed at the stables,' the voice said. 'It's that bloody Arab stallion. It's gone mad, and my son's trapped.'

I waited until the sound of hooves disappeared before I climbed down the ladder. Sukie was standing with Michael in her arms, looking at the table. I followed her glance, and saw what, in our panic, none of us had thought to hide: three half-finished plates of food. My stomach turned over: if Sir Peter hadn't been in such fear for his son, it would have been obvious that there was someone else in the house.

'He was standing right there,' said Sukie. 'If he'd seen…'

She was shaking. I made her sit down and cleared away the plates; neither of us had the stomach to finish our dinners. I started to say I was sorry for putting them in danger, but she glanced at Michael, and shook her head.

'He understands more than you think these days.'

When Jeremiah came back, we found out what had happened. Sir Peter had bought a new horse for hunting; it was big, and powerful, and he'd banned his son from riding it.

'But the boy's not used to the word no,' Jeremiah told us. 'When we'd bedded the horses down for the night and left, he sneaked into the stables, thinking to take it out and prove he could master it.'

'What happened?' asked Sukie. 'He said the boy was trapped?'

'He let it get between him and the door of its stall. It reared up, and he got a bad kicking. And then the poor lad was there for over an hour before anyone realised he was missing.'

'Is he all right now?' I asked.

'He couldn't move his legs, they had to carry him into the house. The master said he thought it was a break, but I've seen broken legs and they don't look like that. The boy had no pain. He just couldn't move.' He shook his head. 'It doesn't look good.'

Sukie stood up and checked that Michael was asleep in his crib, then poked the embers of the fire.

'Gave us all a bit of a fright,' she said, with her back to us both. 'Him coming here like that.'

'I'm sorry,' I said. 'I should never have put you in danger by coming here. I think, tomorrow, I should go.'

'Go where?' said Jeremiah. 'Nat, it's not safe for you out there, you know that. We couldn't live with ourselves if they took you, could we, Suk?'

Sukie gave a little shrug, which Jeremiah seemed to interpret as agreement.

'We'll have to be more careful, that's clear,' he said. 'But you're staying here.'

I didn't argue with Jeremiah, but I didn't change my mind either. I was scared at the thought of leaving, and I had no idea where I might go. But I'd brought this danger on myself.

They'd done nothing and they didn't deserve to be living in fear because of me. So two weeks later, when the moon was full and I'd have the best chance of finding my way, I waited until I heard Jeremiah's rasping snores, and crept down the ladder. Carrying my boots, I padded across the floor and put the note I'd written for them on the table.

My hand was on the latch when their bedroom door opened. I knew it was Sukie: Jeremiah was still snoring.

'Where do you think you're going?' she said quietly.

'It's better if I leave,' I said. 'You know that.'

'We've managed this far. We were careless, the other night. We won't be again. But Jeremiah's right. We couldn't live with ourselves if anything happened to you.'

'But—'

'I mean it. We want you to stay. Both of us.'

'Are you certain?'

She nodded.

'And besides,' she said, 'you've just about got the hang of peeling a turnip. So get back up that ladder and let's hear no more about leaving.'

I won't tell you Sukie never snapped at me again – she was a snappy kind of woman – but we rubbed along better after that. Which was lucky, because there seemed to be no end in sight to my stay with them: the newsbooks barely mentioned the king now, all we read were proclamations from Parliament and the county committee, forbidding us to celebrate saints' days, imposing fines if we didn't fast once a month and threatening prison for anyone still using the old prayerbook.

A week before Christmas, Jeremiah went into town.

'You wouldn't believe it,' he said when he came back. 'Not a sprig of holly anywhere. I was going to buy myself a nice mincemeat pie, but the baker said they've been forbidden to make them, can you credit that? And they've to open on Christmas Day, all the shops, just as though it was any other day.'

There were rumours, he said, that the mayor was sending out soldiers to knock on doors and check that people weren't feasting on the day. After our scare with Sir Peter, we all thought it prudent to take no chances, so on that Christmas Day in 1646, we sat down to a very ordinary dinner of mutton pie, our only act of rebellion a toast in small beer, mouthed so Michael wouldn't hear and repeat it, to happier days and the hope of a better year to come.

Chapter Fifty-two

What we didn't know then was that the king's fortunes were about to take a turn for the worse. By the middle of January, the newsbooks were reporting that the Scots had handed him over to Parliament. Reading between the lines, it sounded like they'd got fed up with him trying his old trick of saying yes, and then no, and then maybe, as if he could bamboozle them into thinking they'd got their way when actually he'd got his. Now it was Parliament's turn to see if they could get any sense out of him.

On the estate though, the talk was of something else entirely. Two months after being kicked by the horse, Sir Peter's son still couldn't walk, despite the ministrations of the best doctors in the county. And once it was clear the local ones were getting nowhere, doctors were even being summoned down from London, Jeremiah told us.

'One bled him, twice a day for a week, another one said to bind his leg to wooden splints. But it's made no difference at all. The master's beside himself. Him having only daughters otherwise, Robert is the apple of his eye.'

Jeremiah was afraid that, having advised the master to buy

the horse, he'd be blamed for the accident. And for once, his forebodings proved accurate. When a third doctor from London pronounced that the boy would probably never walk again, Sir Peter marched down to the stables.

'Yelled out for me, in front of everyone,' said Jeremiah, rubbing his brow with his big old hand. 'Said I was a fool. Said I should have known the horse was dangerous. And plenty more besides, including words not fit to repeat in front of a woman.'

'But it wasn't your fault, was it?' I said. 'The boy shouldn't have sneaked in there.'

'No, he shouldn't. But he's just a boy, and boys are headstrong. I should have made sure Sir Peter understood he couldn't be let near that horse. If he's minded to get rid of me, I wouldn't blame him at all, though what we'd do then, I don't know.'

Sukie's hand flew to her mouth.

'He didn't say that, did he?'

'Not in so many words, no. But I think to myself, what would I do if I thought someone was to blame for hurting little Michael? I wouldn't want them in my sight, and maybe he won't either.'

Despite our efforts to reassure him, Jeremiah remained in a constant state of anxiety about losing his place on the estate, terrified of making the smallest mistake in case it proved the last straw. So when, one day that spring, we saw him coming home, head down and steps heavy, in the middle of the afternoon, both of us feared the worst. Sukie flew to the door.

'What's happened?' she asked.

He shook his head and said, 'Let me get inside, and I'll tell you.'

We both stood and watched as he pulled off his boots and then buried his head in his hands.

'What is it?' said Sukie, kneeling by his side. 'Jeremiah, tell us.'

He looked up, and his big face was sadder than I'd ever seen it.

'I've to shoot the horse,' he said. 'The Arab stallion. Sir Peter says he's got to go, and I'm the one has to do it.'

For a moment, I thought Sukie was going to hit him.

'Jeremiah Hobley,' she said, 'do you realise what you had us thinking?'

He looked at her blankly.

'We thought you'd lost your place.'

'Oh,' he said. 'Well, that's it, you see. I told him, that horse doesn't deserve to be shot. It's done nothing wrong. Sell him, I said, anyone'd be pleased to take him from you. But don't punish the horse for what wasn't the horse's fault.'

'You said that?' said Sukie. 'To Sir Peter?'

'It just came out of me, Sukie. That beautiful horse, it just wasn't fair. I knew, soon as I said it, that I shouldn't have, but it was too late. That's when he said it had to be me. You do it, he said. Shoot the horse, or go.'

We tried to say that the horse was going to be killed anyway, and its best chance was in the hands of someone who'd take care to be sure it didn't suffer. But he was inconsolable. That evening, having taken a good few mugs of beer, he said:

'It's all my fault. I should never have deserted the king and queen.'

'What?' said Sukie. 'What are you talking about?'

'We should have gone with them, like Nat did. She was good to me, the queen. Wasn't she, Nat?'

'Well, yes, she was good to both of us.'

'And if we'd gone along, gone with Nat, none of this would have happened. I'd have been there to stop him killing the Crofts boy, and we wouldn't have come here, and I wouldn't have got us into this terrible mess, when we might be thrown onto the streets, with no job and nowhere to live, and nowhere to hide Nat. The young master would still be striding round in his boots and that horse…' A fat tear slid down his cheek. 'That beautiful horse would be somewhere else, with people who'd take care of him.'

Sukie patted his huge hand with her little one and said, 'It's not your fault. And tomorrow, you'll do your best for that poor horse and give it a quick end. There's nothing else you can do.'

'I don't deserve you,' he said mournfully.

'Probably not,' she said. 'But here we are, so take yourself off to bed, or you'll have a sore head in the morning.'

After Jeremiah had dried his eyes and lumbered off to bed, we sat up a little while.

'You notice the animal's predicament got the tears?' she said. 'Not ours. That man and his horses.'

'He does have a special way with them,' I said. 'It's like he speaks their language.'

'Oh, I know. First time I saw him with a horse, that's when I knew he was the one for me. He was so gentle with them, big as he is, and I thought, only a kind man could be that way with an animal.'

A rasping snore erupted from the bedroom, followed by a series of snorts and mumbles. She smiled.

'I didn't know about the snoring then.'

'You seem very happy together,' I said. 'It's nice to see.'

I hadn't meant to sound wistful, but it came out that way and of course, as women will, she noticed.

'What about you?' she said. 'Did you leave a sweetheart behind in France?'

'Why would you think I have a sweetheart?' I asked.

'You get a moony look on your face sometimes.'

I looked down at the table.

'Women aren't interested in me.'

'Because you're small?'

'Yes.'

'Well, I don't want to swell your head, Nat, but I've come to know you pretty well these last months. You're a good man, and they're not easy to find.'

'But women want a man who's tall and strong. You must know that.'

'Have you met every woman in the world?'

'No, of course not, but—'

'Then how do you know there's not one for you?'

'It's obvious.'

'Jeremiah used to think no one would love him,' she said. 'But someone does.'

'Yes, but it's different. You wouldn't want him if he was like me.'

'Well, that we'll never know. But I'll tell you this. I'd love that man if he had three heads, and he'd love me if I had four. Love loves where it loves, Nat. And I don't believe there's no one to love you.'

Once I'd got over my surprise at Sukie allowing herself to issue so many words in one conversation, I thought about what she'd said. She wasn't one to offer false flattery – she was a bit like Arabella in that respect. If she really thought a woman could love me – and she was one, after all – was there a chance it could be true? And if it was, had there ever been a chance that person could have been Arabella? If I hadn't pushed Henry towards her, was it possible she might she have tired of him, and thought of me? And then I would see how ridiculous that was, and tell myself to stop being so stupid.

Chapter Fifty-three

Jeremiah went off the next day, and did what he had to do. When he came home, he didn't want to talk about it, and after that he was quiet in the evenings, and in the mornings, instead of striding off to the stables whistling, he walked with his head down and his shoulders hunched, as though he was headed for the last place he'd ever want to go. What had happened to the boy played on his mind constantly. Why hadn't he made it clearer to Sir Peter that the horse was too strong for a boy to ride, he'd ask himself. Why had he even advised him to buy the horse at all?

Both of us told him, over and over again, that it hadn't been his fault, but it made no difference.

'The boy's taken to his bed now, I heard it from one of the maids,' he told us one evening. 'Won't speak to anyone, won't take his lessons. And Sir Peter, he looks like all the sadness in the world just came and settled on his table.'

I'd had an idea going round in my mind, over the past few days, and that seemed as good a time as any to come out with it.

'There is something you could do to help the boy,' I said. 'You could teach him to ride again.'

'What?'

'He can't use his legs, can he? Well, remember when you taught me? I couldn't use my legs when I was riding either, not the way other people do. So if you taught me, couldn't you teach him?'

His face lit up.

'Do you really think that could work?'

'Of course it could. And you said – he loves horses. You'd be giving him a bit of his life back.'

'That's true enough. There was barely a day went by when that boy wasn't out on a horse.'

'Well, there you are then. If anything's going to get him out of his bed, it's that.'

For a second, he looked thoughtful. Then he shook his head.

'It's a nice idea, but no.'

'Why not?'

'Because I can't be sure I could do it. And if I get their hopes up, and fail, what then? I'm on thin ice already, Nat, I can't take that chance. Better to keep my head down, and hope this all passes over, one way or another.'

All in all, we had a gloomy few months, with Jeremiah miserable, and no end in sight to my time in hiding. But one day that summer he came home from a trip into Canterbury brandishing a newsbook, a great big smile spreading across his face.

'Look,' he said, showing me the page. 'Look what it says here.'

The army had snatched the king away from Parliament and offered him some proposals of their own. He'd have to accept that he wasn't in charge anymore, but they'd let him keep his bishops, and the old prayerbook for those who wanted it. If he said yes, they'd guarantee his safety, and the queen's, and their children's – and there'd be a pardon for everyone who'd helped the Royalist side during the fighting.

'You'll be safe,' said Jeremiah. 'We'll all be safe. And the queen can come home again – you'll be back at Whitehall before you know it.'

We celebrated that night, with a flagon of cider that made even Sukie giggly. And as I fell asleep, I thought about how it would feel to step outside and feel the sun on my face again.

Chapter Fifty-four

I should have known. The king had barely shown an ounce of good sense in his life; why would he start now? He turned down the army's proposals out of hand, saying they needed him more than he needed them, which was a bit like a fish telling a fisherman it'd be choosing what time dinner was. And so nothing changed; I was still stuck and Jeremiah and Sukie were still stuck with me.

We were approaching our second Christmas together when Sukie came back from market saying there'd been a strange feeling in the city.

'People were grumbling about having no Christmas – saying it out loud,' she said. 'The mayor's said the market has to open as well as the shops, since Christmas Day's a Saturday. The knife sharpener told me he won't do it, and he says he's not the only one.'

'You don't want to be getting into conversations like that,' said Jeremiah. 'You don't know who might be listening.'

'I keep myself to myself, as you well know,' she said. 'I didn't venture an opinion. But plenty of people were doing. I

317

heard one woman say it was about time we got the old ways back.'

'And nobody spoke against her?' asked Jeremiah.

'Nobody. There were no soldiers near, mind you, I doubt they'd all have been so free with their tongues if there had been. But all the same, it felt to me like there was something afoot.'

Sukie was right: something was afoot. We didn't hear until afterwards, but that Christmas Day, the people of Canterbury decided enough was enough. Those stallholders who'd opened up were made to close, and men with sticks stood outside the church, so the minister could give his flock a proper Christmas Day sermon.

'This'll end badly,' said Jeremiah. 'The mayor won't put up with it. Why can't people just keep their heads down and wait for things to sort themselves out?'

'They're not sorting themselves out though, are they?' I said. 'All this time, and nothing's changed. They can't make the king agree to anything, because they can't agree among themselves. So no one's got what they fought for – not us, and not them either.'

'That's true enough,' he said. 'But what can we do about it, the likes of us? Pray that wiser heads than ours work out a way to bring this country back to peace – that's all sensible folk can do.'

But the sensible folk of Canterbury had other ideas. They got up a petition, saying they wanted the king back, and the old ways of religion. We could hardly believe our eyes when we got our hands on a newsbook and read the words they'd written.

'Cockatrices and vipers,' said Jeremiah. 'That's what they're calling the Members of Parliament.'

'They won't stand for that, will they?' said Sukie. 'So what's going to happen now?'

To our astonishment, what happened was that the fighting started up again. Once news of the Canterbury petition got out, other places took heart from it. Half of Wales rose up against the army, calling for the king to take his rightful place again, and news came of riots in London and Norwich, and sundry other places I don't recall.

'They've gone too far, that's what it is,' said Jeremiah, as we pored over the latest news. 'People thought they wanted change, but now they've got it, they see the old ways weren't so bad after all.'

For a couple of months, we didn't know whether to live in hope that the tide was turning our way, or fear that the fighting might drag on for years, like the first time round. But it turned out to be neither. At just about the same time we started hearing news that the uprising in Wales had been crushed, the army marched into Kent. The scratched-up bands of rebels didn't stand a chance against Cromwell's soldiers; hundreds died in the space of a night.

From everywhere, the news was the same: Cromwell's army couldn't be beaten. Last time round, captured soldiers had been given parole, and released once they swore not to bear arms against Parliament again; that was what I hoped had happened to Sam. But anyone who'd fought this time had broken that oath, and now they were being made to pay. We heard stories of rebels beaten to death, of tongues cut out and feet hacked off; those who survived to be captured were being sent to the Barbados in their thousands and sold as slaves.

By the end of August all the fighting was over. A month later, Jeremiah was arrested.

Chapter Fifty-five

He'd left that morning for Canterbury, to see a horse Sir Peter was interested in. He wasn't in the best of humours, because Sir Peter had said one of the grooms was to go with him and give his view on the mare. The son, Robert, still couldn't walk, and the master was still taking his anger out on Jeremiah.

'He knows full well Dan Butcher doesn't know horses like Jeremiah does,' Sukie said, as we watched Jeremiah trudge off, head bowed, from the window. 'This is just to make him look a fool.'

As it turned out, it was lucky the other man did go, otherwise I don't know how long it'd have been before we found out what happened. That afternoon, Sukie was sitting by the window, mending a blanket, while I played on the floor with Michael, when she suddenly said, 'Up the ladder – now. Someone's coming.'

Michael wailed as I jumped up, and Sukie had to grab him as his little arms clung onto the ladder. I pulled it up behind me, but he was still crying when the knock came on the door.

'Dan,' she said. 'Where's Jeremiah?'

'Can I come in?' he said. 'I've bad news, I'm afraid.'

She couldn't say no, it would have looked odd.

'I won't beat about the bush,' he said. 'He's been arrested.'

I strained my ears to hear over Michael's cries.

'The city was full of soldiers,' he went on. 'Walking about, listening to what people were saying. I saw them stop a few people, and ask them questions.'

'What's this got to do with Jeremiah?'

'We were walking back through the market, he stopped to buy a pie. The stallholder was talking about that petition thing, saying it was about time Parliament listened to the people. A few others started joining in—'

'But Jeremiah wouldn't—'

'No, he didn't join in, he was just eating his pie. But they were right beside us, and they weren't keeping their voices down either. I said to him, let's walk on, but he said he didn't like to walk and eat at the same time.'

Sukie groaned and, up above, silently, so did I.

'Four soldiers came out from behind another stall – they must have been listening, but they couldn't know who'd said what. So I said to him, run, but when I looked back, they'd got hold of him. And they took him off, with the stallholder and the other ones.'

I slid down the ladder as soon as the latch rattled shut.

'A pie,' she said. 'He gets himself arrested because he's got to stop and eat his pie.' She unhooked her cloak from behind the door. 'I'll leave Michael with you,' she said. 'I can be quicker on my own.'

'Where are you going?'

'To the gaol. You heard Dan, there'll be a fine to pay. If I go now, he needn't spend the night there.'

I had heard him say that. And it had sounded to me like he was telling her what she wanted to hear, so he could get out and have nothing more to do with it.

'It's just a mistake,' she said, as she threw on her cloak. 'But I don't suppose there'll be any point me telling them that. So that'll be the money for his new boots gone.'

I wasn't sure if she really believed what she was saying, or she was trying to convince herself. She wasn't silly, Sukie, and we both knew the Canterbury authorities would come down hard on any new signs of support for the king. But anyway, she went off, and as I played with Michael, I prayed she was right, and that when I saw her next, he'd be with her, getting a telling off about the pie.

It was nearly dark when she came home, and he wasn't with her.

'He's to be put on trial,' she said. 'They're saying he said Parliament are going against God's laws.'

I tried to stop the shock showing on my face, but she saw it.

'This is serious, isn't it?' she said. 'It's worse than we thought.'

Those words were treasonous. Jeremiah wouldn't have said them, but according to Dan's account, the soldiers couldn't have seen who did. So wouldn't it be easiest to pin them on the man who stood out because he looked different? 'The big fellow,' one would have said. 'He said it.'

'If they find him guilty, they could send him to the Barbados, couldn't they?' she said. 'It was in the newsbook, that's what they're doing now.'

I'd been thinking exactly the same thing.

'It won't come to that,' I said. 'Like you said, it's all a mistake. There won't even be a trial, we'll get him out before then.'

I couldn't think how though. And if we couldn't, if Jeremiah was tried, it would be his word against theirs: the strange-looking man who people had called a monster, against four of the men who represented the law of England now.

We sat up late that night. Sukie said she wouldn't be able to sleep, and so we talked until the rushlights I'd lit burned down, and then lit some more. To try and distract her from the worry, I got to talking about the old days at the palace, and she told me then about how people had reacted when she said she was going to marry Jeremiah.

'Oh, there were jokes, of course. And one or two people said nasty things. But it surprised me to find that I didn't care. I just used to think to myself, if they could find a husband or a wife as good and kind as the one I've got, they'd be very lucky.'

In turn, I told her about how kind Jeremiah had been to me when I first arrived at court, and felt so lost and alone. And how he'd changed my life by teaching me to ride.

'He often talked about that day you rode in that race,' she said. 'He told me once he couldn't have been prouder of you if you'd been his own son.'

'He's been more of a father to me than my own father was,' I said. 'I don't think I've ever told him that. I will, when we get him home.'

We both stared at the embers of the fire for a bit, and then she said, 'He will come home, won't he?'

'Of course he will,' I said. 'They'll see he's innocent.'

But I didn't believe that, and the fear in her eyes told me she didn't either.

Sukie went back to the gaol three times over the following week. She couldn't get them to let her see Jeremiah, but on the third visit, she found out when the trial was to be held: it was eight weeks away.

She looked at Michael, playing happily on the floor.

'If they send him away, we'll never see him again, will we? People don't come back from there.'

'We're not going to let that happen,' I said. 'I've been thinking – couldn't Sir Peter do anything? He's in with the mayor, isn't he? And he must know the justices.'

'I should think he could. They'd fall over themselves for a friend of Cromwell. But do you really think he'd help Jeremiah, after what happened with his boy?'

I didn't know. But if Sir Peter had enough influence to get Jeremiah out, that was a start. What we had to do was find a reason for him to use it. That night, a thought kept turning itself over and over in my head. There was something I could do, something I could offer. It was dangerous, for all of us. But if I could use it to drive the right bargain, there might just be a chance to get Jeremiah out before he had to stand up and call four of Cromwell's soldiers liars.

Chapter Fifty-six

I gave myself another day to think it through before I told Sukie; I didn't want to get her hopes up if it couldn't work. Her eyes brightened when I said I had an idea, but the light faded when I continued, 'Do you remember I said to Jeremiah that he should teach Robert to ride again? Teach him the way he taught me?'

'Yes...'

'Well, I think I could do it. I think it's what we can use to bargain for Jeremiah's freedom.'

'Are you mad? We're trying to get Jeremiah out of gaol – if Sir Peter finds out you're here, the pair of us will be put in there with him.'

'You'd have to take Michael and go to your mother's. They won't pursue a woman and a child all the way to Essex. They've got enough to do at the moment, keeping the peace.'

She narrowed her eyes at me.

'And what about you?'

'I'm the other bit of the bargain. If I do what I promise, he gets Jeremiah out. And if I fail, he gets to hand me in. I'm still a prize – he'll recognise that.'

'You've lost your senses. What's to stop him handing you in straight away?'

'That's the chance I'll have to take. But if Jeremiah's right about how much he loves that boy, I think he'll want to see if I can help him.'

'And after? Even if you manage it, you don't know he'll keep his word.'

'Jeremiah said he was a fair man. And besides, by then he'll have been hiding me himself, won't he? He'd have to explain that.'

'I don't know. It's so ...'

'I know. It's not a great plan. But we don't have anything else.'

We talked it over, long into the night. She didn't want to leave, but I knew Jeremiah wouldn't want me to do anything that put her and Michael in danger.

'But he wouldn't want you to put yourself in danger either,' she said. 'If Sir Peter hands you in, now, with all that's going on, they'll make an example of you, you know that.'

'And if we don't get Jeremiah out, they'll make an example of him.'

We went round and round in circles but in the end she agreed.

It was strange, saying goodbye to Sukie; our prickly relationship in the early days seemed like something I'd imagined, and I realised I'd miss her as well as Michael. I'd have to stay in hiding even when I'd revealed my presence to Sir Peter – I couldn't risk someone else turning me in – so she'd been to town to buy as much flour and oats and beans as she could, and before she left, she gave me instructions about what to pick and when from the vegetable patch, and where I was likely to find the new-laid eggs each night.

'Leave a candle in the window, so you can see what you're doing,' she said. 'And keep those chickens alive, they're good layers.'

I watched her and Michael from the window until they disappeared. We'd agreed I'd wait till the next morning, to make sure they were well on their way, before I presented myself and my plan at the big house. To distract myself, I made some bread, the way she'd showed me, and cooked it on the griddle. It was as hard as a rock, and I'd forgotten the salt so it tasted of nothing. It didn't seem a good sign.

As it happened, the first part was easier than I expected. I didn't know how I was going to get to Sir Peter; if the servant who opened the door turned me away, I wasn't sure what I'd do. But as I approached, my heart pounding, there was a coach outside, with four perfectly matched chestnut horses in front. They were tossing their heads, the way coach horses do when they've been kept waiting; someone was about to leave. The coachman was sitting up on top, with his back to me, and I was almost at the door before he turned and saw me. He yelled out, but at that moment, the door opened.

I knew Sir Peter as soon as I saw him; Sukie had described him: short and stocky with red-brown hair. Quickly, I stepped forward, swept off my hat and bowed.

'My name is Nat Davy,' I said. 'Perhaps you've heard of me?'

* * *

'You've got something to offer *me*?'

He stared down at me, his face puzzled. He had recognised my name, and he knew very well there'd be prestige in handing me over. But I'd managed to persuade him to let me in and hear what I had to say.

'That's right,' I said. 'You're a man of business, you know how it works – I do something for you, you do something for me.'

It felt strange, playing the cocky court dwarf again, but I remembered the merchants the queen had sold her jewels to in Amsterdam. They didn't go in for deference and fawning, and the more the queen showed how desperate she was, the harder the bargains they drove. He'd very likely be the same, so with only one chance to convince him I had something he wanted, I'd have to do it the way men like him did it, with bluff and boldness.

'I heard what happened to your son,' I said. 'And I think I can help him.'

He stared at me incredulously, then laughed.

'What have you got? A magic potion to make his legs work again? I've had the finest doctors here, and—'

'I can't help him walk,' I said. 'But I could help him ride a horse again.'

'Ride a *horse*? Is this some kind of a joke?'

'He loved horses, didn't he? It would give him a reason to come out of his room and start living again.'

I've got him interested. I saw it in his face, just a flicker but it was there. *Now convince him.*

As concisely as I could, I explained how I'd been taught to ride, even though I was too small to use my legs the way other people did. And how I thought I could use the same method with Robert.

'I'm certain I can do it,' I said. 'And surely it's worth your while to let me try?'

He looked at me for a long time. Just when I thought he was going to say no, he folded his arms and said, 'You said there was something you wanted in return. Money?'

I shook my head.

'I understand you're a man of influence in the county,' I said.

He cast a glance around the room, as if the paintings and the porcelain and the silk carpet made the answer obvious.

'I hold a certain position in society,' he said.

'The man who taught me to ride is Jeremiah Hobley.'

'My head groom?'

'The same. You won't have heard yet, but he's in gaol, in Canterbury. I want you to get him released.'

He listened as I explained what had happened, and that Jeremiah would never have said the words he'd been accused of. He asked if the Hobleys had been sheltering me, and I said yes: he'd guessed anyway, and if I wanted him to trust me, it seemed better to be honest.

'Can you do it? I asked. 'Can you get him out?'

He shrugged.

'Of course. If I swear to his good character, that'll settle the matter. But it would have to be before he's tried. Once a jury's given their verdict, there'll be nothing even I can do.'

I'd have less than eight weeks. If he even agreed.

'But why would I want to help the man who advised me to buy that murderous horse?' he said. 'He's lucky I didn't turf him out on his ear before now. And then there's the matter of you. A traitor. Who my conscience tells me I should hand over to the authorities, today, to be dealt with as they decide.'

'You could do that,' I said. 'And you could leave Jeremiah to rot. But if you do, you'll never know if I could have helped your son, will you? So here's the arrangement I'm proposing.'

I was sweating as I walked back to the cottage, even though the morning was cool. I'd played my role well, but inside, I'd been terrified. By the time I'd delivered my proposal, it was all I could do to keep up the bravado and stop my knees from shaking. But he'd agreed: if I succeeded in teaching his son to ride again, before Jeremiah's trial, he would get him out, and give me twenty-four hours to leave Kent. If not, he'd turn me over to the authorities in Canterbury. I had no way to be sure he'd keep his word to let me go even if I succeeded, but I couldn't worry about that now; I had to get the job done.

Chapter Fifty-seven

We agreed it would be best if as few people as possible knew about me. One of the coachmen had already seen me: he and a second one were warned to stay quiet if they wanted to keep their jobs, and were instructed to bring Robert to a fallow field not far from Jeremiah's cottage each morning, assist as needed, and take him back again after his lesson. And Robert, who was too young to know who I really was, would be told I'd been recommended by one of the doctors, and was being paid for my services.

So, the following morning, I waited, just as I had before that first lesson with Jeremiah, only this time what I felt was not excitement, but cold, hard fear. It had taken months and months for Jeremiah to teach me to ride. Robert wouldn't be starting from scratch, like I had, but even so, I had no idea if I could do it in the time. Or even if I could do it at all. Perhaps my way wouldn't work for someone who couldn't move their legs, or perhaps I'd just been lucky to have Jeremiah as a teacher, and I wouldn't be able to repeat what he did.

They arrived in a small trap, the boy sitting slouched in the seat. The second coachman was riding a fine-boned grey, and leading a chestnut mare; I'd asked for the two gentlest horses in the stables. Robert had his father's red-brown hair, but where Sir Peter was stocky, the boy seemed skinny for his age, and his face had a pale, unhealthy look. As the trap approached, he sat up and stared, looking me up and down as though he couldn't quite believe his eyes.

Well, I'd seen worse looks than that and survived. I stepped up to the trap.

'Good morning,' I said. 'My name is Nat, and—'

'This is ridiculous,' he said to the coachman. 'Take me back to the house.'

The two coachmen looked at each other.

'Sir, it's what your father wants,' said the one driving the trap. 'We had instructions—'

'And now I'm giving you new ones,' the boy said. 'Take me back.'

Don't lose this chance.

'Sir, would you at least let me show you how I ride?'

'What do I care how you ride? Look, I don't know why my father agreed to this, but there is nothing I can learn from a creature like you.'

'Don't you want to be able to ride again?'

'I can ride! I will be able to, when I can walk again. This is a waste of my time. Tom,' he clicked his fingers at the coachman, 'drive on.'

I took a deep breath.

'Your father thought you'd find it quite easy to learn,' I said. 'But if you don't think you could manage it…'

His face reddened.

'Manage it? I've ridden horses you wouldn't dare get within

a mile of, you stupid little squirt.' He rolled his eyes. 'Right. Go on then. Show me. And then I'm leaving.'

I mounted the smaller horse. In the years since I'd learned to ride Shadow, I'd mastered the art of showing a new horse what I needed from it, but you never knew with horses. If she decided to ignore me now, my chance would be lost. But when I signalled for her to move off, she did. I walked her for a minute to get her used to me, then urged her on. She hesitated, just for a second – *come on, don't let me down now* – but then she took off and we raced round the field at full tilt. It felt so good to be as one with a horse again that for a moment or two I lost myself in the ride. I glanced back; Robert was sitting forward, watching, but the look on his face was still hostile. I had to do something more if he was going to believe I had anything to offer.

The far end of the field was bounded by a hedge, a high one. *Can I do it?* Jumping with an unfamiliar horse was risky, but she was keen, this one, I could feel it. I steered her round and back down to where the trap was waiting, as though I was going to pull up beside them, but then I kept going, turned her to face the far end and let her have her head. She soared over the fence, as though we'd been together for years.

He couldn't hide his surprise as we rode up to the trap.

'People said I'd never be able to ride,' I said, reining the horse in beside him. 'I couldn't use my legs, just like you can't. But I learned, and I can teach you to ride again in just the same way.'

He shrugged.

'I doubt you can teach me anything. But since my father wants it ...'

'Right,' I said, trying not to let my relief show in my voice. 'Do you want to take the chestnut, or—'

'No,' he snapped. 'Just explain what you do.'

'But you'll pick it up more easily if you—'

'My father is paying you for this,' he said. 'So we'll do things the way I decide.'

He watched as I showed how I got my balance in the saddle and communicated with the horse through my movements. When I'd explained all I usefully could, I suggested he try for himself.

'The chestnut's a calm horse,' I said. 'Perhaps, just to start with, you could try sitting on her back, getting your balance?'

It was the wrong thing to say. Of course.

'You think I need a calm horse? A horse for a child?'

'No, I just—'

'I rode my father's hunters, I'm not afraid.' He sat back, and said to the coachman, 'Enough for today, I'm tired. Take me back to the house.'

It was the one eventuality I hadn't considered. I knew there was a chance Jeremiah's method wouldn't work for Robert, or that I just wouldn't be good enough at teaching it. But it hadn't occurred to me that he would refuse to co-operate. After all Jeremiah had said about how much he loved horses, I thought he'd grab at the chance to get back to them. But I should have realised. At the cottage that evening, eating my solitary supper of bean stew and stale bread, I thought back to the night he'd got trapped in the stable with the Arab stallion.

'The horse must have been rearing up, and kicking out,'

Jeremiah had told us when he returned. 'He was still in a right old lather when I got there – in all my days, I've never seen a horse's eyes so wild. Took me a good half an hour to calm him enough to lead him out, and then there was the poor lad, right in the far corner of the stall, all shrunk up against the wall with his hands over his head.'

No wonder he didn't want to get close to a horse again; for all his bluster, the boy was terrified.

As I expected, Robert did everything he could to avoid getting on a horse. The second morning's lesson was missed; Tom the coachman brought the message that Robert was suffering with a violent headache. The day after, I showed him again how to settle in the saddle, how to move off, and how to steer the horse, but when I suggested he try for himself, he snapped that I'd taken too long with my explanations; his father was going away to the north for a month, and he needed to get back to say goodbye before he left.

Every morning that week, I demonstrated how to get the horse to walk, to trot and to gallop; he watched, and occasionally asked questions. But there was always a reason why he couldn't try for himself: he felt unwell; the horse looked a little lame; the ground was too soft. On the Friday, the excuse was that a new doctor was coming from London.

'My father says this one attends all the best people,' he said. 'He'll have the answer. So this is really just a waste of my time.'

Whatever the doctor's answer was, it didn't work. We spent a second week with me trying to teach and Robert putting up a pretence of learning, and at the end of it, with less than six weeks left to Jeremiah's trial, it was obvious we were getting nowhere.

Chapter Fifty-eight

There was no hope of teaching Robert to ride if I continued with what I was doing. Sir Peter was still away, and even if he hadn't been, I doubted very much it would help my case, or Jeremiah's, to go and tell him his son was too scared to get on a horse. I spent an anxious Sunday alone in the cottage, turning over and over in my mind what I could do. And in the end, I decided my only hope was to take a risk.

When the trap pulled up the next morning, I felt sick with fear.

If this goes wrong, it's finished.

As usual, the second coachman got down from the grey, and went to lead her over to me.

'You can let her graze,' I said. 'Both of them, in fact. We won't be needing the horses this morning.'

Robert leaned forward.

'What are you talking about?'

'We won't be riding,' I said. 'Today I want to tell you a story.'

'I hope this won't be a waste of my time,' he said, but

there was relief in his eyes. For once he didn't need to find an excuse.

I told him how, when I was ten, I thought a faerie could make me grow. How I thought, every day, about what it would be like after she cast her spell and I became like other boys. And how she'd turned out to be an ordinary person, not a faerie at all.

'I was stupid to believe she could do magic. Or that magic could make me grow. But I wanted it so much, I would have believed anything.' I took a deep breath. 'And you're the same. You want to believe the doctors can make you walk again. But how many have there been? Your father would pay a fortune to the doctor who could cure you, yet none of them have. And that's because they can't.'

Robert's face reddened.

'Are you calling me stupid?'

'Not stupid. Just desperate, like I was. But they can't make you walk, just like nothing could make me grow. And while you go on believing they can, you're wasting your life.'

The two coachmen looked at each other. Robert was stiff with anger, his hands gripping the sides of the trap.

No point stopping now.

'If you learned to ride again,' I said, 'you could go out with your father, you could even hunt. You wouldn't be mouldering away in that room, just—'

'Enough,' he said. 'My father wouldn't expect me to stand for this. You can consider yourself dismissed. Tom, take me back.'

'If you give up now,' I said, 'you'll be stuck with this half-life for ever. Or you can stop being afraid and learn to be your father's son again. It's up to you.'

With that, I turned and walked away.

By the time I got back to the cottage, I was certain I'd gone too far. Did I really think Robert would listen to me? Wasn't it far more likely he'd wait till his father got back and tell him what I'd said? And how would Sir Peter react when his beloved son reported that I'd suggested he was stupid, and taunted him about his fears? He'd be away for another few weeks: I should leave now, just get away, and take my chances on the run. I'd tried to save Jeremiah, and if I'd failed, he'd want me to try and save myself, I knew that. But I couldn't do it. I didn't think there was much chance of my plan working now but, if nothing else, I could make one last plea to Sir Peter for Jeremiah, who'd done nothing wrong.

I took a long time to find sleep that night and, as a consequence, the dawn light slanting through the windows didn't wake me. So when there came a knocking on the door, I was still asleep, and for a few moments, it worked itself into my dream: I was back at the palace, we were all in the chamber but Jeremiah was outside the door, knocking and knocking, but no one else seemed to hear it.

Then I woke and realised the knocking was real.

They've come for me.

As I tried to think what to do, a voice shouted my name. It took me a moment to recognise it: Tom, the coachman. But they wouldn't send him to get me...

I hurried to open the door.

340

'The young master's waiting,' he said. 'We've been out there twenty minutes.'

His face was so pale as the two coachmen lifted him onto the horse. His poor legs hung uselessly, and he gripped the reins so hard the veins in his hands stood out. Like mine, that first time I sat on Shadow, when the slightest movement seemed certain to send me tumbling to the ground.

I mounted the other horse.

'Right,' I said. 'We'll start with how to sit.'

Robert never once mentioned the conversation about the faerie, and I didn't either. But now he was willing, I pushed him as hard as I could, knowing the weeks to Jeremiah's trial were slipping away. He was a difficult pupil; when things went wrong, it was always my fault, and more than once I was threatened with his father's wrath for pointing out his mistakes. But he didn't give up. As he regained his confidence, some of the bitter anger left him, and when he mastered something that had been giving him trouble, he'd forget his dignity enough to give a whoop of delight. It made me smile, because I knew how that felt; Jeremiah had given me the same gift, all those years ago.

We did it in four weeks. One crisp November morning, I watched him trot the chestnut around the field, and held my breath as he urged her on. As she surged forward he sat tall in the saddle, and I couldn't help letting out a cheer as he circled the field twice, his hair flying in the wind.

'My father will be back tomorrow,' he said as he pulled up. 'Wait till he sees what I can do.'

'He'll be proud of you.'

His cheeks flushed red.

'It will serve a purpose, until I can walk again,' he said. He seemed about to ride off, but then he stopped and looked down at me. 'I wanted to say ... I hope my father pays you well.'

I think it was as close to thanks as he could let himself get, but that was closer than I'd expected.

'So do I,' I said.

Now I had to see if Sir Peter would keep his word. I sent a note with Tom the coachman, simply stating that payment was due, just in case Robert should catch sight of it. It was two days before he brought a message back.

'The master's had to leave for London – important business. He'll see you on Tuesday next.'

That was only a week ahead of Jeremiah's trial. What if he hadn't remembered the date?

'No,' I said. 'I need to see him before that.'

'Can't be done,' said Tom. 'He left at first light.'

Chapter Fifty-nine

All I could do was wait, and hope. Confined to the cottage, alone, I couldn't distract myself from worrying about what was going to happen. In the space of an hour, I would go from telling myself that surely Sir Peter was a man of his word, and soon Jeremiah would be free, to being certain that when I went to the house, I would be met by soldiers and taken away.

When Tuesday came, as Tom had instructed, I presented myself at the front door, squaring my shoulders, ready to play my role again. A maid showed me into the same room where I'd made my bargain with Sir Peter.

He was standing by the fireplace, reading a document, and he turned as I walked in.

'You've come for your payment,' he said.

'I kept my part of the bargain,' I said. 'I trust you'll kee~ yours.'

'I'm a man of my word. But in this case, the term~ changed.'

My heart plummeted.

'But I did what I promised. I taught your son

'Do you want to know where he is now?'

Surely he hadn't hidden himself away in his room again?

'He's out on his horse,' said Sir Peter. 'I'm making him take a groom with him, just for now, but that's more to calm my fears than anything. He's riding as well as he ever did.'

'Then you'll get Jeremiah out?'

'Already arranged,' he said. 'He'll be on his way home this morning.'

I've done it. Jeremiah's safe.

He looked down at his feet, and scuffed the toe of one boot on the other.

'And you can tell him his place here is secure,' he said. 'I was, perhaps, a little unfair to him, before. My son is very precious to me, and I was angry. But what happened wasn't his fault.'

'Thank you. I know he'll be relieved.'

What did he mean then, about changing the terms?

Don't let him see you're afraid.

'As to the other part of our bargain,' I said, 'you'll honour your promise, I hope? I'll leave the county, and you can forget you ever saw me.'

'Well, that was what we agreed, yes.'

He's going to hand me over to them.

'But it turned out that I've been able to do better than that.'

He handed me the paper he'd been reading. I looked at words, but at first I couldn't take in what it said. When I stood there, rooted to the spot, scanning the document over again, in case there was a trick that I hadn't

more than you promised – you gave me my son

back,' he said. 'And I pay well for good service. So I made some enquiries in London. With all the fighting this summer, money's short. You'd be surprised who they're willing to come to terms with, if there's a substantial fine in it. And it *was* a substantial one, you being a friend of her Catholic majesty, but fortunately I'm a man of means. So your crimes are paid for. You're a free man.'

At that moment there was only one place I wanted to go. My face turned to the wintry sun, I headed for the Canterbury road. I hadn't gone far when I saw him in the distance, loping along on those long, spindly legs. I ran to meet him, waving my arms, forgetting that for Jeremiah, potential disaster lay round every corner. By the time I reached him, worry was written in every line on his face.

'What is it?' he said, when I was close enough to hear. 'Is it Sukie? Is little Michael ill?'

'They're fine,' I said. 'I'm sorry, I didn't mean to alarm you.'

'Then why … what are you doing out here?'

'I'm safe,' I said. 'I'm free, and you're free, and we're all safe. At last.'

We spent a last evening together in the cottage. Jeremiah was keen to fetch Sukie and Michael home, and now that I could travel safely, I'd decided to head for Oakham, in the hope that Sam was back there. We planned to set out at dawn, and journey as far as London together.

'There's no need for you to leave us,' he said, as he set down his bowl after a third helping of bean stew. Food had clearly been scarce in the gaol.

'There is,' I said. 'You've been more than kind to me, you and Sukie, and I'll miss you. But you don't want a cuckoo in the nest any longer.'

'Well, after what you did for me, Nat, there'll be a home with us any time you want it. And Sukie would say the same.'

He smiled when I told him what I'd said to Robert to get him on a horse.

'That's most likely the first time anyone's told that boy a truth he didn't want to hear,' he said. 'About time too.'

'Well, it did the trick, anyway.'

'Do you ever think, Nat, about how things would have gone if she really had been a faerie? I mean, if there were such things, and she could have granted your wish?'

'I stopped believing in faeries a long time ago.'

'Because the way I look at it now, if we'd been just like other folks, what kind of lives would we have had? Not the ones we got, that's for sure. I'd never have met my Sukie, or got myself a good friend like you.'

'I don't suppose I'd ever have left Oakham,' I said. 'I'd never have had any reason to.'

Even as the words came out of my mouth, the truth of it seemed astonishing, that I could have stayed in that little town, seeing the same faces I'd always seen, and never knowing what else there was. I'd wanted the faerie to grant my wish so badly, but what a life I would have missed if she had. And it's hard to explain what happened in that moment, but the best I can tell you is that it was as though I'd been looking in a mirror, and then Jeremiah tilted it, showing me a different reflection – but one that had been there all the time. For as long as I could remember, I'd longed to be like everyone else, but everything good in my life had come from being just as I was. All the people I'd met, the friends I'd made, the things I'd done. And most of the bad things had come from my own stupid shame over the way God had made me. Even Crofts' taunts and jibes had only struck home, with all the terrible consequences of that, because I believed them.

'I don't say it's been easy,' Jeremiah went on. 'We've both had our troubles, and I'll speak the truth to you, because you understand – I'm glad Michael's not the way I am. It'll make life easier for him.'

'But you don't wish things had been different for you?'

'No, do you?'

'No, I don't,' I said. 'Not anymore.'

We parted at Southwark, where the first stage of our journeys ended. The wagon had been noisy and bumpy, so we'd talked very little on the way, but there was one thing I wanted to say to Jeremiah before I left him.

'You've been more than a friend to me,' I said, as we stood in the courtyard of the inn that was the wagon's last stop. 'You've been like a father. And a better one than the one I was born to.'

'Well, if your father didn't appreciate what a fine son he had, then I feel sorry for him,' he said. 'And if there's anything I want for Michael, it's that he grows up to be a good man like you.'

I thought about my father, on the long journey to Oakham. I didn't feel sorry for him. He'd been ashamed of me beca· I was small, and he'd made me ashamed of myself. But set me on the path to the life I'd had, and though h his own reasons, perhaps there'd also been a part of him that really did believe he'd found a good chance for me. I'd never know, now, but if I chose to believe it, well, that was up to me.

Chapter Sixty

I took my time walking through the town to Sam's cottage, because I was afraid. All through the journey, I'd pictured his face when he saw me, but I didn't know for sure that I'd ever see it again. My hope was that he'd surrendered to the other side and been given parole. Plenty had. But plenty had died too.

I could have asked someone, but I couldn't bring myself to. If my brother was dead, I didn't want to hear it from someone who'd be itching to tell the neighbours who they'd just seen, and how I'd looked when they told me.

Lucy was outside the cottage, playing with a ginger cat. She looked up and saw me. I didn't expect her to remember me but of course I was quite difficult to forget.

'Uncle Nat,' she shouted. 'Papa, Uncle Nat's here.'

From inside the house, a voice I knew said, 'Don't be silly, pet. You know your mother doesn't like you telling stories.'

I put my finger to my lips, and walked the last few yards to the open door. He was standing with his back to it, my big, tall, little brother. Lucy giggled as I knocked, and he turned round.

'It's me,' I said. 'I've come home.'

* * *

If Sam said 'I can't believe it' once that evening, he said it a dozen times. My ribs were still sore from him throwing his arms round me when I walked through the door, and even hours later, he would look at me every so often, shake his head, and say, 'I can't believe it. You're back here in Oakham, at last.' It was so good to see him again, and no longer in the stiff tunic of a soldier, but sitting by his own fireside, with Lucy leaning against his knee.

'Got my parole after we fought at Newbury,' he told me. 'And I was happy to have it, I can tell you. There were sights on that battlefield I never want to see again. Good men lost on both sides, and if you know what it was all for, Nat, then you can tell me, because I don't know.'

'Well, if Nat knows, he can tell you another time, because I won't have talk of fighting when we're eating,' said Sarah, dishing up bowls of chicken stew, the unfortunate bird having met its end that afternoon, in my honour.

She hadn't looked quite so pleased as Sam to see me, but then I wasn't sure Sarah was given to looking very pleased about anything. Nevertheless, she made a good chicken stew, and when I complimented her on it, her mouth very nearly approximated a smile. Lucy, on the other hand, was a cheerful little girl, who wanted to know everything I could tell about the queen, and what dresses she wore, and how people danced at the palace.

'Ah, but you should have seen her when she was with her ʝldiers,' I said, after I'd run out of dresses I could remember, ⸱ich didn't take long. 'Sitting outside with them, eating ⸱ the fire. She was like a lady general.'

'And you saved her from the people who wanted to kill her,' said Lucy. 'Papa told us.'

'And then your papa saved me,' I said. 'He was very brave.'

Lucy beamed up at Sam, and he reached down and rumpled her curls.

'She's heard that story a few times too,' said Sarah, but there was pride in the glance she gave Sam. It pleased me to see that. She might not be someone I'd want to wake up beside, but it was plain to see she loved my brother and so he was right; he had been lucky.

Before we went to bed, I reassured them that I wouldn't be staying too long; I hadn't missed Sarah's pinched look earlier, when Sam said I had a home with them for as long as I wanted one.

'As soon as the winter storms are over, I'll be on a ship back to France,' I said. 'The king can't hold out much longer. He'll have to agree to go, and I'll go too.'

The following day, Sam and I took a walk; it being a Sunday, he had no work, and I had a fancy to see the woods where we used to play. We got to talking about the Oxford days and – quite in passing – I mentioned Arabella. He stood stock still, and clapped his hand to his mouth.

'What?' I said. I remember I laughed, because he looked so daft.

'I forgot, with all the excitement of you being home. What an idiot, I should have told you.'

'Told me what?'

'Arabella – she came here.'

'Here? To Oakham?'

'Year before last, it was. She came back to England to nurse her father – poor soul was wounded right at the end of it all. And one of the brothers was killed the same time.'

All that time I'd been picturing her and Henry in France, they'd been here in England.

'She'd promised the queen she'd try and find you. They'd all been worried, she said, when you didn't write.'

'What did you tell her?'

'What could I tell her? I didn't know where you were either. But you can go and find her now, can't you? They're living back in the village she came from, she said.'

I shook my head.

'I can't face it.'

'Face what?'

'Seeing them together. Her and Henry.'

'No but that's the thing! She didn't marry him. Said they were never really suited, and she'd broken it off not long after you went away.'

She's not married?

He winked at me.

'Seemed to me she was quite keen for me to know that. Seemed to me she'd want you to know it too.'

But it's hopeless. You know it's hopeless.

'Stop it, Sam. She wasn't interested in me then, and she wouldn't be interested in me now.'

'You know what?' he said. 'I always thought you were the ˄ver one, but when it comes to women, you're as a stupid ˄sheep.'

˄and you know so much about them, do you?'

˄hat's just it – I was as stupid as you are. If Sarah

hadn't asked me to the fair that day, I'd never have dared to speak a word to her, and I'd have lost her to the cowman. But seeing that I'd been so daft, I thought you'd make sure you didn't make the same mistake.'

'It's not the same.'

'Well, I think you should go and see her.'

'Thank you for your advice. Now can we talk about something else?'

I can't remember what we did talk about on the rest of that walk; I don't suppose I heard half of what Sam said anyway. The same thoughts kept going round and round in my head.

It's not too late.

So what? She'd never want you.

But what if she did? What if Sam's right, and I had it all wrong?

No. Don't be an idiot. Forget it. Don't let yourself go there again.

That night, as I lay curled up on the kitchen floor, after Sam and Sarah had gone to bed, I thought and thought about what I should do. For so long, I'd tried to keep Arabella out of my head, believing she was Henry's wife. But she wasn't, she never had been. So now, I let the thoughts come back, and remembered all the things I'd loved about her: her smile, her quick way with words, even her kindness to the queen's smelly old dog.

I remembered Sukie's words too: 'I'd love that man ' had three heads and he'd love me if I had four.' A was beautiful – but I'd have loved her if she had f too. Had there ever been a chance she could lov if there was even the smallest possibility of it, shouldn't I find out?

I woke, in the early hours, drenched in sweat. Over the time I'd spent in Kent, my nightmares about Crofts had gradually left me, but for the first time in many months, I'd dreamed about that morning in the forest again. Except that this time, when I stepped towards the body on the ground, it wasn't Crofts lying there, it was Arabella. As my terror faded, I saw how stupid I'd been. I couldn't go to her. It didn't make any difference whether there was a chance for me or not: my foolishness in falling in love with her had caused Crofts' death. How could I think I deserved to be with her, knowing that?

Chapter Sixty-one

Those first few weeks back in Oakham were cold and very
wet, and with the roads impassable, no news reached us. As
far as anyone knew, the king and Parliament and the Scots
and the army were still arguing about who'd have the final
say on taxes, and whether the bishops were to stay or go. But
then, one icy morning just before Christmas, I went to the
market to pick up some provisions for Sarah, and saw people
standing around, in little groups, reading the newsbooks over
each other's shoulders, or listening as someone else read aloud.
There was shock on their faces, all of them.

I couldn't see the seller; by the looks of it, he'd sold out
and gone. I joined the edge of a little knot of people standing
round the blacksmith, who was reading out loud, his finger
tracing each line as he spoke it. For once no one looked twice
at me, they were hanging on to his every word.

'…broken the sacred covna… covee…'

'Covenant,' said a woman, reading over his shoulder.

'…the sacred cov-en-ant with his people,' read the bl
smith, 'and put himself above the law.'

'What's happened?' I asked.

'They're trying him. For treason,' said the woman.

'Trying who?'

'The king.'

It had all happened in a matter of days. He'd made a treaty with Parliament, the newsbook said, but the army didn't trust him: he'd already surrendered once and then gone back on it, what was to say he'd keep any promises after they'd put him back on the throne? So they'd taken matters into their own hands: declared the king an enemy of the people, for causing the war in the first place, then picked off the Members of Parliament who didn't agree with them, and arrested them.

'That can't be true,' said Sarah, when I ran home with the news. 'They can't do that, can they?'

'I don't know,' I said. 'But it looks like they have.'

You'll know, of course, what happened after that. The news from his trial travelled fast, even to Oakham; he'd told them, on the very first day, that they weren't fit to sit in judgement on him, and he wasn't going to dignify the proceedings by even answering the charges. You could see then how it was going to end. They wouldn't stand for that, not now.

All the way to London, I told myself perhaps I was wrong. Perhaps they'd still let him go, pack him off to France and ᵗell him not to come back. But at every inn, the news was the ᵐe; he was still telling them they couldn't sit in judgement ᵗim, even as witness after witness stood up and said it ᵈ his fault that so many people had died. I don't know ᵈld have made any difference, by then, if he'd behaved

356

differently, but I never met anyone who was as good at making a bad situation worse as he was.

Perhaps you think it strange that I travelled to London to see it? I know Sam thought so, but I had a stupid idea he might like to see a face he knew in the crowd. Mostly though, I went for her, because she couldn't be there to say goodbye to him.

When I stepped off the coach at Cheapside, it was already over. The day before, they'd found him guilty of treason and sentenced him to death. That night, for the first time in quite a while, I prayed – for the king, who'd been a fool, but who didn't deserve this, and for the queen, whose agony I could hardly even imagine.

The day dawned bitterly cold, and my breath billowed out in front of me as I followed the crowds to Whitehall. My old home was a barracks now, run-down and shabby. They'd built a scaffold outside the banqueting hall, level with the first-floor windows, and hacked a rough opening in the wall. The platform was draped in black, and the block was in the middle, so low he wouldn't even be able to kneel, but would have to lie flat. On either side were thick metal staples; a man standing near me told his daughter he'd be tied to them if he struggled. They knew, anyone who'd ever had dealings with him would know, he wouldn't struggle. But someone had decided to put them there anyway.

Across the road was an elm tree; half a dozen boys ha climbed it and I did the same, finding myself a broad bra to sit on so I could see over the crowds. They must been fifty deep, and people were hanging out from v too, and even standing on the rooftops. A row of stamping their feet against the cold, stood with their backs to the scaffold, keeping the crowds at a distance, as though even now, someone might try to rescue him. But I heard no one speak against the proceedings, and the people around me showed nothing more than curiosity: speculating about how the thing would be done, whether he might say anything, even what he would wear, as though it was a new form of entertainment that might or might not catch on, depending on how well the first performance went.

A murmur ran through the crowd as two figures stepped onto the platform, wearing hoods that showed only their eyes, one of them carrying the axe. The rumour in the taverns was that the executioner of London had refused the task, and they'd had to promise his replacement, and his assistant, that they could conceal their identity. Like stage actors pretending to chat among themselves while the main character makes a speech, they busied themselves with checking the position of the block, placing the axe down and picking it up again, and trying the unnecessary staples for strength.

When he appeared he was dressed in black. It shocked me to see his beard grizzled with grey. The crowd fell silent as he looked out over them. Behind him came a short man in the robes of a bishop, and two pikemen. The king began to speak, but I couldn't catch more than the odd word, and judging by the puzzled faces in the crowd below, they couldn't either. But he had that look he always had when he was explaining someone why they were wrong and he was right. The poor didn't see, even then, that that was what had put him e was.

the executioner started testing the edge of the axe

on his own hand, the king caught the movement out of the corner of his eye and lost his thread for a moment. But then he carried on, and when he got to the end of what he had to say, his gaze swept from left to right, over the crowd, as though he'd just taught them something and he was checking to see if they understood. I hoped he didn't realise most of them hadn't heard a word of it.

The bishop stepped forward, and they spoke a few words together – I supposed it was a prayer – and then the king took off his hat. The executioner's assistant put a white cap on him, pushing all his hair up inside it, but he couldn't have made a proper job of it; the king felt the back of his neck and then gestured to the bishop, who stepped up and tucked some last bits in. My stomach turned over then; what must that feel like, to stand there and know in a few minutes someone's going to cut your head off? And yet he stood straight, he didn't tremble. She would have been proud of him.

He waved the executioner over, and pointed towards the block. I think he must have been asking if it could be raised; the executioner shook his head. The king took off his cloak, removed his high-necked doublet, and put his cloak back on. Then he folded his hands together and prayed, and when he'd finished, he lay down with his head on the block. And when you see something like that, when it's right in front of you, you can't believe it's really going to happen but it did. The axe swung down, blood sprayed out and the crowd let out a groan like a wounded animal. It was as though up till that point they really had thought they were at the theatre, and it h only just dawned on them that this time the lead char wasn't going to get up and take a bow. The king was d

* * *

I got very drunk that night. I went back to the inn where I was staying, took a flagon of wine up to my room and drank my way through it. When you're my size, it doesn't take much to set the room spinning, but I had to get the axe and the blood and that terrible groan out of my head. I'd never had much love for the king, I've made no secret of that, and I still think he was a fool. But he was an honourable man too and seeing him stand there, brave and dignified, when they'd done all they could to humiliate him in his last moments… well, I thought he acquitted himself better in death than he'd ever done in life. And of course, I thought of the queen. She wouldn't know yet he was dead. But there was such a bond between them I wondered if she might feel it anyway. It was a fanciful notion and I'm generally not given to those, but it had been a strange day and I'd drunk a lot of wine.

The one good thing I could find in the whole story was that at least he'd gone to his death knowing she was safe. But for that there'd been a price: all those years spent apart. She told me once that when she was away from him, it was like having less air to breathe. And now they would never see each other again.

What was it all for?

All that blood spilt, all those lives lost. I didn't believe the king's cause to be right in every degree, but it was far from clear to me that the people who'd put themselves in his place would make the country better, or happier, or help us rub along more easily when we differed. And whether they were right or wrong that it was his fault so many lives were lost, his wasn't going to bring any of those men back. They'd turned the world upside down, that day, and it was hard to see how they could set it to rights again.

When you've seen something like that, stood there and watched it happen in front of you, it can't help but make you think. And what I thought of was another death, on a misty morning in the woods outside Paris. I would never lose my guilt about killing Crofts, and I didn't seek to. But I couldn't bring him back either. And if that day had taught me anything, it was that life is precious and none of us should waste a second of it.

Before my eyes closed and the flagon slipped to the floor, I had decided; the very next day, I'd travel north. God had given me one life, and I wasn't going to waste whatever might be left of it. She might not want me. There was every chance she wouldn't. But I had to try.

Chapter Sixty-two

The coach north took three days, and by the end of the third one, I was more nervous than I'd been since the day I was put in that pie. I arrived around the middle of the day and found a room at the village inn, telling myself I wanted to smarten myself up. What I really wanted was to put off the moment. And when the coachman shouted 'Ready to leave', it was all I could do not to rush outside and climb back in.

It wasn't hard to find her; everyone had known the Denhams when they had the big house. The woman I asked gave me a strange look: what, it said, what does the likes of you want with her? But she told me to look out for a green gate and a big apple tree in the garden, so I spotted the cottage easily.

There she is.

She was hanging out some washing, with her back to me, and singing quietly to herself. I stood still for a moment, just ɔoking at her, and then took a deep breath. My hand was on gate when I realised she wasn't singing, she was talking. little girl, playing on the ground beside her. She bent ɔ the child, tickling her so she wriggled and squirmed.

I stepped back, out of sight. How could I have been so stupid? She hadn't married Henry, but that didn't mean she hadn't married someone else. It had been over two years since she'd come to Oakham. And in that time, someone else had found her.

I was too late after all. Sick at heart, I trudged back to the inn. I had to get away. The village was small; if I stayed overnight, she was sure to discover I was there. One day, perhaps, I might be able to sit in the same room as her husband and child, but not today. The church bells struck two; the last coach out would be going soon. I broke into a run, but as I reached the inn, it was disappearing down the road.

The best I could do then was order food in my room and stay there until the first coach left in the morning. I didn't care where it was going; I'd take it and make my way back to Oakham by whatever route I could find.

Next morning, I was stuffing the last of my things into my bag when there was a knock on the door of my room. The innkeeper, curiosity seeping from every pore, informed me that I had a visitor. Of course. Someone was bound to tell her.

'Waiting outside the door when we opened, she was.'

'Is anyone with her?' I asked, eyeing the window and wondering if I could I climb out of it. But when he said she was alone, I told him I'd come down. In truth, now she was there I couldn't resist the chance to see her face again.

Chapter Sixty-three

As I came down the stairs she turned and smiled, and my heart flipped over.

'So it *is* you,' she said. 'I thought it must be, but... Where have you been? The queen tried to find you—'

I told her a shortened version of my story.

'We had no idea,' she said. 'All that time...'

'What about you?' I said. 'I heard about your father, and your brother. I'm sorry.'

'Poor Ed, he'd only married a month before. That stupid war – in the end, I don't think any of them knew what they were fighting for.' She shook her head. 'But let's not talk about that now. It's good to see you. You'll stay a while, won't you? The cottage isn't very big, but we can make room.'

'No, I have to get back to Oakham.'

'But you've only just got here. You can stay the night, ~urely?'

'No, I can't,' I said. 'I'd like to meet your husband but—'

'~hat husband?'

'~ husband.'

'~'t got a husband.'

'But yesterday I saw you. In the garden with your child.'

She frowned, and then laughed.

'That wasn't my child, you idiot! That's my niece, Alice. Ed's daughter. Ed's wife and Alice live with Father and me.'

I think I must have stared at her like a fool as the thoughts tumbled round in my head.

She's not married. She's still free.

But that didn't mean she could love me, did it? She was pleased to see me, that much was obvious, but we'd been friends; she might have been just as pleased to see Susan or Elizabeth. Or Bonbon.

I couldn't say it, not now, not just like that. Maybe if I stayed a while, I could see how things went? And then I remembered the king, and all the time he and the queen had lost.

'Could you... could you come here?' I said, beckoning her down towards me. I reached out and took her hand.

'What are you—'

'That's good news,' I said. 'About you not being married. Because the thing is, I love you.'

'You... What did you say?'

I took a deep breath.

'I love you. I think I've probably loved you since the day I met you.'

'You... well, that just about takes the biscuit.' She snatched her hand away, stood and looked down at me, her hands on her hips, her face reddening. 'Of all the... You come here now and tell me you *love* me?'

I looked down at my feet.

You fool.

I was right all along. She thought the idea was ridiculous, of course she did.

'Why didn't you say so before?' she said.

I looked up.

'You idiot,' she said. 'All that time... I nearly married Henry because of you! You bloody well broke my heart, Nat Davy.'

'But you loved Henry. I saw the way you used to look at him.'

She rolled her eyes.

'Still this? You numbskull, I wasn't looking at Henry. Who was usually standing beside him?'

She was looking at me? That day, when we left for Oakham, that look was for me?

'You loved me since the day you met me?' she went on. 'Then why didn't you ever do anything about it? Oh yes, you said, Henry will make you a very good husband. Why would you say that if you loved me?'

'But why did you say yes to him if you loved me?'

'Because I thought... this is so embarrassing... I thought it would make you jealous. And then you might—'

The door opened and the innkeeper came in, casually drying a tankard and trying to look as though he hadn't been listening outside.

'Coach is here,' he said. 'Will you be wanting—'

'What we want is a bit of privacy,' she snapped, and he backed out, carefully leaving the door ajar.

'Let me see if I understand this,' I said. 'Are you saying you ~ed me too?'

'~ut you know that! I told you everything in my letter. you didn't reply, I thought—'

'I didn't read it,' I said. 'I thought you were just saying goodbye, and I couldn't bring myself to hear it.'

'It took me hours to write that letter! I said I thought you should know I loved you, and if you thought you might love me, you only had to write and tell me where you were, and I'd come to you. I said I'd live in a cave, if it meant we could be together. And I've spent nearly three years, up to and including the last ten minutes, thinking I'd embarrassed myself and that wherever you were, you were laughing at me for being such a fool.'

'You'd live with me in a cave?'

'Obviously I was hoping it wouldn't come to that.'

'So when you say you loved me back then...'

'Yes?'

'Do you by any chance think you might still love me?'

'As it happens, I do.'

From outside the door came the clang of a pewter tankard hitting the floor.

She folded her arms and frowned at me.

'Well?' she said. 'Are you going to give this village something to gossip about, and ask me to marry you, or not?'

'Isn't it usual for the lady to be a bit less forward?'

'I think we've established that if I wait for you to take the initiative, I'll be ninety before I get a ring on my finger.'

She crouched down again, and looked into my eyes.

'I love you, Nat Davy,' she said. 'Even if you are the bigg idiot in England.'

Epilogue

London, 1663

For years and years I haven't thought about those long ago days at the palace. And then Sam wrote, and said I had to come to London, there was something I should see.

Tradescant's cabinet of curiosities, they call the place – all manner of strange and wonderful items, collected from across the world, just for people to come and gaze at them. Sam and Sarah having already made a visit, and Sarah none too keen to pay twice, my niece Lucy came with me that morning. A grown woman now, she looks more like my mother than ever, and she has my brother's sweet nature.

'Shall I take you to it?' she asked. 'Or do you want to find it for yourself?'

'Will I know it when I see it?'

She laughed.

'Yes, there's no mistaking it.'

So I looked around at the wonders on display. In the first ꓳ alone, I saw a piece of the true cross, a mermaid's hand ꓲcene from *Hamlet* carved on a cherrystone, but they ꓳe what Sam meant. Along one wall was a bank of ꓲl of little drawers, and a couple of elderly ladies were poking about in one and exclaiming over the contents, so I went to have a look. But inside the drawers was just a collection of gemstones carved into animals.

'I couldn't believe my eyes when I saw it,' Sam had said in his letter. 'If you won't come to London just to see us, you've got to come and see this.'

She wrote it of course, Sarah. Sam never did get to grips with the alphabet. But she's a clever one, I'll give her that. It was her idea to come to London, and it'll be her pushing that got Sam a good job at the fish market -- though by the way she wrinkles her nose at the smell of his clothes, I'd bet she's got plans to move him on soon. And now she wants Lucy to get a place at the palace, which I've no doubt is the real reason she welcomed me so warmly to their home for the visit. But I don't mind. Lucy's a lovely girl, and if I can help her by a word to the queen, I will. My own two boys are country lads, they'd no sooner live in the city than on the moon, and though she loves the queen as dearly as I do, Arabella would go mad with boredom if she had to live at court. She's as happy as a dog with a bone running the estate for her father, and if the new house is smaller than the old one, well, she doesn't mind and nor do I.

Lucy smiled at my puzzled expression, and nodded at the next room. I walked through, and there it was. In a corner, in a glass case: the suit I wore when we were painted by Mr Van Dyck. Even after all these years, the red velvet glowed at me across the room; the queen always did insist on the best. When I got closer, it was threadbare in places, but the la around the neck was still white, and the gold buttons d the front were all there. And beside it, my boots, all s round the toes from the gravel in the palace gardens

How old was I then? Twelve, perhaps? And the queen, standing beside me, was still only seventeen. What would we have thought, back then, if anyone had told us what would happen to us? And yet we've come through it all, both of us. When she came home from France to join her son, the new king, people cheered in the streets. And me? I've got everything I ever wanted, and more.

Then I saw there was a label, saying who I was – as if you could get a life like the one I've had into five words. That's when it came to me that I should write this all down and tell my story properly. Show people that, on the inside, I'm as big as anyone else. Just like my mother said, all those years ago.

Lucy stooped to read what the label said.

'Costume worn by Nathaniel Davy, the Smallest Man in England.'

She turned and looked at me.

'Is that what they used to call you, Uncle Nat?'

'Yes,' I said. 'That's what they used to call me.'

Author's Note

When I read a historical novel that features real events, the question in my mind is always 'How much of this is true?' Nat Davy is a figment of my imagination, but his story was inspired by that of Jeffrey Hudson, court dwarf to Queen Henrietta Maria, who became what these days we'd call a celebrity, thanks to his tiny size, doll-like looks and ready wit.

Like so many figures who lived on the edge of great historical events, Jeffrey's life is documented only in snatches, but thanks to Nick Page's excellent biography, *Lord Minimus*, we know that he was presented to the queen in a pie, and that he accompanied her to Holland to buy arms for the Civil War, putting him by her side during the attack on Bridlington – and yes, she really did go back for the dog (which fans of the period may know was actually called Mitte – my excuse for the change is that people kept asking me why a French queen had a dog with a German-sounding name). Jeffrey was wit¹ her on the journey down to Oxford, when a kidnap plot ᵥ rumoured; we don't know how far the plot went, so the dᵗ of the one described here come from my imaginatioᵣ Arabella and the Dunham family. He then accompᵣ queen to France and there killed a man in a duel; it's not known why.

This is a novel though, not a fictionalised biography or a history textbook, so not everything that happens to Nat happened to Jeffrey Hudson and, here and there, I've changed the order of events, or their locations.

After being banished from France, Jeffrey was kidnapped en route to England by the infamous Barbary pirates, who roamed the seas around Europe capturing ships and their passengers; the wealthy were ransomed, the rest sold into slavery in North Africa, which is what seems to have happened to Jeffrey. Nothing is known of his life there, but it's thought he may have been held for as long as twenty-five years, and eventually freed, with hundreds of others, as a result of a scheme to use a percentage of customs takings to pay for the release of Barbary captives.

Unlike Nat, as far as we know, Jeffrey didn't get a happy ending – his biographer found no record of him marrying, and believes he died, alone and poor, back home in Oakham. As there's no record of that either, I like to think there's at least the possibility that Jeffrey found his own Arabella – but we'll never know.

Acknowledgements

There should really be a five-author credit for this book, because it wouldn't have got finished without my amazing writing buddies, Kate Clarke, Lucy Smallwood Barker, Amy Hoskin and Clêr Lewis, who read endless drafts, brainstormed ideas and got me out of some very deep plot holes. You four are just the best – thank you doesn't even begin to cover it.

Thanks to Jan Bhend, Sarah Giles, Ian Kirkpatrick and Julie Ball, who read early and frankly terrible drafts and gave me useful feedback; to Ollie Rice, my mentor and cheerleader for longer than either of us care to remember; to Sheila Saner from Riding for the Disabled, and Jo White, who helped me figure out how Nat might learn to ride; and to Dave Harris of Kent Fire and Rescue, for answering my hopelessly vague questions about how quickly a fire in a seventeenth-century house that he'd never seen might spread, and in which direction. And thanks to my friend John Garvie for the picture of Jeffrey Hudson that ⟨ on my desk as inspiration while I wrote the book.

Thank you too to the people who made my story i⟨ book: my super-smart editor Clare Hey, possibly the on⟨ in the world who I could still like after they'd asked ⟨

away 30,000 words and write new ones to replace them (she was right); my sharp-eyed and wise copy-editor Susan Opie; cover designer Emma Ewbank; proof reader Seán Costello; and all the team at Simon & Schuster, especially Marketing Director Hayley McMullan and Publicity Managers Jamie Criswell and Jess Barratt, who pushed Nat out in the world. And huge thanks to my fantastic agent, Alice Lutyens, for spot-on advice, irrepressible enthusiasm and especially for taking a punt on Nat, and me, before his story was even finished.

At the risk of this turning into an Oscar speech, thank you to my mum and dad, for giving me the love of reading that made me want to write, and to my teachers at St Angela's Ursuline Convent School for Girls in Forest Gate, East London, especially Mrs Atherfold, Miss Turvey and Dr Betts, for showing me that being able to string a sentence together gives you more options in life than I'd ever imagined.

Last but definitely not least, thanks to my long-suffering husband, Mike Jeffree, for everything else.

Q & A with Frances Quinn, author of *The Smallest Man*

How did you come across the true story that inspired the novel?
I was researching a different book – later abandoned – and wanted to feature a character with a disability. A bit of googling and up popped Jeffrey Hudson's Wikipedia entry. He drew me in immediately, as someone who'd had a difficult hand in life and made the best of it, and I knew I wanted to try to tell his story.

But *The Smallest Man* isn't Jeffrey Hudson's story?
No. Originally I intended to fictionalise the real story, and for Jeffrey to be the main character, but the problem I discovered was that real life, however dramatic, doesn't usually have the right shape for a novel – it meanders about instead of heading towards a conclusion, there are boring bits, and too many characters come in and out, especially in a life as colourful as Jeffrey's.

The other thing was, his name really got in the way – it sounded to me like an accountant from Pinner (no offence to accountants from Pinner!) and made it really difficult to shape the character I wanted him to be. It was only when I decided to create a character inspired by Jeffrey, and came up with the name Nat Davy, that he started to come to life for me.

How did you decide what real history to include, and what to make up?
Obviously, the main historical background had to be correct. But because Nat tells the story himself, I felt I could leave out certain details that wouldn't have been important to him, so if you were to read a textbook on the Civil War, there would be events in there that don't appear here. In particular, the run-up to the war involves an enormous amount of political manoeuvring between the king and Parliament that really wouldn't make good fiction – and that I genuinely believe Jeffrey Hudson himself wouldn't mention if you

bumped into him in the Red Lion in Oakham and he told you his life story.

In terms of making up events, my rule was that I could include things that aren't documented as happening, but that feasibly could have happened. So for example, there was a rumour of a kidnap plot against the queen during the journey down to Oxford, and certainly the Parliamentarians would have been able to get the king to do anything if they'd captured her. There's no evidence that there actually was an attempt, but there's no evidence that there wasn't either. Not everyone will agree with that approach – I know some people like their historical fiction to be purely dramatised fact – but my priority was to write a good story, not a history textbook.

Did you talk to people with dwarfism as part of your research?
No, I didn't. I read some books by people with dwarfism, to get a sense of the practical difficulties Nat might face, but he lives in a very different time to ours, and so his experience would be very different to that of anyone I could talk to today. Also, Nat's feelings about his dwarfism are Nat's – it's not an attempt to say, 'This is what it's like to have dwarfism,' because as with any disability, each person's experience of it, and attitude to it, will be different.

Having said that, I hope that spending some time inside Nat's head might make people think twice about staring at someone with dwarfism, or any visible disability, or making jokes about it – we may have come a long way since the days of the freak show and the court dwarf but, as anyone who has a visible disability knows, not nearly as far as you might hope.

Do you have a favourite character?
Well, Nat, of course – I lived with him for so long, and we went through a lot of ups and downs together, so he feels quite real to me and I missed him when the book was finished. But also Arabella – she's based on a very good friend of mine, Angharad Rhys (not the actress), and as soon as I realised that's who she was, she was easy to write, which as an author, you're very grateful for!